ᵂHITED SEPULCHRES

A MEDIAEVAL MYSTERY

WHITED SEPULCHRES

A MEDIAEVAL MYSTERY

C.B. HANLEY

For P.A.E., P.C.S.

and our friend from Fenoli.

First published by The Mystery Press, 2014

The Mystery Press, an imprint of The History Press
The Mill, Brimscombe Port
Stroud, Gloucestershire, GL5 2QG
www.thehistorypress.co.uk

British Library Cataloguing in Publication Data.
A catalogue record for this book is available from the British Library.

ISBN 978 0 7509 5682 6

Typesetting and origination by The History Press
Printed in Great Britain

Ye are like unto whited sepulchres,
which appear beautiful outward,
but are within full of dead men's bones,
and of all uncleanness.

Matthew, ch. 23, v. 27

Conisbrough 1217

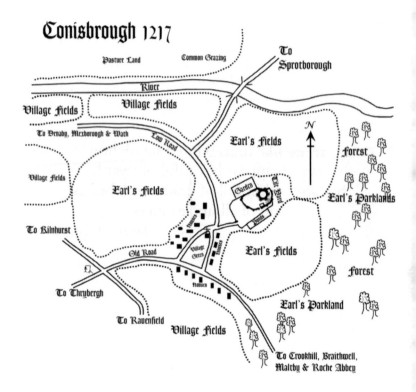

Pasture Land   Common Grazing

To Sprotborough

River

Village Fields   Village Fields

To Denaby, Mexborough & Wath

Low Road

Earl's Fields

N

Forest

Village Fields

Earl's Fields

Garden

Earl's Parklands

Park Hill

To Kilnhurst

Old Road

Village Green

Houses

Houses

Earl's Fields

Forest

To Thrybergh

To Ravenfield

Houses

Earl's Parkland

Village Fields

Earl's Parkland

To Crookhill, Braithwell, Maltby & Roche Abbey

Chapter One

Conisbrough, June 1217

The wedding was only a week away, and there was still so much to do. Edwin splashed some water on his face and hands, pulled his new tunic over his head, grabbed the piece of bread his mother held out to him and ran out of the door, knotting his belt around his waist as he went.

It was high summer, the feast of St John the Baptist, and even at this early hour the sun was bright. As he jogged up the village's main street towards the castle, Edwin appreciated the cool morning air, knowing that it wouldn't last, and that it would be another blazing day later on. It wouldn't be pleasant sitting in the steward's cramped office, which tended to get a bit airless, but he supposed he should be grateful that he wouldn't be out toiling in the furnace-like fields like most of the other villagers. And, thank the Lord, there would be no violence, no danger, and no death. It had been four weeks since he'd returned from Lincoln, and he could still smell the blood.

Since he'd been back, everything had been different. He hadn't managed a whole night's sleep, for a start, which was making him jumpy and increasingly lightheaded. He spent his nights tossing and turning on his straw palliasse, trying to blot out the visions of battle which filled his head. The heat didn't help, but for the first summer in his life he wouldn't leave the cottage door open overnight to let in some cool air. Instead he shut it fast, and had even fitted a wooden bar. His days weren't safe, either: he couldn't get over the feeling that he needed to look over his shoulder all the time, that horrors were hiding just out of his field of vision, reaching for the corner of his eye. Every shadow made him jump.

He shivered, and found to his surprise that he was already outside the door to the earl's council chamber: he'd walked right through the castle wards, into the keep and up the stairs without even noticing. He was breathing heavily and the headache which had been hanging around for days was making him feel dizzy. He stood for a moment, leaning his head on the stone wall to soak up some of its coolness, before standing upright and inhaling. He smoothed down his hair and his tunic, and knocked.

The door was opened from within and Edwin was greeted with a smile by Adam, the earl's junior squire, as he entered. Adam closed the door behind him and Edwin stood in silence until such time as the earl should notice him, exchanging a glance with Martin, who was looming in the corner. Martin nodded to him briefly, but he was busy trying not to make a noise as he scolded the new young page, who was fidgeting.

The earl was in the middle of a conversation with Sir Geoffrey.

'... and so it is the only honourable thing to do.'

The old knight gestured. 'But surely, my lord, a little unnecessary? After the recent events in Lincoln, the regent will be well aware that you have returned to his fold, and so will Prince Louis. There could be no doubt.'

Edwin felt a jolt at the mention of the word 'Lincoln'. He had to get over this. It was a place which would doubtless be mentioned frequently in the months and years to come. He needed to put the terror behind him and be proud that he'd managed to serve his lord so well. He needed to drown out the sight and smell of the blood by thinking of the one more pleasant memory from his time away. He let his mind drift a little, encouraging it to recall the face, the summer-blue eyes … he sighed, and then remembered where he was and hoped that nobody had noticed. Fortunately the earl hadn't, and was continuing.

'No, I think it must be made more formal.' His tone was firm. 'I will send a letter to Louis over my seal, informing him that I am leaving his camp and have returned my allegiance to its rightful place with our lord king and his regent. A copy of this should also go to the regent himself, so that there can be absolutely no doubt about my loyalty. I don't want questions to arise later which might endanger us all.'

Edwin could see that Martin was looking at him with a questioning expression, having finished his whispered rebuke of the page, and he surprised himself by realising that he knew exactly what their great lord was talking about. He was involved in affairs of the realm. How far he had come ... he tried to intimate with an inconspicuous nod of his head that he would explain it all later, and Martin seemed satisfied.

The earl had moved on to brusque instructions to Sir Geoffrey. 'Have Hamo arrange the scribing ... oh no, better not to take him away from his other duties just at the moment, or this wedding will never happen. Father Ignatius will have to do it. Damn it!' He slapped the table, making them all jump. 'I need a dedicated clerk these days now that we all have to do so much reading and writing. I thought you were going to send to the abbey for someone?'

'I did, my lord, and he should be here within the next few days.'

The earl looked as though he was going to make an angry retort, but he reined it in and merely nodded. 'Good. And the sooner the better, although now is not an ideal time to be adding someone new to my close household.' He poked at the pieces of parchment in front of him in a lacklustre fashion. 'Anyway, speaking of household ...' He turned briskly and Edwin was glad he'd been paying attention.

'Weaver, good.' The earl always called him that, and Edwin was more or less getting used to it, although it was his father's name, not his. Which was odd in itself, as he didn't think his father had ever actually been a weaver, but he didn't have time to think about it as the earl was continuing. 'I have no particular duties for you this morning, so I'm sure you'll be wanted down in the steward's office. Is William still ailing?'

'Yes, my lord. His injury is healing, but slowly.'

'Hmm. Well, no doubt Hamo is doing an admirable job covering for him.'

Edwin couldn't think of a polite answer to that, but he had to say something. 'Yes, my lord.'

The corner of the earl's mouth twitched. 'Very tactful. And no doubt he is scratching everyone the wrong way as he goes about his business, and most men are looking for an opportunity to push him down the stairs as well?'

Edwin opened his mouth but it wasn't his place to criticise a senior member of the household, so he said nothing and felt awkward.

But it seemed the earl was not testing him; he laughed and waved Edwin away. 'Off with you, then. I trust you to keep some sort of order in my household. If I need you for anything I'll send Thomas.'

Edwin bowed – he was getting slightly better at it but it still wasn't perfect – and left the room.

———

As Martin watched Edwin leave, he thought to himself what an unusually good mood the earl had been in since he'd arranged a new marriage for his sister. It wasn't as if he was a bad master at any time, really: it was just that he had an unpredictable temper – not surprising given that he was a Plantagenet, a family said to descend from the devil – and he tended to get irritated by small things, which didn't make life easy for his squires. Still, at the moment all was sunshine, and the earl was full of smiles and carefree movements.

Martin wished his own life could be carefree, but it certainly wasn't at the moment. He had two main problems which filled his thoughts from morning until night, and often during the hours of darkness as well. Firstly there was – but before he had time to dwell on it, his attention was distracted by Thomas, who seemed completely unable to stay still. And that, of course, was his other difficulty. If only the boy –

But his mind had wandered from the earl. Now he was the senior squire he needed to concentrate more on what his lord was talking about, for he had nobody to explain it to him in greater detail afterwards unless Edwin happened to be there, which he wasn't all the time. How he longed to be out in the tiltyard practising his horsemanship or weapons training, but strength and skill alone didn't make a good knight, or a good servant to his lord for that matter. He needed to have his wits about him. He put a firm hand on Thomas's shoulder in an attempt to stop him squirming, and turned his attention to the earl and Sir Geoffrey.

The old castellan was speaking. 'So you are expecting them all tomorrow, my lord?'

'Yes. The guest quarters and the hall are going to be crowded, so you'll have to arrange an encampment outside the walls as well. God knows that my dear sisters don't like to travel without their attendants and their comforts.'

Martin glanced at him sharply in case the smile was about to disappear, but the earl still appeared relaxed. Martin felt some of his own tension ebb away – if the earl could be sanguine about having all his sisters and their families under the same roof at once then it wasn't his place to worry about it. Although it would mean that –

The earl sounded satisfied. 'After all that's happened recently I should give thanks that we're all still here to celebrate. It's good to be home, with family about me, and to be among people I know I can trust.'

He settled himself back in the room's one fine chair and flicked his fingers at Thomas, who stifled a yawn and moved with irritating slowness to the wine flagon on the side table. Martin watched as he tried to lift it, realised that he needed both hands to do so, replaced it, fetched a cup, thumped it down and then managed to spill the wine everywhere while trying to pour it. Then he handed the cup, still dripping, to the earl. Martin saw Sir Geoffrey's hands twitch and almost felt him quell the urge to administer a cuff round the ear, but as the earl didn't seem bothered, merely drumming his fingers on the arm of the chair and then taking the wine without comment, he could do nothing. Thomas smirked at Martin as he resumed his place, licking some drops off the back of his hand. Martin felt his own temper start to rumble. Honestly …

But the earl had drained the cup and was already standing again, dismissing Sir Geoffrey with a wave. 'Good. I leave the morning's arrangements to you. Meanwhile I shall go for a ride,' – Martin straightened, hope rising – 'Adam, you can come with me. Go and saddle Gringolet.' Adam was almost out of the room before he'd even finished bowing, grinning all over his face, and Martin watched him with resignation. The earl turned to him. 'Martin, my sword wasn't cleaned properly yesterday. I expect better of you – take Thomas and do it again.'

There was much that Martin could say on that subject, but the earl's tone was verging on being clipped, so he bowed swiftly with a simple 'Yes, my lord,' and left the room, pulling the page with him.

Now he was really annoyed. Yesterday he'd been all set to give the earl's sword a proper clean and polish, a job he enjoyed, but Thomas had begged to be allowed to do it, pleading to such an extent that Martin had given in – after all, the boy needed to practise. But then he'd left him to it, and he hadn't checked that the task had been carried out properly. Obviously it hadn't, but much as he wanted to lay the blame with the page, he recognised that it was his own fault for not making sure the work had been done.

He considered sending Thomas up to the earl's bedchamber to fetch the sword, but realised that he'd probably have to wait all day, so he bade him stay where he was while he ascended himself, loping up the stairs two at a time. When he returned they both went to the armoury, where Martin pointed out – again – where the fine sand, the rags and the oil could be found. He watched as Thomas took his time selecting what was needed, and then they both went outside to find a quiet corner of the inner ward.

As soon as Martin withdrew the sword from the scabbard it took barely a glance to see why the earl had been so annoyed. 'You didn't clean this very well, did you?'

The boy said nothing, but the impudent what-are-you-going-to-do-about-it look said it all.

A suspicion was growing in Martin's mind. 'In fact, did you work on it at all?' The grin got wider. 'You didn't, did you? You begged me to leave you with it, and then you did nothing, just to get me into trouble. You little …'

He started to raise his hand, but Thomas skipped back and stuck out his tongue. 'You can't touch me!'

Martin let his hand drop. 'Of course I can – I'm our lord's senior squire and I'm supposed to be in charge of you and Adam.' But even as he spoke, he knew it sounded defensive and that the boy, curse him, had got the better of him again.

'Senior squire? You're a nobody. But *I'm* my lord's nephew, his *oldest* nephew, and when I'm grown up I'll inherit lots of lands. If you hit me, I'll tell my uncle about it and it'll be you who gets punished, not me.'

Damn it, he was right. When Thomas had arrived, his mother had taken Martin to one side and explained in no uncertain terms what would happen to him if he laid a hand on the boy, and Martin knew that he had no choice but to obey. After all, who was he? And he'd have to try and stay out of the Lady Ela's way once she arrived in case she started on the subject once more and began spoiling her brat again. No wonder he wasn't looking forward to her arrival. But Thomas was such a wretch! It wouldn't have been so bad if he'd made a few mistakes through lack of experience, but he was deliberately disobedient and malicious, playing on his position. But there was nothing to be done. He was of higher rank and that was how the world worked. Sighing, Martin picked up the rag and prepared to do the cleaning himself.

'Right, I've had just about enough of this.'

Martin leapt to his feet, for the speaker was Sir Geoffrey, who had appeared without warning. The knight was carrying a bunch of birch twigs, which Martin recognised well from his youth. He hadn't been subjected to it for many a year now, though, and the thought of being humiliated like a child again, and especially in front of the smug little imp, was almost too much to bear.

But Sir Geoffrey was speaking to Thomas. 'You might think you're too high and mighty to be disciplined, boy, but I've been training pages and squires all my life, and I know that nothing ruins a man so much as being spoilt when he's a child. I beat our lord when he was younger, and I'm not afraid to do it to you. Our lord will want you to grow up into a respectable man and a good knight, and he won't thank me if I let you get away with these games.'

For the first time Thomas lost some of his poise and began to look worried. He started to back away as Sir Geoffrey swished the birch.

'But my mother ...'

Sir Geoffrey snorted. 'Your mother? What does she know of the raising of men? I'm well aware that she cosseted you until you were more than old enough to serve as a page – you're nearly ten years old, in the Lord's name, and most boys are sent away at seven – but that doesn't mean that we need to bow to her wishes now.'

Thomas looked really panicked now, his voice squeaking. 'But our lord is my *uncle*!'

'Yes, your uncle. So you keep saying. But who's your father? William Fitzwilliam of Sprotborough? Hardly a name to strike fear into our hearts. And besides, now that the Lady Isabelle is marrying again, your father is yet further removed from the earl and his estates. So *you* need to know that your whining about family and rank will serve you naught – you'll be treated the same as every other boy who's been in the earl's service. Now, act like a man for once and take off your tunic.'

'You're not really going to beat me?' The boy was tearful now.
'No, I'm not.'

Thomas was so surprised that he stopped crying, and a look of cunning came over his face. 'That is well, because – '

The knight interrupted him. 'I said *I* wasn't going to. Martin is.' And he turned and thrust the birch at Martin, who took it in his hand before he had a chance to think about it.

'Me, Sir Geoffrey?' He stared stupidly at the twigs.

'Yes, you. I've been watching you as well, and you need to take a firmer hand now you're the senior. You're a good lad, but I think you're in danger of being a bit soft. Giving Thomas his long-overdue beating will do you good.'

'But – '

'Get on with it!' The voice, whip-sharp, had ordered his life since he was a small boy, and he had no choice but to obey. He was taller by nearly a head than the knight, but there was no question as to where the authority lay.

He reached down with his left hand and took a firm grip of the snivelling Thomas's arm. Then he raised the birch and brought it down across the boy's back, not very hard. Thomas howled, much too loudly for Martin's liking, and certainly disproportionate to the force he'd used.

Sir Geoffrey nodded. 'Good. Again. Six strokes should do for now.'

Despite his earlier anger, Martin now felt like a bit of a bully as he raised the birch and brought it down five more times on the small back. Thomas's wailing had drawn an audience, and he was now surrounded by men-at-arms and curious serving men, most of them smiling and cheering. Once Martin had finished, he was seized by an urge to throw the birch as far away as possible, but he took a deep breath and handed it back to Sir Geoffrey.

The knight took it but didn't move. 'And?'

It took Martin a moment to work out what he meant. He turned to Thomas, who had collapsed into a weeping heap, and towered above him as he spoke. He tried to keep his voice firm. 'Now, you will clean and polish that sword as you were meant to, and I will inspect it before it goes back to the earl's chamber. If it isn't done properly then there will be consequences.'

Thomas stopped wailing and turned his head, and Martin could see that his eyes were completely dry. They stared at each other for a long moment. Martin hoped that he would never see a look of such venom directed at him again.

Shaken, he turned to leave the boy to his task, but had to push his way through the onlookers who were still gathered. Swearing under his breath, he used his greater size to shove them all aside; one or two of them started to protest, but their words died on their lips – there were, after all, some advantages to being the earl's senior squire who would be a knight one day – and he felt a rough satisfaction. He still wasn't looking where he was going, though, and before he knew it he had laid his hand on the arm of a much smaller figure. Horrified, he realised that he had been on the verge of pushing Joanna to the ground. As her eyes met his, startled, he could feel the redness burning in his cheeks, and he lengthened his stride and ran off without a word.

Damn it! He hardly ever got to speak to her without the Lady Isabelle being present, and now he'd missed his chance due to his own inability to control himself. Dear Lord, what was he going to do? This was, of course, his main problem, the one he'd been dwelling on for some time. As the Lady Isabelle's companion, Joanna would have to accompany her away to her new home once she married, and then Martin would never see her again. The thought of this made him want to curl up and sob, but he had to keep his feelings in check. This was what life was like, and what could he do about it, in truth? He was only a squire, and although he was in one of the best positions in the country, his prospects were still fairly limited, with several more years of training before he would eventually become a knight and hopefully have a portion of his father's estates settled on him. No, he had no hope of being able to support a wife in the near future, especially one who belonged to one of the realm's nobler families. Moreover, his father and her cousin would never arrange such a match, and it was up to them, not him, to decide who would marry whom. And anyway, what if she didn't even feel the same way about him? What if …?

His eyes started to prickle, and he knew he had to get away from all the people in the bustling inner ward. He was seventeen years old, a man, part of the earl's personal household, and he should be acting like it, but he was going to lose his grip here and he needed to do it in private. He hurried away.

Edwin's aching head was full as he left the council chamber and made his way down and out of the keep. He slowed and stopped as he reached the bottom of the outside staircase, blinded by the reflection of the sun off the bright stone. He sat on the last step and shielded his eyes for a moment. The inner ward was quieter than it had been in the last few months, for the masons had stopped work until the festivities were over, and they had all dispersed, travelling to their home villages and towns to see their families. They had now finished the kitchen – and thank the Lord for that, for Richard the cook would not have wanted the building work going on while he was trying to cater for a wedding – and apparently would move on to the great hall next. Edwin had no idea how that was going to work, or where everyone would eat while the work was going on, but fortunately that wasn't for him to organise.

He forced himself to stand up. He was downcast at the thought of the day ahead. For all that he needed the peace and quiet and routine of normal life for a while, he was finding things strangely … dissatisfying. He didn't know why or what exactly was bothering him, but it was like an itch he couldn't reach. He'd always quite liked spending time in the steward's office, helping William with his accounts; the scent of the room with its spice chests was as much the smell of home as the wood smoke and pottage of his house. But now the thought of being cooped up in that little room all day just didn't appeal. Of course it didn't help that the gruff but pleasant William wasn't there, having injured his good leg in a fall: he was now completely unable to walk until it healed. He was laid up in his house in the village, driving his wife to distraction, and his place in the steward's office had been taken temporarily by Hamo, the earl's marshal and therefore the man who normally made his travel arrangements and dealt with the outdoor staff instead of organising domestic matters at the castle.

As Edwin entered the great hall he was enveloped in the pleasant aroma of the fresh rushes on the floor which had been strewn with sweet-smelling herbs, and he almost began to brighten as he inhaled the scent. He allowed himself to stop and close his eyes for a moment, but he could hear Hamo's high-pitched voice emanating from the steward's office, as he berated some luckless individual about the wrong type of wine having been brought up from the cellar that morning, so with a sigh he began to make his way past the bustling men in the service area at the back of the hall. He slowed, wondering if he could possibly think of an excuse to delay his entrance. He stopped entirely, letting the serving men move around him as they started their preparations for the mid-morning dinner, and thought that maybe if he just turned and crept out again, nobody would –

'Ah Edwin, finally. Where have you been, boy?'

Hamo had emerged from the office, pushing another man out before him, and he was already plucking at Edwin's arm. There would be no escape now. And being called 'boy' irked him more than he would like to admit, particuarly after all he'd been through in recent weeks. Still, orders were orders and the earl had instructed him directly to be here, so he should go with a cheerful heart. There was no point in getting ideas above his station about being given more interesting tasks to do, as though he were a squire or a man of rank. He should be grateful for the lot the Lord had provided him with. And he should keep telling himself that. Besides, interesting tasks involved danger and violence ... he shivered and allowed himself to be shepherded into the office.

Once he got started it really wasn't all that difficult, despite the headache. Hamo had been planning the meals for the next week, both for the wedding feast itself and for the days afterwards, but he was having difficulty adding up all the quantities of everything that would be needed. With the castle's usual population swollen by guests, and the extra extravagance which would result from a wedding, an awful lot of provisions would be needed, and they weren't all available in the castle's stores – some would need to be sourced from further away. The ordering would be Hamo's business, but nobody had a head for figures like Edwin, and he was often called upon by William Steward in this regard anyway. Generally he didn't mind – he could never understand how others couldn't do what he could do, to see all the neat columns of numbers in their head, and calculate and reckon while barely having to think about it. Glancing at the figures which Hamo had written on scraps of used parchment, he foresaw no problem. Now let me see, if you're going to provide *that* many mutton pies and *this* much barley pottage for *that* number of people, and the ingredients are *these*, you're going to need ...

He hummed to himself as he went down the list, adding his own notes with a pen which wasn't really sharp enough and which spluttered ink all over his hand. As he went through the plainer items which would be the fare served to the guests' servants and retainers, he let his mind wander slightly. The wedding ... the more he thought about it, the more odd it became. He just couldn't believe who it was that the Lady Isabelle was marrying. Honestly, why would –

'I tell you, you're not having it!'

Edwin was distracted by Hamo's voice as he squared up to a man whom Edwin recognised as one of the kitchen hands.

'But I must take it – master cook has told me not to come back without it!' The man's voice had an edge of desperation, and Edwin could well understand why: Richard Cook was a large, red-faced man who had a choleric temper at the best of times, but the current added strain had caused all sorts of problems in the kitchen, and several of the scullery boys – and some of the higher-ranked cooks, for that matter – had been seen around the place sporting nasty bruises. The scene this man would encounter if he went back to the kitchen without whatever it was that Richard had demanded didn't bear thinking about.

But Hamo had folded his arms. 'I tell you, he is not having any more. This is the third time since yesterday morning that he has asked for more sugar – what is he doing, eating it raw? No, it is staying here and you will have to tell him to do without for today. He'll need the rest for that big marchpane.'

'But ...' The man was almost speechless. Edwin's eyes went over to the chests stacked against the far wall where he knew the most precious spices were kept, and he could see that they were all firmly locked. Of course, this was normal – nobody would keep anything so valuable in an open area such as the kitchen, and the sugar, cloves, saffron, ginger, pepper and so on were always stored here under lock and key, under William's personal supervision. But William and Richard, hard men both, had a kind of gruff agreement where William would basically give him whatever he asked for, knowing that the talented cook would get good value for money out of it and would produce delicacies which were appreciated by the earl and his family.

The man's voice really was desperate now. 'Then perhaps you would like to go to the kitchen and explain that to him, master marshal?'

Hamo assumed a supercilious air and drew himself up to his full height, which wasn't much. 'I? *I* go to the kitchen and speak to the cook? I think not, my man.' He leaned forward and jabbed the other in the chest. '*You* will tell him, and *you* will take the consequences. If he doesn't like it then he can complain to the earl himself if he wants to.' He rocked back on his heels and smirked, and the man, admitting defeat, turned and shuffled out of the room, shoulders slumped.

Hamo span and saw that Edwin had stopped work and was watching. 'Well? Have you finished, impudent boy? You might think you're important now, but I know where you've come from and it would be easy to send you back out to the village if you don't look sharp.' He snapped his fingers under Edwin's nose, forcing him to grit his teeth in an attempt to stay silent. 'Let me see what you've done.' Hamo snatched the parchment from Edwin's hand and sniffed as he looked at the scrawls. 'From what I can make out from your appalling hand, these look adequate, but you really need to work on your penmanship. How William puts up with you, I don't know.' He handed it back. 'But you haven't finished yet – get on with the reckoning for the earl's own table before you think of moving anywhere.' He sniffed again and stalked out of the room, leaving Edwin to grumble and draw his eating knife in order to sharpen the quill before he started again. As he started to do so his rope belt, which had been fraying for quite some time, snapped and fell to the floor, taking everything that was hanging on it with it.

Sighing, Edwin got down on his hands and knees. His purse – which wasn't exactly heavy, containing only a couple of halfpennies and a small wooden spoon – and the eating knife in its plain leather sheath were right next to him, but he had to crawl under the table to get to the larger dagger in its ornate scabbard. This was probably what had caused the break: it was far too heavy for a piece of old rope, and should by rights have a proper leather belt, except that he didn't own one. He'd only had the dagger a few weeks, but since the day he left Lincoln he somehow hadn't felt able to take it off. Even when he lay down at night he kept it where he could put his hand on it at any moment.

Edwin sat back and drew out the dagger. He weighed it in his hand and stared at the blade, moving it from side to side so the light caught it. His hand was a little too small for the hilt, but it had a fine balance. Once more, memories leapt unbidden into his mind …

He had no idea how long it was before he realised that he was sitting on the floor under the table, and that questions were sure to be asked if anyone came in and saw him. He sheathed the dagger once more and threaded the rope through the scabbard loops and those of his eating knife and purse. He knotted the frayed ends together as best he could and hoped that would suffice until he could get hold of something more substantial.

Right. What was he supposed to be doing? Oh yes, the meals for the earl's own table. Concentrate, now. At least this part of the list was interesting. The earl and his noble guests would be eating some real delicacies, and Edwin's mouth watered at the mere thought of the quails, the capons, the venison, the marchpane and sweet custards.

But his other thoughts couldn't be kept away, and his mind went back to Lincoln again. This time he managed to force away the blood and recall more pleasant memories. He wondered if he was in Alys's thoughts as often as she was in his. He hoped so, but he couldn't be sure. He was tortured by the thought that she would have forgotten him already, although deep down he knew that wasn't likely after what they had been through together. But how would he ever see her again? It was a ride of two or three days back to Lincoln, and it wasn't as if he was free to go gallivanting around the country whenever he pleased anyway. But still … the remembrance mingled in his mind with the pleasant perfume of the spices and the agreeable background of the delicious dishes he was reading about, and he was comforted a little. Whatever happened, he would always have his memories, and would be able to summon the image of her face and her smile …

He finished the list and put down the pen. He was about to wipe his inky hands on his tunic before he realised that it was the new one which his mother had made for his birthday today. She remembered every year that he had been born on the auspicious feast of St John the Baptist, and never failed to give him a gift and to remind him of how happy his arrival had made both her and his father, who had been much older than his wife and who had all but given up on the hope of a son. Knowing this always made Edwin feel safe and loved. He wiped his hands on his hose instead.

It was with an almost-cheerful whistle that he pushed back his stool and moved towards the door. He had been at the table a little longer than he thought, and men were already shuffling into the hall for dinner. The service area was crowded with servants bearing large platters, and Edwin stepped carefully around them to ensure he didn't knock anything out of their hands. But not all was calm there: he could hear Hamo's voice again, berating someone for something at the other side of the room.

He was determined not to let anything spoil his unaccustomed mood of complacency and made up his mind to ignore it, but the conversation of two of the servants nearest to him caught his attention. He knew really that they were speaking only in jest, but he'd seen so much bloodshed recently that the words couldn't help but chill him.

'He gets worse and worse every day. I don't know how much longer anyone'll stand it.'

The other nodded as he shifted the weight of a stack of trenchers in his arms. He leaned over and spat on to the floor. 'Not long. I'd certainly like to see 'im dead, and I'm not the only one, I can tell you.'

The room started to spin for a moment and Edwin stood still with his eyes closed until the men had moved away.

Chapter Two

Once Edwin felt calm enough to move, he made his way into the hall and found a place at one of the lower tables. Now that the hall was full of people, the scent of the herb-strewn rushes was buried under the smell of the dense crowd of hot, sweaty men, and the air was stale. He and the others stood while the earl entered, and once grace had been said and those at the high table were seated, he sat down himself and waited for the table servants to enter. As he waited he surveyed the earl and his party. The high table was relatively empty today, although of course it would be full once all the honoured wedding guests arrived. While they were here there would also be entertainment during the meals, which would provide an unusual and welcome change from the normal routine; Edwin had seen a minstrel arrive the day before, and wondered what sort of stories or songs he would perform. But for this meal the high table contained only the earl, the Lady Isabelle and her companion Mistress Joanna, Sir Geoffrey, Father Ignatius, and, in the place of honour at the earl's right hand, Sir Gilbert de l'Aigle, the Lady Isabelle's betrothed.

Edwin still couldn't quite believe it. During his recent adventures in Lincoln and on the subsequent journey back to Conisbrough he'd become quite close to the knight, and the new situation seemed odd. He couldn't quite work out why to start with, but after a while he'd realised it was to do with the way he ordered things in his own mind. He'd known vaguely that Sir Gilbert was a landowner, and not just a household knight, but he'd been fooled by the knight's down-to-earth behaviour into thinking that he was almost a mere mortal like himself. So to find suddenly that he'd been sharing his journey with a man who apparently owned much of the realm's south coast, and who was considered a worthy match for no less a wife than the earl's sister, was something of a shock. Immediately Edwin had felt a chasm opening between him and his former companion, and they hadn't spoken since the announcement of the forthcoming wedding had been made. Sir Gilbert was now a distant figure at the high table to be viewed from afar, not a man to whom one could chat about everyday matters.

Those at the high table were served first, of course, and Edwin watched as dishes of delicacies were brought in by servants, to be placed on a board to one side and carried to the table by the squires and pages. Sir Gilbert's squire, Eustace, was a sober fellow who, as Edwin had noted on his journey north, performed his duties with a minimum of fuss, and he, Martin and Adam were moving around each other adeptly with the various foodstuffs. Martin was finally getting over his clumsiness, caused by growing so fast and being all elbows and knees, and Edwin noticed Sir Geoffrey casting an approving glance at him. Thomas the page, however, seemed to be getting in everyone's way, much more than necessary. As Edwin watched, Thomas moved behind Martin and jostled his arm just as Martin was pouring wine for the Lady Isabelle. Some of it splashed on to the white tablecloth, and she admonished him sharply. Martin hung his head and mumbled something to her before stepping back. Edwin heard an intake of breath from next to him and turned to see that Richard, Sir Gilbert's senior sergeant, was next to him and had noted the incident. He murmured something about what would happen to any boy under his command who did such a thing, and Edwin silently agreed, feeling sorry for his friend.

Edwin's thoughts were interrupted by the arrival of a large trencher of pottage and a cup of ale. He drew out his spoon and attacked it with gusto as he pondered the best method of staying out of Hamo's way during the afternoon. Perhaps he would slip away quietly and go to survey the crops in his parts of the fields, as he hadn't done that for a few days.

Despite the fact that he was now to be awarded a substantial wage – about twice what he'd earned while standing in for his father as bailiff, an amount which in itself had been twice what a labourer would be given – as a reward for his position in the earl's household, the winter would still be bleak for him and his mother if he didn't manage to get his crops harvested properly in a few weeks' time, and he couldn't just leave it all to the man he'd hired to take his place in the fields.

The men at the lower tables finished their simple fare and got up to go back to work, leaving those at the high end of the hall to continue their meal, more courses of which were still arriving. Edwin gulped the last of his ale and wiped his mouth on the back of his hand as he filed out into the bright sunshine. He took a surreptitious glance around him to ensure that Hamo wasn't watching – hopefully he'd still be inside supervising – and hurried off towards the gate. There he almost ran into Hamo himself, but fortunately the marshal was busy overseeing the unloading of some barrels from a cart. One of the barrels, a smallish one, slipped as the men manoeuvred it off the tailgate, and Hamo shrieked in alarm.

'Be careful, for God's sake! That's the special hippocras for the wedding, to be drunk only by the bride and groom. We can't get any more of it in time, and it's worth more than you – I'll see you flogged if anything happens to it!'

Edwin watched as the chastened men lifted the barrel very, very slowly and carried it with aching care towards the kitchen.

Hamo was outraged again. 'No, not that way! Put it in my office behind the hall. Then I can keep my eye on it to make sure none of those thieving kitchen hands get near it.'

The men changed direction and Edwin was able to slip past behind Hamo, unnoticed. He hurried out of the inner gate. *My office*, thought Edwin, he's already considering it his own. This didn't bode well for William, and Edwin made up his mind to seek his uncle out later to check on his recovery. But first, the fields.

After about a mile and a half he was almost regretting his decision. Of course the idea of going to look at the strips which were furthest away from the village had been to stay as far away from Hamo as possible, but the disadvantage was that it was a long walk under the hot sun. He could feel the heat beating down on the back of his neck as he plodded up a hill, and his rather pale face would no doubt soon be burned. His head was boiling under its woollen cap, so he took it off, but then the burning sensation on his scalp got too bad, so he used it to wipe the sweat from his brow and then put it back on again. His headache wasn't improving.

As he reached the top of the hill he had a fine view of the countryside all around. It was about another mile to the furthest fields, but he could see them from here: long strips with the golden grain baking in the sunshine, people moving to and fro among them as they pulled out the weeds which could choke the precious crop. He could see another figure on the road making its way towards him; squinting in the bright light, he thought it was a monk. Yes, it was, walking by the side of a horse – no, too small for that, a mule. Most monks in the land wore the black of the Benedictine order, but this one was in a white robe, meaning that he was a Cistercian, probably from the local abbey at Roche. Whoever he was, he was setting a good pace and their paths would soon cross. Between here and there the road dipped again and went through a thickly wooded area, and as he saw the monk enter it on the far side, Edwin thought that it might be a good place to dawdle and enjoy the shade for a few moments. He would probably meet him there and would have an excuse to stop and pass the time of day.

But wait, what was that? As he looked at the near side of the woods he became aware of movement which didn't seem natural. Several men were crouched in the undergrowth – one of them had just stood up and that was what Edwin had noticed. They hadn't seen him, but were looking the other way, towards the monk and his laden mule. Dear Lord.

Robbers, and within a couple of miles of the castle itself! This was unheard of: he would have to tell Sir Geoffrey about it when he got back, but right now there was no time – he had to warn the monk. He drew his dagger and started to run.

He gathered speed as he went down the hill, but he wasn't going to get there. He still had a good quarter of a mile to go. As he pounded along the road he shouted as loud as he could, making himself hoarse as the dust flew up and caught in his throat, and waved his arms to try and alert the monk's attention. The robbers broke their cover as they heard him, and came into the road – three of them. They looked round, but saw how far away he was and turned towards the monk anyway. He had seen them now and had stopped, his mule shying in fright as armed men ran towards it. He had the presence of mind to throw the rein into a thick bush so that it caught there before he turned to face the oncoming attackers. Edwin could see the whole picture laid out in front of him, but he was never going to get there. A man of God! How could they? His chest felt as though it was going to burst, but he tried to increase his speed, pumping his arms and sucking in huge breaths. It was no good. The men reached the defenceless monk.

And then something so extraordinary happened that Edwin wasn't quite sure whether he'd seen it correctly. Maybe it was the effect of the sun, the dust and the midges clouding his eyes, or the headache, but as he watched, the monk reached round to the back of the mule, which was shying in fright but unable to pull its rein away from where it was entangled, and yanked. For one bizarre and dizzy moment Edwin could have sworn that he'd pulled its leg off. He skidded to a halt, gasping, and shook his head. As his vision cleared he could see that what the monk had in his hand was in fact a stout cudgel, two or three feet long. Well, thank the Lord he wasn't seeing things, but really, a lump of wood wouldn't be much use against three armed men – he had to get there and help. He gulped a huge breath and started to jog forward again. But as the monk stood to receive the assault, he swung the stick expertly in his right hand and stepped into the attack.

The first man, slashing a dagger wildly, went down with a crack to the head before he'd even got close. Then the monk took on the other two together, twirling the cudgel at such speed that Edwin could hardly see it, although he heard the thump as it connected with something, followed by a scream. The second man was staggering back with blood streaming from his face as the third, armed with a sword, tried to lunge forward. The monk feinted to one side and then brought his weapon down precisely on the man's elbow. He shrieked in pain and dropped the sword, clutching at his injured arm. The monk watched him calmly, still swinging the cudgel, and took a single step forward. The man fled, followed by the one with the bleeding face, and they both disappeared into the undergrowth. The entire encounter had taken less time than it would take Edwin to say a paternoster.

Edwin slowed as he finally reached the scene. The monk turned to him and he suddenly realised that he might look like another attacker, so he flung his hands into the air and stopped, gasping that he'd been on his way to help. The monk smiled. '*Benedicte*, my son. I know you were, and you have my thanks for warning me.' His voice was calm – he wasn't even out of breath! As Edwin stood puffing and blowing with his hands on his knees, the monk flicked the massive cudgel nonchalantly up and looked with no trace of concern at the blood and hair stuck to it. He walked over to the first attacker, who was still lying prone in the road, and poked him with one sandalled foot. 'Not dead, but it will take him a while to wake up.' He used the unconscious man's tunic to wipe the blood from the cudgel before returning to stow it in the mule's pack. He stroked the animal, which was still looking wild-eyed, and spoke soothingly to it.

How could he be so calm? Edwin's own heart was still thumping hard inside him, as much from the shock as from the running. 'But how – why – what I mean is, how did you do that?'

'I wasn't always a monk.'

Edwin looked at him properly and noticed for the first time how tall and powerful he was; if it hadn't been for the obvious signs of robe and tonsure Edwin would never have placed him as a member of the clergy. He opened his mouth to question further, but before he could say anything the other held out his hand. 'Brother William, late of the abbey at Roche, but now sent by Abbot Reginald to be a clerk to the lord earl.'

Edwin shook his hand, wincing as his own was crushed in a powerful grip, and belatedly remembered his manners. '*Benedicte*, brother. I'm from the earl's household myself.' Lord, but it still sounded strange to say that out loud.

The monk was looking him up and down with a quizzical expression. 'Not one of his squires, I take it?'

'No, brother, just a – ' He wasn't sure what the right word would be. 'I'm just a man who serves him.'

'And yet you were running to take on three armed men with only a dagger? I hope you know how to use it!'

For the first time Edwin realised what an unbelievably foolhardy thing he'd done. Honestly, how could he have thought of fighting against three men? But he hadn't even considered this as he'd run to help. He could feel his face growing redder. 'Well, I've had one or two lessons.' He fumbled as he sheathed the dagger, his fingers suddenly not wanting to work properly.

There was a moment of silence before Brother William clapped him on the back. 'You're a brave lad, and if I have the opportunity I'll tell the lord earl so. Now, can you tell me whether I'm on the right road for my lord's castle at Conisbrough?'

'Yes, just head this way past the fields and through the village. The road will take you straight there.'

'Good.' Brother William turned to go.

'But what about him?' Edwin asked, pointing at the man on the ground.'

Brother William looked at the man and sniffed. 'Well, I certainly don't want to carry him, and I've nothing to tie him up with. We'll just have to leave him here and hope he doesn't wake up before someone can come and get him.'

'But I should come back with you, to report this to Sir Geoffrey. And there might be others around.'

The monk considered. 'No, I'd guess they were on their own, so there's no need to fear. If there were more near here, we'd know about it by now. But don't worry, I'll report it as soon as I get there, so you can be on your way.' He turned again.

As he was about to speak, Edwin heard the sound of voices and he stiffened, hand reaching for his dagger. But these sounded familiar, and as he looked up the road he could see four other men from the village. They were all carrying tools and were probably on their way from one set of fields to another. They called out a greeting as they saw Edwin. He told them briefly of what had happened and they all expressed surprise and some fear at there being outlaws so close to the castle. But work in the fields couldn't stop, so it was agreed that they would all walk there together, while Brother William continued his journey to the castle. They set off, tools grasped tightly, peering about them in case of further danger. Edwin went with them, but kept twisting round to look back at the extraordinary monk, until he and his mule had disappeared from sight.

Joanna stood in the great chamber and looked around with some satisfaction. The large room had been cleaned more thoroughly than it had been in ten years, the hanging tapestries taken out and beaten, the floor scrubbed and strewn with fresh rushes and herbs, the walls washed and the sconces cleaned of their old wax and filled with fresh new candles. The bedchamber which was partitioned off at the end of the room had received similar treatment and was adorned with an extravagant new coverlet for the bed, one of the fine gifts which the earl had given his sister. Joanna was just watching a serving man lay a fire in the hearth – not that they needed it now, for certain, but it might be wanted later if the evening became cool – and then everything would be ready. And thank the Lord for that, for she was exhausted. She made a small adjustment to one of the new chairs and then, checking to see that the man had left the room and that she was alone, she sat down on it. How comfortable it was! She wasn't used to sitting on a chair which had a back, and the support it offered was wonderful, the soft cushion plump and yielding.

She was just about to sink back into it when the Lady Isabelle swept into the room. Joanna leapt up, her face becoming hot, expecting a rebuke. But Isabelle had softened in the last few weeks, and she merely seated herself, adjusted her gown, looked around, and said 'Very nice.'

Hardly able to believe her good fortune, Joanna hastened to fetch a footstool and arrange it to Isabelle's satisfaction. Once her mistress had made herself comfortable, she explained that everything had been made ready here, but that the guest chambers still needed their final preparations. 'But that can wait until later, my lady, as your sisters will not arrive until tom – '

The door burst open and Thomas hurled himself into the room. He skidded to a halt in front of Isabelle, but before he could say anything, the old Isabelle returned for a moment. 'Stop!' She held up her hand and he stood with his mouth open. 'I have told you before that you must seek permission before you enter my chambers. Go back outside, knock, and wait for me to reply.'

'But my lady …'

She slapped him on the back of his head. 'Don't you dare talk back to me! Go and do as I say at once, or there will be trouble.'

He turned, shoulders hunched, and sulked his way back to the door. He hovered near a stool and for a moment Joanna thought that he might kick it, but fortunately for him – and his health – he decided against it. He left the room and pulled the door closed behind him, and then Joanna heard an impatient knock. She looked at Isabelle, who was examining her fingernails with some care. There was silence for a moment before the pounding sounded again, just as insistently. Isabelle still said nothing.

'My lady, should I – '

'No, Joanna. He'll get the idea in a moment.'

Joanna waited, and then after a pause the knocking came a third time, controlled and polite. Now Isabelle looked up. 'You may enter.'

Thomas came in, walked steadily up to Isabelle, shot her a look of venom, and bowed. 'My lady.' Joanna hadn't thought it was possible to bow sarcastically, but evidently it was.

'Yes, what is it?'

'My lord sends me to tell you that a messenger has arrived, and that his sisters will be arriving this afternoon instead of tomorrow. They will be here within the hour.' He bowed again, smirking now.

Joanna nearly jumped from her seat. But the rooms weren't ready! They still needed the mattresses airing and the bedclothes setting out. There would need to be water for washing, and the kists for the guests' clothes would need to be checked to ensure that they were clean and sweet-smelling. And then ... but Isabelle looked equally rattled and needed her attention. She waved Thomas on his way and stood.

'Oh Lord, will you look at me! I need to change my gown and put on a better headdress before they get here. Quickly now!'

Edwin wiped his sleeve across his forehead as he returned from the fields. In the wide open spaces the heat had been even greater than he'd expected, bouncing back off the ground and turning the fields into a shimmering furnace, and he could feel the sweat pooling under his arms and trickling down his back as he trudged towards the village. Some of that, he admitted to himself, may have been from fear; every rustle in the undergrowth, every movement of a branch, had startled him and made his hand fly towards the dagger. He was walking slowly, but his heart felt as though he'd been running non-stop for miles. He tried to remain calm – after all, he'd seen two separate groups of men from the castle riding out in search of outlaws, so surely they would have run away by now – as he longed for some ale to wet his dusty throat, a cool cloth to put on his pounding head, and some shade to stop his pale skin from burning. Still, the walk had been worth it: his barley and oats in the south field were fine and he seemed set for a good harvest, which would provide for him and his mother through the winter as well as something of a surplus if they were lucky. Of course, no man counted his harvest until it was successfully gathered, so he would have to watch the weather carefully over the next few weeks; he muttered a brief prayer to ask the Lord's blessing on their efforts and for the avoidance of the hard winter which would follow if the crops failed. It had happened only once in his lifetime, but he remembered the gaunt faces and the endless succession of funerals.

He shuddered as he entered the village, either from the thought of winter or at the relief of being safe from attack on the open road, and his head began to clear. Yes, say a harvest of two dozen quarters of grain in total, minus the tithe, save, say, six quarters for next year's seed, allow ten to feed the family and animals over the winter and spring, and that would still leave ... oh, wait. They wouldn't need so much now. They were no longer a family of three, but only two. A dark shadow hovered at the corner of his eye; he turned quickly to try and catch it, but it was gone.

He had arrived home. He stood across the street and contemplated it. In the weeks since he'd been back he'd been able to attend to some of the repairs which had been needed, and now the cottage – one of only three in the village with more than one room – looked more like the residence he remembered and less like it was starting to become derelict. Of course, all the things which were women's work – the garden, the livestock, the cleaning inside – had been perfect all along, but the male tasks had been neglected during his father's last illness. He sighed as he started to cross the road, only then realising that the sound of hoofbeats was close behind him. He turned to find himself almost under the horses of several men in livery, the advance riders of a large party which was raising a huge cloud of dust as it ploughed through the village's dry street. He skipped across quickly and flattened himself against the fence to let them pass.

Behind the advance riders came two men in rich clothing. One was very thin and looked as though he might also be tall once he got down from what was a very fine horse; the other was much burlier and had a huge beard. He was laughing at something the other had said, throwing his head back with mirth, his face lighting up. He then turned to the small boy riding behind him on a pony, to include him in the joke. The boy smiled back but he looked tired, concentrating on sitting up straight and staying on his mount. Edwin could sympathise with that – he still winced when he thought of the long ride to Lincoln and back. If the boy had been a villager, Edwin would have said he was about seven or eight years of age, but given that he was a noble and therefore bigger and more well built, he was probably only about six: he really would be glad to get to his destination. Still, they weren't far from it now, for surely these were the earl's relatives who were arriving for the wedding.

His guess was confirmed when he saw the sumptuous covered wagon which followed the men on horseback. It creaked along, pulled by four heavy-looking horses who seemed to be struggling even though the ground was dry and hard, and as it passed him Edwin saw another boy peering out the back of it. He was slightly older than the one on the pony, and he bore a striking resemblance to Thomas. As the boy saw

Edwin he made a rude gesture and pulled his head back inside. As the coloured hanging fell back into place Edwin caught a glimpse of the bright clothing of some ladies inside the wagon, no doubt being jolted by every tiny movement.

Behind the nobles came a large number of packhorses, servants and guards, some looking curiously around them at the village, others staring doggedly ahead towards the castle gate. Coughing at the dust which had been raised by such a large party, Edwin waited until they had all passed – which took some time – before he stepped out into the street again. A number of other villagers had emerged from their houses to watch the spectacle, and he waved to Agnes, the old woman who was the priest's housekeeper, as he turned to go into his garden. Before he could get there, however, he was accosted by Godleva, the daughter of one of the village labourers. She bounced in front of him, barring his path, and spoke.

She sounded out of breath. 'Oh, Edwin, did you ever see anything so fine? How lovely it must be to travel about the country in such a cart, with so many servants and men around you!'

Actually Edwin thought that the wagon had looked pretty uncomfortable, but out of politeness he agreed that it had been fine, and made to move on.

She put a hand on his arm. 'And how fortunate the ladies are, to have such rich husbands to provide them with such finery!' She smoothed down a fold of her rather ragged gown and her eyelashes fluttered. He wondered if she had something in her eye.

'Edwin! Are you coming in?'

It was his mother, coming out of the garden and across the street to him. Godleva scowled but then assumed a sweet smile as she turned. 'Good day, Mistress Anne. How well you are looking today.' Her voice was so honeyed you could have put it on bread.

Edwin's mother bobbed her head briefly. 'Good day. I'm sorry I have no time to stand and talk, for there's always so much to do in the home. Can I not hear your mother calling for you?' Godleva turned and Edwin took the opportunity to disengage his arm and move towards his mother.

'Well, it was nice to speak with you, but I must be going.'

She took a step towards him. He took a step back.

'It was lovely to speak to you too, Edwin. We must do it again *very* soon.' Her eyelashes quivered again as she swirled her skirts to walk away, revealing one dirty ankle as she did so.

Edwin's mother grumbled to herself as they went into the house, but Edwin didn't catch any of it. Once they were inside he sat as she fetched a cup of ale; as she brought it over he opened his mouth to speak but was surprised when she banged it down on the table with unnecessary force.

'Mother!'

She looked at him.

He was confused. 'What?'

She sighed. 'You really must make more of an effort not to keep getting caught by these girls.'

'What?'

She made a tutting noise. 'Ever since you came back from Lincoln, or more specifically, since you were employed by our lord earl, every girl in the village has tried to throw herself at you. Obviously you'll have to marry one day, but I'll be in my grave before I let the likes of Godleva get hold of you!'

Edwin choked on the ale he'd just sipped. He coughed and then spluttered as some of it went up his nose. 'Married? But …' He tried to set the cup down again without spilling anything, and took a deep breath. 'Me?'

His mother rolled her eyes. 'Yes, you. You've always been a good steady lad, and now you're earning a fine wage and you have the attention of the lord earl himself, you're the best prospect in the village.' She softened and smiled for the first time. 'Hadn't you noticed?'

'Well, no. But I mean … that is to say, what I mean is … married? Me?'

'It comes to us all, Edwin, and you must put your mind to it. There are one or two suitable girls in the village, so you'll have to choose from among them.'

Strangely, the room seemed to look different from usual. Was it spinning slightly? He stood and drained the rest of his ale. 'I have to go to … well, I'm in a hurry. I'll talk to you later.' He left the house.

Joanna had no idea how an hour could have gone by so fast – even though it was midsummer so the hours were longer than at any other time of year – but it seemed like no more than a few moments before she was standing behind Isabelle as the heavy covered wagon creaked to a halt and the accompanying riders pulled up in the inner ward. The earl stepped forward to greet his guests as they alighted: first the Lady Ela, shaking out her skirts and pushing away the spindly arm of her husband William Fitzwilliam as she took her brother's hand instead; next her younger son Roger, who jumped nimbly down – Joanna saw the earl frown slightly and wondered that a boy of eight should still be carried in the wagon like a child instead of riding a horse – and then the Lady Maud, short and plump, smiling as ever as she disembarked. The ladies' companions followed, looking pleased to be out of the wagon, as well they might. Little Pierre had already dismounted from his pony and now he skipped forward to hold his father's stirrup; Henry de Stuteville smiled at his son through his beard as he stood to await his turn to shake hands with the earl. Then they were introduced to Sir Gilbert and the group ascended the steps to enter the great chamber.

Once inside there was a flurry of activity as the various squires and companions sought to make their masters and mistresses comfortable. Joanna was able to steal several glances at Martin as he directed them all to the wine and helped them to move chairs around. Once he looked back at her and her heart leapt so much that she thought she would drop the cup she was holding. But she managed to complete her duties and then retreated to the corner of the room along with Matilda, who was the Lady Ela's companion, and the vivacious girl who had accompanied the Lady Maud, whom she hadn't met before.

It was strange how they seemed to become invisible so quickly. When Isabelle and Joanna were alone they spoke often, but now that there were other people of rank in the room, the companions – and the squires for that matter – were unnoticed as their betters chatted among themselves. Or at least, they were unseen until they were needed: soon both Matilda and the other girl, who had briefly introduced herself as Rosamund, had been dismissed and sent to unpack in the guest quarters. Joanna hoped they wouldn't notice that the final preparations for the rooms had been a little rushed – she would go over there as soon as she could and see if they needed anything else. In the meantime she took up her embroidery and continued with it while the nobles caught up with each other.

Isabelle was in her element, and why shouldn't she be? She was about to regain the precedence over her sisters which had disappeared when she was a childless widow. She sat between them, the skirts of her new crimson gown spread out in a seemingly carefree manner, but one which was designed to show off the eye-catching colour to best effect. Joanna had laboured for many hours on that gown, although mainly on the seams, while the professional seamstress who was summoned twice a year from York had fitted the bodice. It was a shame the colour wouldn't last – like all bright things, it would fade over time – but just now it looked magnificent, putting the slightly drab travelling clothes of the other two ladies into the shade, as did the new gold filigree headdress holding Isabelle's wimple in place, which both sisters had dutifully admired. And if you think that's lovely, thought Joanna, then wait until you see what she'll be wearing for the actual wedding. She'll outshine you both.

Joanna tried to work out what was going on in the Lady Ela's mind. Both sisters were sipping wine while they spoke with Isabelle, but whereas Maud seemed fully engaged, Ela's eyes kept turning to where Sir Gilbert was sitting with William Fitzwilliam and Henry de Stuteville. The afternoon sun slanted in from the windows which faced the inner ward and illuminated his profile. He was certainly more handsome than Lady Ela's skinny husband, but she didn't seem to be admiring him in that way. So what was it? Joanna realised she was staring, and turned her eyes back to her embroidery in case anyone had noticed. But after a few moments she risked another glance at the Lady Ela, who was still flicking her eyes between Isabelle and Sir Gilbert. And then she realised why the look was familiar – it was the one Isabelle wore when she was looking over new goods to buy, assessing their worth. The Lady Ela was sizing her sister's bridegroom up as though he were no more than a new set of hairpins.

Before Joanna could explore this thought further, her attention was distracted by a squabble which had broken out between the boys. At first she thought it was the two visitors, but little Pierre was standing attentively beside his father. No, it was Roger and Thomas. Thomas really ought to have been standing around the edge of the room with the squires, but he'd given up on his duties once his mother had arrived, and sat down with his brother to play at merels and filch from one of the bowls of dried fruit which was set out. It would appear that they now had a disagreement over the game, for Thomas had picked up the board, scattering the pieces everywhere, and was trying to hit the smaller boy with it. Roger started shrieking and crying to his mother, and soon both boys were rolling on the floor striking at one another.

William Fitzwilliam leapt out of his chair and waded into the fray, telling them to stop and trying rather ineffectually to separate the boys as he was kicked by their flying feet, looking all the while at the earl, who remained aloof. Sir Gilbert looked rather startled, not having heard such a commotion in these chambers before; Henry de Stuteville gave a tolerant shake of his head, slapped his hand on the arm of his chair, stood, looked appraisingly at the two rolling, scratching children, and then swooped, catching each by the neck of the tunic and lifting them into the air.

Their father smoothed the front of his clothing, which had become ruffled, and opened his mouth to speak. But he was interrupted before he could start.

'William!' The Lady Ela had risen from her chair and was looking through narrowed eyes at her husband. 'Don't bore us all with another of your lectures. They're just in high spirits, that's all.' She looked with fatuous devotion at the boys. 'Come now, apologise to your lord uncle and play quietly.'

Apologise to your uncle, thought Joanna. Yes, but not to your father, who was the one who got kicked. That's the Lady Ela for you. She looked as Henry de Stuteville gave the boys a little shake and then put them down, clapping them on the back. He spoke in his pronounced Norman accent – 'Yes, yes, just boys playing' – as he patted Thomas on the head. 'Come now, come and tell me about being a page here.' He moved him away from Roger, who went to sit with his mother, and peace reigned once more.

Joanna looked at the earl, who throughout all of this had remained silent and almost motionless. His face held no expression, but his hands were gripping the arms of his chair, and behind him Martin looked worried. She was relieved when Sir Geoffrey stepped into the room and bent over the earl to speak quietly in his ear. With a very brief and hardly muttered 'excuse me', the earl stood and followed Sir Geoffrey out of the room. There was a short pause in all the conversations as he left, but then everyone returned to what they were doing, and there was a comfortable buzz about the chamber.

From her corner of the room, Joanna could see out of one of the open windows into the inner ward, and she watched as both men emerged from the building. She couldn't hear what they were saying, but she saw Sir Geoffrey gesture, and then both of them moved towards the centre of the ward. Some guards were dragging something towards them, and she had to stifle a gasp as she saw what it was – an unconscious man with blood on his face. The guards dropped him on the ground while the earl and Sir Geoffrey stood over him and spoke. Eventually the earl nodded and Sir Geoffrey signalled to the guards to move the man away again. This time they pulled him by his feet, and as his head was dragged along it left a trail of blood in the dusty earth.

Chapter Three

Refreshed by his ale, although not by the conversation, Edwin left his mother's house. Marriage? He hadn't really thought of it before, or had he? Perhaps it had been at the back of his mind since … strange, as soon as his mother had mentioned the word, Alys's face had appeared before him, her summer-blue eyes smiling. She was so different from any of the girls he'd grown up with. Well, of course she would be, she was from a different part of the country and she lived in a big city, but even accounting for that she was still … but there was Godleva again, lurking at the side of one of the houses. She looked as though she was about to step over to him again, so he hurried across the green to the street on the other side, entering the yard of one of the village's other larger houses and calling out a greeting before he stepped over the threshold.

The door stood open in the warm weather, and the windows were uncovered, but still it was darker than the bright sunlight outside so he stopped to let his eyes become accustomed to the gloom. As he did so, his aunt bustled forward and embraced him, smelling as always of the fragrant herbs with which she often worked. She stepped back and patted him on the cheek, but had barely started on an offer of refreshment before a harsh voice came from the cottage's other room, demanding to know who was there and what was going on. Cecily rolled her eyes at Edwin and said he'd better go in.

Edwin stepped into the bedchamber and leaned over to shake the hand of the man in the bed. William cheered up on seeing who his visitor was, but it was almost grudging – he'd probably been looking for an excuse to take his temper out on anyone else unfortunate enough to get in his way. He motioned Edwin to a small stool which was overturned by the side of the bed, and Edwin righted it and sat down to ask him how he was.

He expected something of a rant and he wasn't disappointed. He let it wash over him – the normally even-tempered William was probably entitled to be irritable given his current situation. He'd been crippled ever since Edwin could remember: he'd once been a soldier in the service of the old earl, and had returned from a long-ago campaign with part of his left ear missing, a horrific scar which disfigured the entire left side of his face, and a maimed and twisted leg which caused him to limp heavily. Normally he managed to hobble about fairly well: as the steward his work was almost entirely in the castle rather than out on the estate, and he hauled himself up the hill and back once every day. However, two weeks ago he'd fallen down the stairs which led up to the entrance to the keep, and he'd injured his good right leg. There it lay on top of the bed, the ankle swollen and purple, causing him great pain and preventing him from walking altogether. There was of course a good chance that he would recover, so the earl hadn't dismissed him from service, but William was both frustrated by his enforced inactivity and worried about his future, so his outbursts were regular.

After he'd calmed down slightly he asked for news, so Edwin tried to give him an idea of what was going on outside the walls of the cottage. He decided that any mention of the outlaws or their attack on the monk would cause far too much excitement, so he restricted himself to speaking of the crops and the weather. William seemed content and started to lie back on his pillows and smile, so Edwin moved on to describe the wedding preparations at the castle. It was only after he'd been talking about the details for some time that he realised that William's face was growing blacker and blacker, and that this was particularly pronounced whenever he mentioned Hamo. He tailed off in the middle of a sentence, deciding it was probably unwise to recount how Hamo had refused to provide sugar to the cook.

It was too late. William was already struggling to get out of the bed, cursing at the pain. 'Help me will you, for God's sake!' He held out his hand as he tried to push himself up.

Edwin wasn't at all sure that this was a good idea. He tried to make soothing noises and press William back down, but this was the wrong approach.

'Don't talk to me like that, boy – I'm not a child! Just get me out of this cursed bed and get me up to the castle.' William's face contorted as he managed to swing his leg over the side of the bed but then he cried out as his foot touched the floor. Cecily hurried in and attempted to help Edwin calm her husband down, trying to push him back on to the bed, but it wasn't going to work.

'Get off me!' William shook off their arms. 'Edwin, get outside right now and find some men to help. I am going up to that office whether it kills me – or you, for that matter, or both of us, and I am going to tell that Hamo what's what.' His face was growing purple. Edwin looked at his aunt, shrugged and went outside to find some help.

Within a short space of time Edwin found himself at the head of a procession, as Alwin and Osmund, two of the burlier villagers, carried William on a seat made from their intertwined hands. They were followed by all the other men who happened to be around, not to mention a number of curious children; the village women came out of their houses and gardens to watch. They struggled up to the castle's outer gate, where the man on guard thought better of trying to halt the furious steward. He did manage to prevent the hangers-on from accompanying them, though, so Edwin, William and the other two continued up into the inner ward alone.

When they reached the great hall, Edwin hoped that they would find the service area and office behind it empty, and then they could all calm down and go home, but his luck was out. Hamo was in there, wagging his finger in the face of one of the servants.

William roared. 'Hamo! You son of a ...'

Hamo turned in alarm as he heard the bellow, and had Edwin not been worried about the scene in front of him he might have laughed, for he had never seen anyone look so surprised. The marshal took a step back at the sight of the enraged steward and his hefty bearers, and that was his undoing.

'Aha! You know you're in the wrong, you little toad! Taking my duties behind my back and destroying all the goodwill I've spent years building up. How dare you!' William removed his arm from around Osmund's shoulder and tried to lunge forward, but as his foot made contact with the floor his leg collapsed under him and he was forced to grab Alwin's arm, allowing Hamo to back away further until he was against the wall. He stood there while William launched a stream of oaths against him, and Edwin tried unsuccessfully to shut the office door and keep out the crowds of onlookers who were gathering. Most of them were smiling, happy to see the pompous marshal on the receiving end for once.

William was trying ever harder to hobble forward until eventually, still being supported by the off-balance Alwin, with Osmund trying to catch hold of him, he managed to grab a fistful of Hamo's tunic. The muscles in his burly right arm bulged through his sleeve as he all but lifted the smaller man off the floor. 'If you don't start putting this right, I'll kill you, d'you hear? I'll wring your scrawny neck!' He shook Hamo but the effort made him overbalance completely and he fell, pulling both Hamo and Alwin with him. Just to complete the scene, Osmund couldn't stop himself tripping over them, and soon they were all in a heap on the floor.

Edwin ran forward to try and restore some order, shouting at the laughing onlookers behind him that they should either help or go away, or he'd have something to say about it. They remained where they were, though, including a small figure at the front who was doubled over with mirth, tears streaming down his face. Edwin had no time to wonder what Thomas might be doing there, however, and he leaned down to try to help the men untangle themselves before anyone more senior came along and found out what was happening. William would be lucky to keep his position after this, even if his leg did recover, and if he lost his place he could well end up a destitute beggar. Not that Edwin would let it come to that, of course, but how William would *hate* being a burden on his nephew. There must be some way of smoothing this over. Finally Edwin managed to get everyone sorted out, and, leaving Hamo to dust himself down, he helped the two men to pick William up and carry him out through the cheering throng, the page's cackles still echoing in his ears.

Martin turned his face up to the sunshine as he strolled through the inner ward. After they'd seen the unconscious outlaw safely locked away in a cell, the earl had released him and Adam for an hour as he intended to speak with Sir Gilbert, no doubt hammering out the finer details of the marriage settlement. Martin was glad to be able to get out into the air instead of having to stand and listen to all the talk about inheritances and dowries. He was off to the tiltyard to practise his horsemanship, and nothing could have made him happier. He picked up his gear from the armoury, and headed out to the inner gate and down towards the stables.

As he passed near to the castle's outer gate he saw a small group of people arriving – three men and a small boy, with an extra packhorse. The man on the lead animal caught his eye and waved. Martin waved back and changed direction to greet him, for it was Sir Roger, one of the earl's knights and the man who would act as Sir Gilbert's groomsman at the wedding. He was accompanied by two men-at-arms, one of whom carried on the back of his horse the boy Peter, formerly a villager of Conisbrough and now Sir Roger's servant.

As Martin reached the group he put out his hand to hold the head of the knight's horse. It looked tired, and so it might, for it was a more elderly mount than you would normally see carrying a knight. He patted its neck as Sir Roger swung easily to the ground with his customary grace. The sunshine had if anything made his hair even blonder, and it glowed like a halo around his head as he smiled his thanks. Then he handed the reins of the horse over to Peter, telling him to follow the two men to the stable and see the animal looked after. After watching them go he turned to Martin.

'Well met. A happier occasion than when we last parted, I think?'

Martin smiled. 'Undoubtedly, Sir Roger. Would you like to go and greet my lord straight away? He's in conference with Sir Gilbert, but I could go and tell him that you're here, if you like.'

The knight shook his head. 'Oh no, I wouldn't think of disturbing him while he speaks of business. No doubt they'll emerge when they've finished and I can offer them both my congratulations at the same time. But perhaps Sir Geoffrey is around for me to pay my respects?'

'Yes, he's about somewhere. He was up near the inner gatehouse last time I saw him.'

'Well then, I'd better head that way. Perhaps you'd like to join me?'

Martin weighed up the opportunity to go out and ride with the chance to spend some time with a knight whom he admired. But the pull of the open space was too much, so he reluctantly bade farewell to Sir Roger and turned back towards the stables.

Once his courser was saddled, he led it out of the gate before mounting and proceeding at walking pace around the outside of the castle wall towards the flat ground on the eastern side. He held his padded gear in front of him and felt the warmth of the sun upon his face as he smiled and relaxed for the first time in days. Thank the Lord, a chance to get out and do something physical for a change. Being the senior squire was turning out to be much more difficult than he'd anticipated. Of course, it hadn't helped that he'd had the position thrust upon him so suddenly, but there was no point dwelling on that. It wasn't so much the extra duties regarding the earl, his clothing, his armour, his horse, or serving at table – he was used to that kind of thing and it was just a case of there being more of it. It wasn't even the responsibility of training the little devil Thomas, although that certainly wasn't his favourite part of the job. No, it was the *politics*. Suddenly he was expected to attend meetings and councils with the earl and Sir Geoffrey, where he was expected to know who everyone that they were talking about was, which side they were on in the war, who they were allied to in marriage, and so on. He couldn't keep up and it made his head hurt.

As he nudged his horse past the fishponds, shrunken in the summer heat, he let his mind wander over some of the more tedious conversations he'd heard recently about tax revenue, scutage, tallage and other such financial matters. Surely he didn't need to know all this? While he was a squire there would always be the earl and Sir Geoffrey to tell him what to do, and once he was a knight, he wouldn't exactly be part of the noble circle – his father held reasonable lands that he'd probably have to manage in due course, but it was hardly of importance when compared with the earls, barons and great landowners who ran the kingdom.

But anyway, no need to worry about that now. He had reached the flat ground outside the walls, where a large area was roped off. Adam was already there, his own pony tethered to a rail, with a pile of blunted lances. He was busy erecting the quintain, and Martin dismounted to go and help him.

The main post on its pivot was already in place, and Adam was struggling to fit one of the arms to it as the socket was too high up for him. Martin helped him to heft it into place and secure it, and then made sure the shield was hanging correctly off the end. Then they moved to the other side to affix the second arm, the one with the heavy bag of sand attached to it by a short rope. Satisfied that everything was ready, they walked back to their mounts.

Adam looked up at him. 'Do you want to go first?'

Martin considered. 'No, you have the first try. We'll get you kitted up, and then I'll watch you to see how you do while I put mine on.'

Adam nodded, and Martin bent to help him into the padded garments which he needed for the practice.

After Adam was ready, he mounted and Martin stood ready with a lance. 'Leave your shield for now – you'll be able to control him better if you've only got to hold the reins in your left hand. Now, take this.' He handed over the lance. Adam struggled with the twelve-foot pole, sliding off balance and making his horse dance. Martin held its bridle until it calmed again. 'All right. You haven't used one the proper length before, have you?' Adam shook his head, his face looking worried inside the padded hood. 'You'll be fine. Couch it level now, before you start, and just canter towards the quintain. You probably won't hit it first time, but we'll see how you get on.'

Adam clasped his right hand around the lance and brought it down so that it lay level, gripping it under his right arm and pointing over the left side of his horse's neck. Martin let go of the bridle and stood back to watch.

As Adam rode forward Martin could see that the lance was wobbling all over the place. There was a huge difference between using one of the eight-foot poles he'd been training with up until now, and a proper one. Still, he was fourteen now and he needed to learn. Martin was unsurprised as Adam missed the hanging shield completely, but he did manage to retain hold of everything as he reined in his mount and turned to come back. The pony remained calm, having done the same exercise with generations of pages and squires over the years; it ambled back and waited for Adam to collect himself and start his run once more.

He missed again the second time. That was the problem with the longer lances – it only took the tiniest tremble of the hand to make the tip of the lance sway quite dramatically from side to side. But Adam would get the hang of it. He had proved himself adept in practice before – not strong, but accurate. He never hit any target hard enough to knock it right over, but he was able to thread the lance through a hanging ring at quite some speed. He just needed to get used to the full-size equipment, that was all.

At his third tilt, Adam managed to graze the hanging shield. It was a glancing blow which hardly made the quintain move at all, but it was progress, and Martin shouted his encouragement. The he realised he needed to get ready himself, so he bent to start putting on his gear. As he pulled the thick gambeson over his body, strapped some padding to his legs and arranged the hood on his head, he watched out of the corner of his eye as Adam rode up and down efficiently.

After a few more tries Martin signalled to him to stop and dismount. Together they moved the quintain's arms up a notch to account for the taller horse, and then Martin told Adam to take a rest as he mounted. All the padding made him slightly stiffer as he settled himself in the saddle, but it was nowhere near as uncomfortable as wearing full mail – he tried to avoid that whenever possible as it was incredibly heavy and he didn't like restricting his movement so much. Anyway, this was fine – a bit warm, to be sure, but still moveable.

Adam tethered his pony and held out a lance to him. Martin hefted the familiar weight, keeping the pole upright until he started moving, then bringing it down level into the couched position. He'd had the instructions drummed into him so often over so many years that he could hear Sir Geoffrey's voice in his head. The weight of the lance should be supported by the palm of the hand, not the fingers. Press your feet down in the stirrups, squeeze your legs tight and allow yourself to go with the rhythm of the movement of the horse. The lance should be held steady at three points: by the hand that supports it, by the arm that holds it tight, and by the chest against part of which it is being held. Focus on the shield – look at the target and don't get distracted by the tip of the lance. And keep your eyes open while you hit it.

He struck the shield a solid blow, remembering to dodge the bag of sand as it came swinging round. Satisfied, he turned and rode back to start again.

He hit the target satisfactorily every time, as he had known he would, feeling himself enjoying the movement of the horse, the co-ordination of the weapon and the force of the blow. He reached his mark once more and turned. Right, enough of accuracy and solidity. This time he was going to be clever. Sir Geoffrey was always telling him that brute strength wasn't enough, that he had to *think* a bit more. This seemed a bit unnecessary to Martin – why not just hit the target really hard? – but if Sir Geoffrey wanted him to be clever, he would try. Up until now he'd been concentrating on hitting the shield right in the middle, with his lance square on to it. This time he would aim to strike it at more of an angle, swerving away from it and dodging the quintain as it turned.

As he rode he brought his lance down in a smooth movement. The target came nearer and nearer, and he urged the horse on. The end of the lance smacked into the shield at exactly the angle he'd planned, and he felt a momentary glee, which he didn't have the chance to enjoy before a huge thump on the back sent him tumbling from the saddle.

As he fell, he remembered what he'd been taught. He kicked his feet out of the stirrups and rolled as he hit the ground. It was hard, baked in the sun, but the thick layers of horsehair and wadding in the gambeson cushioned most of the blow, and he was already starting to rise as Adam ran over. He was ashamed more than anything, which proved he wasn't hurt, so he made light of it. 'That's the last time I pretend he's a Frenchman! Next time I'll tell myself it's Sir Geoffrey, and I'll treat it with more respect!' He stood for a moment and moved his shoulder round, sensing some soreness, but it was fine. The horse, another one used to the exercise, had wandered off to the edge of the tiltyard and was standing still, nibbling at the dusty grass; Martin brushed off Adam's help and ran to fetch it. Important to get back on, of course, and this time he'd take more care. It was still more enjoyable than politics. He rode back to his mark.

———

The hall was absolutely heaving with people when it was time for the evening meal. Outside, the air had cooled slightly, but inside it was hot, sweaty and airless. As Edwin walked in and saw everyone he nearly turned and walked out again: perhaps he might be better off going to see if his mother had any of the day's warm pottage left for him. But as he stood in indecision he was spotted by Brother William, sitting at the end of the nearest long table, who moved up and beckoned him over. Edwin squeezed himself on to the very end of the bench, bracing one leg to make sure he didn't fall off and make himself look foolish. He looked sideways at the monk, trying to see if he could glimpse any sign of the extraordinary behaviour he'd witnessed earlier, but his companion didn't mention it and gave no hint. Edwin began to wonder if he'd imagined the whole episode. But as Brother William pushed back the sleeves of his habit ready to eat his meal, Edwin could see the thick muscle of that powerful right arm. Not many monks looked like that.

Brother William was introducing himself politely to the other men around him, who nodded in greeting. Edwin looked past him and the packed lower tables towards the top end of the room, where the high table was just as crowded, if not even more so, with all the earl's family there. Indeed, it was not one table but two – another had been added to it so there were places for fourteen, and it took up so much space on the dais that there was barely room for the squires and servants to get round it. Thomas wasn't there, Edwin noticed: perhaps he'd been banned after making Martin spill the wine earlier. But as he watched, the page scuttled out from the service area at the bottom of the hall, his mouth crammed with something – some stolen delicacy, no doubt – and made his way to the top table where he slipped into the milling crowd without anyone really noticing. Edwin wondered if any of the nobles would spot that some luxury or other would be missing from their dishes, but decided that they probably wouldn't. Richard the cook had apparently almost had apoplexy when he'd heard that the noble guests had arrived a day early, but somehow he'd managed to produce a meal which would be stupendous, if the smells were anything to judge by. Edwin wondered how the man had fared who had been sent back by Hamo without the sugar. He had a look round in case he could spot him anywhere, but he couldn't – of course, the kitchen staff themselves wouldn't be in here; they'd have a bite to eat while everyone was at the meal, and then prepare themselves for the return of the dirty dishes and the preparations for tomorrow. Anyway, Edwin was profoundly glad that he hadn't been the one entrusted with *that* message.

Brother William was speaking to him, so he dragged his mind back and paid heed. The monk was asking him about the people who were at the high table with the earl. Edwin was some help but not much: he was able to point out the Lady Isabelle and the knights Sir Gilbert, Sir Geoffrey and Sir Roger, and also to note that the earl had two other sisters who were both married with children, but he didn't know which was which. The girls sitting with Mistress Joanna were presumably companions of the noble ladies, but again he didn't really know who they were. Brother William didn't seem to mind, though – Edwin got the feeling that he'd just been asking in order to pass the time while he waited for his meal. Once the dishes for the noble table had gone past them and made Edwin's mouth water, the fare for the cramped lower tables was brought out, and huge quantities of pie, pottage, bread and ale were placed before them. Richard Cook's concentration on the noble dishes evidently hadn't extended to the food for everyone else, and it didn't quite taste up to the usual standard. But Brother William tucked in as though he hadn't eaten for some time, and Edwin wondered what the monks ate at the abbey. Whatever it was, Edwin was fairly sure they wouldn't shovel in quite so much and quite so fast as Brother William was doing now.

As Edwin applied himself to his pie he saw Hamo near him at the back of the hall, flitting around the door to the service area and fussing over the serving men going in and out. He didn't seem to be achieving much except getting in everyone's way, but still he kept buzzing around like a fly on a carcass. Edwin felt a little bit guilty sitting there eating while Hamo wasn't. The man giving out trenchers asked him whether he wanted a place setting anywhere, and Hamo snipped something back at him, presumably indicating that he'd have something later. As Edwin watched, Hamo waved the man away and continued his pacing, but then he stopped, very suddenly, causing a man carrying a tray of pies to swerve around him. One pie dropped to the floor, to be snatched up immediately by someone's dog, which retreated under the table with its prize. Hamo stood completely still, all the colour draining from his face, as he stared at Edwin. Edwin half stood out of his seat, wondering what in the Lord's name he could have said or done which would cause Hamo to look at him in such shock; he thought he'd better go and ask, but before he could move, Hamo turned and disappeared back into the service room. Bemused, but deciding that now wasn't the time to make a scene, Edwin sat down again and continued eating.

The meal went on for a very long time, the hall getting hotter and hotter as time passed. Edwin had eaten his fill but as everyone else around him was still supping and talking he thought it might be seen as uncivil to leave. But then there was a stir of anticipation, and Edwin saw that the minstrel was stepping forward; he decided he couldn't leave now or it might draw attention to himself. Besides, it wasn't every day, or even every month, that such entertainment was to be had. He tried to settle himself more comfortably on the end of the bench.

Edwin looked at the minstrel with interest. He stood in the centre of the hall, in the space between the lower tables and the dais where the nobles sat. He was an average, plain-looking man at whom nobody would look twice if they saw him in the street, but he had a certain *presence* which Edwin couldn't define; a hush descended as he swept off his hat and flourished a low bow towards the earl and his guests. Then he replaced his hat, picked up some kind of stringed musical instrument with a bow, and took a deep breath.

The sound of his voice took Edwin by surprise, for it was huge, filling the room from the rushes to the rafters. Accompanied by a melodious sound from the instrument, he boomed out the first two lines of his performance:

'Carles li reis, nostre emperere magnes,
Set anz tuz pleins ad estet en Espaigne.'

Then he stopped as applause and a roar of approval swept the hall, bowing slightly and waiting for it to subside before he continued.

Edwin was confused. *Charles the king, our great emperor, had been in Spain for seven long years.* What was so exciting about that?

Brother William saw his bewilderment. 'It's *The Song of Roland*, the greatest poem of them all. It tells of the great emperor Charlemagne, his nephew Roland and their battles against the Saracens. Most of the older men here will have heard it before, but they're cheering because they know what's coming up.'

Edwin nodded, still not quite sure why this should cause so much excitement, but he determined to listen. Of course, French wasn't a native language for him as it was for the nobles, but he knew enough of it to be able to understand what was going on, as did all the other men in the hall – they wouldn't be where they were now if they spoke only English. He concentrated on the minstrel's words. The man's performance was extraordinary; he declaimed his lines in a sing-song voice while accompanying himself on his instrument, and held every man in the hall in the palm of his hand. As his voice rose with the tension, all those listening held their breath, only letting it out when the minstrel suddenly dropped his tone to a more normal level. He recited the narrative, but also played all the parts of the men in it, putting on a different voice for each one, to suitable cheers or jeers from his audience. Edwin had never seen such a large group of people – and rough-house soldiers, many of them – so spellbound. But for the life of him he still couldn't make out what all the fuss was about, as the text appeared to consist of nothing but talking: Charlemagne talked to his men, the Saracen king talked to his; they sent envoys to each other who talked some more. Why was this so exciting?

The performance continued for about an hour, with the hall getting hotter and sweatier all the time, and Edwin wondered again if he could slip away without anyone noticing. But the atmosphere was changing: it was becoming tense, even angry, and he could see fierce expressions on the faces of the men who had obviously heard the tale before. Even the earl was leaning forward in anticipation. Edwin turned his attention back to the minstrel as his music and voice reached a climax. Ganelon, one of Charlemagne's lords (and, as far as Edwin could make out, Roland's father), had been sent as an envoy to the Saracens, but he was arranging to betray his lord. No wonder the men in the hall were snarling – in the eyes of the nobles there could be no greater sin. Edwin listened as the final words of the evening were proclaimed: *upon the relics of his sword, he swore treason and swore his faith away.*

The minstrel fell silent. He was sweating profusely as he let his arms drop and lowered his head, his chest heaving. All around the hall men were cheering and banging on the tables in approval, and even Edwin could feel the surge of emotion.

The earl stood and raised his hand, and the noise died down. He turned to the minstrel, flipping him a coin. 'A masterly performance. We look forward to the continuation tomorrow.' He nodded at the rest of the noble party, and they too stood, the men wiping their beards and the ladies shaking crumbs from their fine gowns, and prepared to leave. Once they had exited the hall, people began to discuss what they'd heard, arguing among themselves. But eventually they started to wind down their conversations, and some began to bring out blankets and find themselves places to sleep. Edwin rose and stretched himself, stiff after so long perching on the hard wooden bench, and staggered out into the night.

The cool air hit him as he left the hall, and he felt somewhat revived. It was very late, but there was still a hint of light in the midsummer sky as he passed through the gatehouse and down into the village. He let himself into his mother's house very quietly, knowing she would be asleep in the bedroom, and shut the front door behind him before barring it carefully. The fire had died down, and the last orange glimmers gave little light to see, but he'd lived in this house all his life and needed nothing to guide him as he fetched his straw palliasse and his blanket from the kist in the corner, took four steps back towards the hearth, rolled himself up and fell asleep watching the comforting glow.

It seemed like only moments later when he was being shaken.

'Edwin! Edwin, wake up!'

'What?' He stirred sleepily, wondering if he'd overslept, but it was still dark and the voice wasn't his mother's.

'Come on, wake up!' He was still being shaken, and as he came to himself he realised that the door was open and his mother was hovering in the background. But the figure standing over him was Adam: that roused him quicker than a dash of cold water, for there could be no happy reason why one of the earl's squires should be here in the middle of the night.

He sat up. 'What is it?'

Adam's voice was low but urgent. 'You have to come up to the castle. It's Hamo – he's dead.'

Chapter Four

The moon was on the wane, but there was just enough light for Edwin to see his way as he followed Adam through the still, colourless village and up the path to the castle. Even at this hour it wasn't cold, but he shivered as he remembered another occasion when he'd been woken from sleep by one of the earl's squires with news of a death. The memory of it made him queasy, and he wondered what he was going to have to face once he got there. Had Hamo been stabbed? Would there be blood and flies everywhere? Would there … but he was letting his imagination run away with him. Better to find out the facts rather than allowing his mind to conjure up such images.

Adam was setting a fair pace, and Edwin jogged to catch up.

'So, tell me what's happened.'

Adam looked uneasy, and Edwin recalled that he probably had bad memories of his own. 'Did you … I mean, was it you who found the body?'

'No. It was when he went into the office – '

'Who?'

'The serving man. I don't know his name.'

'And what office?'

'The steward's room. He went in – '

Edwin thought that he needed some clearer information before he walked into whatever situation was awaiting him. He stopped and grabbed Adam's arm. 'Please, just wait a moment.'

Adam halted, and Edwin could just make out his face in the faint light. Was he paler than usual? Or had the moon drained away his colour?

'Just … just take a breath and tell me, from the beginning, what has happened.'

Adam inhaled deeply. 'All right. But we must walk while we're talking, or Sir Geoffrey will wonder where I've got to.'

They resumed their pace and Edwin listened carefully, trying to take in as much as possible.

'Some of the men who work in the kitchen were up early, as they always are, to make the bread. They also wanted to make a start on the dinner for later, as it's Sunday and my lord has guests.'

Edwin nodded. Richard Cook would want to produce something worthy of the company, so that made sense.

Adam continued. 'Cook needed some spice or other, so he sent one of his men to the steward's office to get it. The fellow went there and found Hamo lying dead on the floor. He ran to get the guard, and the guard fetched Sir Geoffrey. I was already up because I'd remembered that I hadn't polished my lord's saddle, which I meant to do last night. So I thought I'd get up early this morning and do it. When Sir Geoffrey saw me he sent me to get you. I haven't seen the body – all I know is that he's dead.'

By this time they were entering the castle gates, and Adam slowed his pace. 'I don't think I want to …'

Edwin understood. 'I can find my own way there. You'd better go and get back to your saddle.'

He turned towards the stables. There were lights over there, and a party of armed men was already assembling, leading their horses out of the building, checking their harnesses and mounting. 'What's going on?' Edwin asked.

'It's another patrol going out to search the area for those outlaws. They haven't been caught yet and Sir Geoffrey is … well, he's not pleased, let's put it that way.'

They both stood as the men rode past them, mail jingling and the horses' breath steaming in the early morning air. Then Adam touched Edwin's arm in farewell and headed towards the stable, while Edwin walked up to the torchlit inner gatehouse. At least he could spare the boy the sight which was about to greet him. The night porter, yawning at the end of his shift, waved him through, and he crossed the ward, entered the hall and moved towards the service area at the back.

He had to push his way through a few curious onlookers, but two guards were keeping people away from the office itself. They parted to let him in, and he stepped inside.

Sir Geoffrey was striding up and down, but he stopped as Edwin entered. 'You're here. Good. What kept you?'

Edwin opened his mouth.

'Well, never mind that, anyway. Tell me what you think.' The knight gestured to the body on the floor. It was lying in the corner of the room furthest away from the door, which was why Edwin hadn't seen it to start with. It was very dark in there, even with three of Sir Geoffrey's men standing around holding spitting torches. Screwing up his eyes to avoid having to look at anything horrible, he edged his way over and looked down.

Well, there was no blood for a start, but there was a horrendous smell. Edwin opened his eyes properly and squinted in the poor light. Hamo was contorted and stiff, hands clawed, a grimace on his face, eyes open and staring. At first Edwin thought they were moving, and crossed himself to ward off evil, but it was just the reflection of the flames from the torches. He looked around. A stool was on its side near him. The smell was coming from the vomit which was all over the front of Hamo's tunic and sprayed around him on the floor, and which was making Edwin start to feel queasy. It seemed fairly obvious that Hamo had eaten something which didn't agree with him, especially given that the remains of a meal lay scattered on the floor, an upturned bowl and wine cup spreading their contents across the flagstones. Edwin tried to contain his bile as he crouched to get a closer look. Maybe if he concentrated on working out what had happened it would take his mind off his stomach.

Yes, Hamo would have sat down to eat, probably after everyone else had finished, as Edwin had suspected last night. He'd brought some food in here, sat down at the table where it was clear, and started. Something in it had choked him? But would he have retched up so much if that had happened? Wouldn't it just have stuck in his throat? Edwin certainly wasn't about to get that close to the body to have a look. No, more likely there was something in the food which had irritated his stomach, which was why he was sick. Perhaps he had delicate innards like some people did? Edwin didn't know, but presumably that wouldn't be too difficult to find out. That would be why it had only affected him and not anyone else who ate the dinner. Then he'd fallen off his stool, spilled his meal and writhed around, knocking the stool over. Edwin felt a small grain of relief. Perhaps this had just been an accident. That would be welcome. Well, he could just tell Sir Geoffrey – oh Lord, but what was that under the table? Oh no, no, no.

Edwin sat back on his heels, overcome as a wave of nausea and foreboding crashed over him. He'd been fooling himself, trying to deny the horrible truth. Nobody would writhe around and vomit like that in his death throes from natural causes, and the contorted form of the dead dog under the table seemed to confirm his suspicions. It must have died of the same cause as Hamo – it certainly hadn't been there yesterday, as he would have noticed it himself when he'd had to crawl on the floor after his belt snapped. He looked up at the figure of Sir Geoffrey looming above him in silence and shadow.

'I'm sorry, Sir Geoffrey, but I think Hamo has been poisoned.'

───────

It wasn't long afterwards that Edwin found himself following the striding knight up the steps of the keep. Dawn had broken, but inside the thick stone walls it was dark, and he tried to concentrate on watching his feet in the guttering torchlight lest he fall. He shuddered as another memory came over him, of a time he had ascended these same stairs to be met with a sight he didn't want to think about, and he shook himself and tried to clamp his chattering teeth together before he came into the earl's presence.

Sir Geoffrey made only the most perfunctory of knocks before sweeping into the earl's chamber, and Edwin hesitated a moment on the threshold, sure that he didn't have the same right to enter his lord's room while he might still be abed. But the earl was up and dressed, Adam and Martin at his side, and he looked so grim that Edwin wanted to flee. But there was no escape, so he wiped his sweating palms on his tunic and went in.

'Well?' Martin had once told Edwin that the shorter their lord's sentences, the worse his mood was likely to be, so that wasn't a good start.

Edwin looked dumbly at Sir Geoffrey, who started for him. 'As Adam has no doubt told you, my lord, your marshal, Hamo, is dead. I was hoping it might be natural, but Edwin here thinks he was murdered.'

The earl whipped round so fast that Edwin had no time to say anything before those slate-grey eyes were boring into him. 'Is this true?'

Edwin wanted with all his heart to say that it had all been a mistake, Hamo had just choked and he was sorry, but there was nothing they could do about it, but he simply couldn't lie to that face. Dear Lord, what would be his punishment for the sin of telling such a huge untruth to his lord and master? Not only in this life, but in the next?

'Well? Speak, man!'

Edwin couldn't stop his voice from quavering. 'W-well, partly, my lord.' The earl's brows drew closer together and Edwin rushed to finish the rest of it. 'W-what I mean to say, my lord, is that he might not have been murdered, but I do think he was poisoned.' He was gabbling. Why did he feel this need to be so exact? Why couldn't he just say yes or no? But –

'Murdered, poisoned, what's the difference?' The earl began pacing across the chamber. Edwin noticed that both Martin and Adam were trying to make themselves unobtrusive, and he wished he could do the same. The earl let fly some colourful oaths, and Adam took a step back. 'I don't need this! Not today, not *now*!'

Sir Geoffrey was probably the bravest person Edwin knew, and he proved it now. He stepped forward and interrupted the earl's rant. 'But my lord, your duty – '

'Don't lecture me on my duty, damn it!' The earl's voice rose in pitch and a candle was knocked flying off the table. Thank the Lord it wasn't lit. Such was the intensity in the earl's face that Edwin honestly thought he might strike the knight; Sir Geoffrey didn't flinch, meeting his lord eye for eye. The earl stopped and locked his gaze on to the older man. Then, unexpectedly, he laughed. 'God's blood, Geoffrey, did you do this to my father as well? All right, I know my duty.' He turned again to Edwin. Fortunately Edwin was expecting it this time and he managed not to flinch. 'This is inconvenient, to say the least, and I'll be a laughing stock if it spoils the wedding and word of it gets out, but I will *not* tolerate such a crime on my lands, in my home. You will find out who has done this, and by God we'll have him hanging at the crossroads before the week is out.'

Edwin gulped. 'Yes, my lord.'

The earl looked him up and down. 'You look like a cornered deer, man. Pull yourself together.' He poked Edwin hard in the chest with one finger. 'You've proved yourself before; you can do it again. Sir Geoffrey will give you any authority you need. You're acting in my name and none will stop you. Now go.' He jerked his head towards the door.

Edwin stumbled out of the room, then stopped to wait for Sir Geoffrey, who was following more sedately with his own instructions ringing out behind him. 'Make sure my household still runs, or my sisters will never let me forget the shame.'

As the door closed behind them, Edwin's knees sagged with relief. But there was no time to rest: Sir Geoffrey was already starting down the stairs. 'Come, Edwin, we have much to do.'

Edwin hurried to keep up and slipped, grabbing at the wall to steady himself before scurrying after the old knight, who was continuing. 'If you don't need to look at him again, I'll send some men to take him down to the church, and I'll have Father Ignatius say a Mass for his soul.' Edwin realised that he'd been so caught up in his own affairs that he hadn't even thought to pray for the dead man, and he asked forgiveness for that even as he implored the Lord to take Hamo into His kingdom, even though he presumably couldn't have been shriven of his sins before his death.

By the time he'd finished his prayer they were outside the keep. Sir Geoffrey was about to stride off when Edwin stopped him. 'But who will run the household, as my lord wanted? Shall I go down to the village and have William fetched, even though he can't walk? At least he knows what he's doing.'

The knight stopped dead. 'No.'

Edwin looked at him, not understanding the expression on his face. Sir Geoffrey sighed, his face looking even more lined than usual. 'Work it out,' he said and strode off.

Edwin thought through the implications, and felt cold.

Joanna awoke, savouring the few quiet moments in the cool of the morning before she had to rise from her bed and start the day. She prayed, as she always did, for the soul of her brother, whom she remembered with pain, and those of her parents, whom she could hardly remember at all. She added a brief request that her own life might be happy, and then she turned to more practical matters. She threw off her blanket, rose, dressed, tucked the truckle bed neatly away without waking her mistress, and then began to lay out the clothing and toiletries which Lady Isabelle would need. Today was Sunday, so she would want something becoming to wear to Mass. Yes, the russet-coloured linen gown over the light summer shift; no need for wool or for fur-lined sleeves in this weather, and the wimple with the decorative lace around the edge.

As she laid out the garments, the hair-comb, the polished mirror and some scent, she enjoyed the silence and hoped that the day would be a pleasant one. Last night there had been some family friction as everyone gathered together after the evening meal: the Lady Ela had complained that one of the dishes had tasted foul, and she had snipped at her husband when he tried to shush her. Then the Lord Henry had made some comment about his nephew Roger being old enough to be sent away as a page, as he was intending to do with his own son Pierre later in the year, and that had started another argument; even the lovely Lady Maud had been shouted at when she tried to intervene to calm everyone down. Still, that was families for you – the first few hours of being in one another's company was fine, as everyone caught up on news, but after that the civilities became thinner as everyone remembered that they didn't really like each other that much, and the enforced proximity became grating. Joanna wondered if married life was always like that. Of course, most people didn't know each other well or even at all before they married, but there must be some who managed to find a degree of contentment. And there were sometimes a lucky few who had the fortune to be able to marry where their hearts led …

Isabelle was awake. Joanna realised that she'd been pushing the same bottle of rosewater around the table for some time, so she left it and went to help her mistress.

Once Isabelle was dressed she wanted something to break her fast; no formal meal was served early in the morning, but the kitchen was normally able to provide the earl's sister with something sweet and light. Joanna opened the door of the chamber and called out for a servant, but the hallway and stairwell were strangely empty. She ventured further, to the outside door, but the inner ward of the castle also seemed devoid of people. How odd. But Isabelle wouldn't want to be kept waiting, so Joanna called back that she would be but a short while, and set out across the yard towards the kitchen.

As she passed the entrance to the great hall she became aware of a crowd inside. As she stopped to look she spotted Adam leaving the building, and beckoned him over. As he came closer she could see that he looked greensick.

'Are you all right?'

He swallowed and nodded. 'Yes, mistress.'

She smiled. 'I've told you before, now that we're in the same household you can call me Joanna. Do you know what's going on in there?'

Adam looked even more sick. 'It's not good news, Mist – I mean, Joanna.'

It's not good news. He couldn't have known that those were the exact words which had been spoken to her on the day she had been informed of her brother's death; an icy hand stole around her heart and began to squeeze. She opened her mouth to question further, but no words could come out. It was then that the crowd spilled out of the door and parted, and four men stepped out carrying a shrouded figure on a stretcher. Dear Lord … but no, it couldn't be him, the body wasn't big enough. Surely it wasn't him.

She managed to speak. 'Who …?'

'It's Hamo, the marshal.'

Joanna's knees started to buckle, but she caught herself and realised it was unworthy to feel such relief when a man was dead. She tried to gather her wits.

'How did it happen? Did he fall? Or have a seizure?'

Adam shook his head. 'It was something he'd eaten. We all wondered if it was just mischance, but Edwin thinks he was poisoned.'

Dear Lord. Another murder. Had the Lord not visited enough strife and worry on them in the last few weeks? But at least this time Martin would be well out of it – there could be no reason for him to become involved in any danger. She hurried to the kitchen to fetch some wafers, sure that the Lady

Isabelle would want to hear the news, but sure also that her mistress wouldn't let it spoil her breakfast.

Up in the earl's chamber, Martin was trying his best powers of persuasion.

'Please, my lord.'

The earl gave him a smile which Martin recognised as tolerant but edging towards impatient. 'No, Martin. There's simply no need for you to get involved in something which will no doubt turn out to be a household matter.'

'But my lord – '

'I said no. No doubt this will turn out to be something very mundane – Hamo has obviously upset someone and they've decided to take revenge, albeit in a cowardly, underhand way. I'm angry that this should have happened under my roof, but I won't let it get in the way of more important matters.'

'But – '

'Enough!' The smile had disappeared completely. Martin wasn't stupid.

'Yes, my lord. Sorry, my lord.'

The earl sighed. 'Good. Now, let's hear no more about it. I can't and won't release you from your duties while there's so much to do.' He took a few paces and became more cheerful again. 'Besides, that Weaver's a clever young fellow and he'll no doubt sort it all out without needing armed help.'

Martin had to agree with that. Why would Edwin need help from someone as unintelligent as him? It wasn't as though brute force would be necessary. He was better off sticking to what he was best at.

The earl had moved on. 'Now, go and fetch my new clerk for me. He and I have much to catch up on, and I have matters of importance to attend to.'

'Yes, my lord.' Martin left the room.

Edwin knelt on the floor of the church and prayed. He was surrounded by the other villagers, some also praying, some staring into space, and some ignoring the priest altogether and chatting among themselves. As it wasn't a feast day there was no requirement to participate in the Mass or partake of Holy Communion, only to listen; however, as most of the villagers understood no Latin, and Father Ignatius was in any case gabbling even more than usual, there wasn't exactly an air of peace or spirituality about the place. Edwin *did* understand the words being spoken, but he was praying for guidance more than anything else, some help with the task which had been laid upon him. But he couldn't concentrate with Godleva kneeling so close, almost leaning in to him, so he gave up and went back to worrying. As he'd walked from the castle back down to the village, he'd realised that he didn't have the slightest clue how to go about finding out who had killed Hamo, and in his heart of hearts he wasn't even sure he wanted to know, for it would almost certainly be someone he knew.

Edwin escaped from Godleva as soon as Mass was finished, wishing he could get away from everything else as well. But he needed to get started. He tried to speak with Father Ignatius, who might know something more about Hamo or where he came from, but the priest barely had time to mention that he had to go up to the castle to say a private Mass in the chapel for the earl and his family before he was puffing his way up the hill with Edwin watching him go.

'Edwin. Are you all right? I wondered what had happened to you when you left so suddenly this morning.'

Edwin turned and smiled at his mother, who was arm-in-arm with her sister. 'I'm afraid it wasn't good – there's been a death up at the castle.' He outlined some bare facts, unsure of how much to say, but certain that news of Hamo's death would have reached the village by now anyway. In fact four men were approaching the church now, carrying a covered form. The villagers stepped back to allow them to pass, the men removing their hats as the body was carried into the church and laid down.

Cecily crossed herself. 'You must come, Edwin, and tell William the news. He was in a foul temper when he returned yesterday, swearing terribly at the men who carried him in, and I couldn't get out of him what had happened. If Hamo is dead, he'll want to hear it from you, not from village gossip and jangling.'

Edwin felt trapped. He'd known that he would have to go and talk to William sometime soon, but he had been hoping to spend a bit more time in thought first, to consider how best to approach the conversation. He needed a delaying tactic.

'I'll come directly, aunt, but first I hope you'll allow me to pray at my father's grave for a few moments.'

'Oh – yes, of course.'

Edwin's mother smiled at him wanly. 'I'd come with you, Edwin, but I have a feeling you'll want to speak to your father in peace. I'll go with Cecily now and you can come along when you're ready.' She squeezed his arm and started to shepherd her sister away.

Grateful for her tact, Edwin bent to kiss her cheek and then turned to walk through the churchyard until he found the place where his father was buried. In the weeks since his death some grass had started to inch back over the grave, but it was still mostly bare soil, a livid scar which would one day fade back into the earth, as the memories of the dead man would fade. Edwin started to kneel, but then just lowered himself to sit heavily on the ground, looking at the simple wooden cross which marked where his father's head lay.

'What shall I do, Father?' Edwin realised that he'd spoken out loud and that the one or two other people in the graveyard were looking at him strangely. He nodded at them before bending his head and crossing himself, hoping they'd go away and leave him to himself. The last thing he needed would be to find himself accused of heresy and communing with spirits. He clasped his hands together and kept his thoughts inside his head. He still couldn't quite believe that the rock of his life, the fount of knowledge and comfort, was no more, and he often still spoke to him as though he expected a reply. But his father had gone to his everlasting rest and would never answer him. Still, Edwin knew that he had been shriven just before his death, so that his path through purgatory would be short. No doubt he was or would soon be in heaven, looking down upon those he loved. Edwin sat in peace, remembering, until he felt he had gathered the strength that he needed in order to obey the earl's orders and find the culprit.

On the way out of the churchyard he passed the boy Peter coming in, and he recalled that Peter's entire family was buried there. Aware that the little lad had lost even more than he had, he stopped to greet him and ask how he was. Peter flinched and looked initially as though he would run, and Edwin remembered guiltily the way the boy had once been treated by the villagers after he was orphaned and forced to beg and steal his food. But Peter puffed out his chest and spoke in a voice which only shook a little, saying he was happy serving his new lord, even as he looked past at the graveyard. Edwin patted him on the head, seeing the tears welling up in his eyes, and left him to cry in peace.

He sighed as he crossed the village green towards William's house. How should he approach this? 'Hello William, did you murder Hamo after you threatened him yesterday?' wasn't exactly going to go down well, was it? It took only a few moments to reach his destination, but he almost balked when he reached the door. Was there anything more important he should be doing ...? Could he possibly ...? But William would be expecting him, and anyway, Cecily had seen him and was already beckoning him in.

He was surprised to find William in the cottage's main room. He was propped awkwardly on a stool, his back against the wall and one elbow on the table, his legs stretched out in front of him.

'Ha! Didn't expect to see me out of bed, I'll wager, but I'd had enough of lying there like a cripple.' He pointed to a pair of roughly hewn crutches which lay on the floor beside him.

'I won't be running races any time soon, but at least I can stand upright as a man should and get myself in here to eat.'

His face was belligerent, and Edwin didn't know where to start.

William picked up one of the crutches and used it to shove another stool towards Edwin. 'But anyway, sit. Tell me of this death. Someone finally had enough of the little weasel, did they, and stove his head in?'

Edwin looked at him sharply before lowering himself on to the seat. He explained that he thought Hamo had been poisoned, watching his uncle's face carefully all the while. But he just wasn't very *good* at reading people's thoughts and emotions, and he couldn't tell whether William was surprised or whether he was simply a good dissembler. But honestly, how could he think that William would be guilty of murder? How could he suspect someone so close to him? It was disloyal just to be considering the possibility. But then again ...

He had missed some of what William was saying.

'Sorry?'

William sighed. 'Can you not hear me? I said, never mind about Hamo, who's serving my lord? Someone is going to have to make sure that things keep running up there. I had best ...' he started to reach for his crutches, as though he would haul himself up and drag himself to the castle straight away.

It was time to release the arrow. 'You can't.'

William stopped. 'Why not?'

'Because Sir Geoffrey says not.' Edwin looked at the floor.

William was balanced precariously, one crutch under his arm. 'Why in the Lord's name would he say not?'

Edwin sat in silence, not daring to raise his head.

The crutch gave way and William collapsed back on to his stool. He sat in stunned silence.

After a few moments he whispered. 'Sir Geoffrey thinks ...?' He looked so lost that Edwin could hardly bear to meet his eyes as he nodded.

William lapsed into silence again. Edwin didn't know what to say.

'But how could he think that? How could he?' Edwin was about to interrupt, but he didn't get the chance as William's voice rose angrily. 'How could anyone think that of me? Dear Lord, I could cheerfully have killed him many a time, but how could anyone think I'd be cowardly enough to use poison? God's blood, if I'd wanted to murder him I'd have walked straight up to him and wrung his scrawny neck!' He thumped his crutch on the floor and leant forward. 'I will *not* have my name smirched like that. You and I are going to find out who did this, by God, and we are going to bring him to justice so that all men know I am innocent. We'll crack every head in the village if we need to.' He sat back.

Oh dear, thought Edwin.

Chapter Five

Edwin was in need of some peace and quiet. There were too many things in his head at once, and he couldn't concentrate on them here, not in William's house with his anger almost lifting the roof. He mumbled something about needing to attend the earl, and hurried out of the door. William's voice followed him, still shouting about the injustice, and Edwin thanked the Lord, somewhat guiltily, that he couldn't follow. The sound died away behind him as he strode up the hill to the castle and through the outer ward, crinkling his nose against the stench from the moat, which was even worse than it normally was in this hot weather. The day porter waved him through the inner gate, and he climbed the steps up to the curtain wall and sat in his favourite embrasure. Up here the air was fresher, free from the smells of tightly packed humanity, and he could look down on the busy world and think.

He let himself drift slightly while the thoughts ordered themselves, and he realised just how little he knew about Hamo. Of course, there was no reason why he should know him well – he'd only been in the earl's household a few weeks, whereas Hamo had been there as long as Edwin could remember. So what did he know? Hamo was the earl's marshal, in charge of his travel arrangements. There were a lot of these – like all the nobility, the earl moved around a great deal, although he did spend more of his time at Conisbrough than anywhere else. What else? Hamo was not the most pleasant of men and was very fussy about details; although, thinking about it, that was probably what made him a good marshal, and he'd have to have been good to stay in the earl's personal retinue for so long. He wasn't married, or at least Edwin couldn't imagine that he was, unless he had a wife somewhere whom he never saw. But where did he come from? He lived with the earl, obviously, but he must have come from somewhere. How would he have got his position? He must have come from a landowning family, maybe some minor nobility? The name Hamo would seem to bear this out.

And that was it. That was all he knew. How in the Lord's name was he going to find out who might have wanted to kill him? Was it someone who had simply got fed up with his behaviour, someone who had suffered at his hands recently, such as the serving men, or Richard the cook, or (God forbid) even William? Or was there something hidden in his past which had come back to destroy him? If there was, he needed to find out more. How would he do that? Well, there was one obvious person to start asking. Somewhat reluctantly he stood up from the embrasure and headed back down the steps, into the full heat of the sun which reflected from the stone and beat on to him, making him squint. The headache, which he'd almost managed to forget about with everything else going on, was back, but now it wasn't pounding – it was drilling into his head. How he longed for some cloud, some shade, a cool breeze, anything.

He heard Sir Geoffrey before he could see him, his voice barking in the armoury. '... and look at the state of this! You'd better get these nicks ground out of the blade before I set you to cleaning out the garderobes for a month! Any more gouges on this and you wouldn't be able to pull it out of the scabbard, and then where would you be? Back in my day you'd have been ...'

Edwin wasn't sure that this was a good idea. But he had nowhere else to start, so he stopped outside and peered round the door. He was looking at Sir Geoffrey's back but the knight had some kind of extra sense.

'What are you doing there? You can't have sorted this out already, can you?'

Edwin inserted himself into the into the dark, stuffy interior. 'Well, no, but – '

He jumped back as the sword came towards him. For just a moment he thought he was being attacked, but Sir Geoffrey had merely forgotten that he had the weapon in his hand as he turned. He looked at it as if seeing it for the first time, grunted, and shoved it hilt-first at the man he had been talking to, who took the opportunity to escape, almost tripping over Edwin's feet in his haste to be gone.

Sir Geoffrey folded his arms. His face was hard. 'So, why are you here?'

Edwin was taken aback – he hadn't expected such hostility. He knew that Sir Geoffrey was a hard man, but he'd always had something of a soft spot for him – maybe because his father had been the knight's oldest friend. But the stone face, so legendary among the castle's garrison, was now turned on him. The room felt even more airless than it had done a few moments ago, and Edwin could feel sweat breaking out on his forehead. The combined smells of metal, leather, vinegar and polish made him feel slightly queasy.

'Well, I was … that is to say …' He cleared his throat. 'What I mean is, I was just wondering if you could tell me anything about Hamo's past – where he came from, when he started working here, that sort of thing.'

'For God's sake, boy, how do you think idle gossip will help you? Our lord earl wants you to find out who killed the man, so get on with it, can't you? He was killed here, now, not twenty years ago in Reigate.'

Edwin pounced. 'Is that where he came from?'

Sir Geoffrey opened his mouth and realised what he'd said. 'Yes. Yes it is, though I haven't thought of it for many years. Why did I suddenly remember that?' He unfolded his arms and hooked his thumbs in his belt. 'And do you really think it matters?'

Thank the Lord, he seemed to have calmed down a bit. Edwin shrugged. 'To be honest, Sir Geoffrey, I'm not sure. I was just thinking about him, and I realised I knew nothing about him. Someone might well have killed him for something he'd done recently, but then again, the key might lie back in his past.'

Sir Geoffrey grunted, losing interest again and picking up a scabbard from the pile which was lying on a table. The stitching had come undone at the bottom end and he ran his finger over it before throwing it behind him. He picked up another. 'Well, whatever you say.' He kept looking at the scabbard and didn't turn to Edwin. 'Thinking about it, though, Father Ignatius might know more – I've seen them speaking together a few times. But don't get too bogged down in all this: our lord wants a quick answer and a resolution to this, and you need to make sure he gets – '

Edwin was shoved to one side by a man who ran in and stood, doubled over from lack of breath and inhaling deeply, before Sir Geoffrey. The knight looked him up and down. 'Well?'

'Nothing, sir. They must have left the district.'

Sir Geoffrey flung the scabbard back on the table. 'Damn it, you'd better hope they have. Three patrols I've sent out since yesterday, and yet none of you can find a small group of ne'er-do-wells? In your own territory?'

Edwin could probably have told the man not to push his luck, but he didn't get the chance. 'Well, sir, we have got the one in the cell ...' Edwin winced.

Sir Geoffrey took one step forward. 'One man? One man in custody? Yes, we damn well have – no thanks to you or the rest of the milksops who call themselves a garrison!' He was starting to bellow, one fist clenched, and the man tried to creep backwards, standing on Edwin's toe. 'Outlaws on *my* ground, and *my* men let them slip out while the only one we have was knocked out cold by a monk. A *monk*!' The man was starting to look desperate, and Edwin thought it might be a good time for him to leave, too. 'And he hasn't even come to himself yet, and the Lord knows if he ever will. And you stand there saying you can't find the rest! Get out of my sight before I do something you'll regret, you pox-ridden –'

Edwin didn't stay to hear the rest. He was halfway across the inner ward before the other man could leave the room. He thought he'd go into the steward's office – after all, there wouldn't be anyone in there, would there?

When he got there he was glad to see – and smell – that everything had been cleared up. He sat down on a stool and tried to marshal his thoughts, but he was disturbed by some whispering from just outside the door.

'You need to tell him!'

'Yes, but what if I get in trouble? It's nothin' to do with me. I was just at this end of the hall …'

'But you'll get in worse trouble if you don't say, won't you? I know you didn't like him – none of us did. But he'll lie uneasy in his grave if nobody finds out who did it, and you don't want him a-stalking of you in the night, do you?'

Edwin got up and walked to the door, finding two men standing outside. They stopped whispering and looked guilty.

He sighed. 'You'd better come in and tell me what you know.'

One man virtually shoved the other into the room. 'Go on then!' He himself backed away and hurried into the main hall.

The man stepped forward as Edwin went to sit back on his stool. It was one of the two he'd overheard the other night in the great hall, the one who'd said he would like to murder Hamo. He looked greensick.

'I didn't do it, sir, honest I didn't. It was just talk, like anyone would do.' He ducked his head.

'I'm not trying to say you did anything, er …' – he dredged his memory – 'Dickon?' The other nodded. 'I just want to know what you heard on the night that Hamo died.'

Dickon looked at his feet.

Edwin prompted him. 'You've already said that you were at this end of the hall.'

'Yes, yes I was.'

There was silence for a moment. 'And?'

Dickon took off his cap, revealing greasy lank hair of an indeterminate colour. 'Well, sir, I can't swear to all this, 'cause I was so tired, like, I was already half-asleep in my blanket when I first heard him. But I needed to get up to – well, to go outside, if you know what I mean. So as I'm goin' past the entrance to the office, like, I hears things gettin' thrown around in the room, so I thinks to myself, there's someone else gettin' in trouble, and I'm not goin' near there. So I creeps out, and after I've had a – well, after I've come back in, I go past the door and it's all gone more quiet, but I hears his voice – '

'Whose voice?'

'Hamo's voice, sir. It was all hoarse, like, but I'm sure I heard just the one word.'

Edwin leaned forward. 'And what word was that?'

'He said "William", sir.'

***

Mass was finished and Martin was ready for his dinner. Actually he'd been ready for his dinner for quite some time – he seemed to be permanently starving at the moment, and his stomach had been growling all through the service. He guessed it must be the effect of all the growing he'd been doing, although, thank the Lord, that seemed finally to have stopped. He was already the tallest man in the castle, and he was having trouble fitting into any of the hauberks in the armoury; he hadn't tried any of the mail chausses for a while, but he reckoned he'd have a hard time getting any of them more than halfway up his legs. He took stock of himself as he went down the stairs in the keep two at a time. There was something to be said for being taller than most, certainly – much better for any man, but especially a knight – but you didn't want to go too far. He had to bend over all the time to serve at table, which made his back ache, and he was starting to have dreams about people laughing at him because his feet touched the ground on either side of his horse. But still …

His thoughts were interrupted as Thomas flew by, tripping him and forcing him to grab at the wall to stop himself falling. People could have nasty accidents on stairs if they weren't careful, as well he knew, and he didn't want to be one of them. Damn the boy. He'd been fidgeting all the way through Mass, and the earl had even had to look behind him to see what the noise was, encompassing Martin in his forbidding gaze as well as Thomas. That was not good. Martin supposed he could sympathise to an extent – it wasn't much fun listening to the priest gabbling away in Latin, which neither of them understood, but it was holy, so the least he could do was stand still and think about God, maybe sending up some prayers of his own. He normally liked to remain motionless in the chapel and enjoy the peace, but not today. Why couldn't Thomas just learn to stay still and do as he was told? Fortunately none of the guests had been disturbed, or Martin might be looking forward to some stern words from his lord later. Mind you, if the earl wanted to berate Martin he'd probably have to queue behind the Lady Ela – as Martin expected, she'd been doting on the boy and spoiling him again, and the brat had been behaving even worse since she had arrived. Martin also had a gnawing suspicion that Thomas had told his mother about the episode with the birch: certainly she was looking daggers at him even more than usual. He couldn't be sure, but to be on the safe side he'd vowed not to go anywhere where there might be the slightest chance of encountering her alone. He winced at the thought of what she might say to him.

He reached the bottom of the stairs and strode out into the sunshine, down the wooden exterior staircase which led to ground level. The nobles were still up in the earl's council chamber, chatting and taking their time, and he was on his way to check that everything was prepared properly in the great hall. Thomas was supposed to be helping him, but he couldn't see him anywhere. He looked around and realised that Adam was following him silently: well, at least someone knew how to go about his business quietly and well. He opened his mouth to make some kind of remark, but he couldn't really think of much to say, so he didn't bother. Adam wasn't the kind for small talk either, so he wouldn't mind.

As they walked through the inner ward, he saw Sir Geoffrey near the gate, and he altered his course, hoping to catch him and ask him about the possibility of going out to the tiltyard later, or maybe even hunting. But then he saw one of the guards greet the knight, and the snarl which came his way in return, so he changed his mind and headed back towards the hall.

Adam had reached it before him, and was already checking the trenchers and dishes on the sideboard by the high table. As he loped up to join him, Martin wondered if he might be able to sneak an hour off that afternoon so he could go and see Edwin to ask how his labours were progressing. He couldn't get as far as being annoyed with the earl – it wasn't his place to judge his lord's actions or motives – but he did feel a little aggrieved that his request to help Edwin had been turned down so flatly. It wasn't as though he'd actually *enjoyed* what had gone on a few weeks ago – nobody could say that – but it had been something very different, and it had given him the chance to make a new friend. Not to mention the chance to spend valuable time talking to Joanna … he sighed as he reached the sideboard and poked at the great salt cellar to see that it was full.

Everything looked all right for the nobles' dinner, and Adam nodded to show him that he thought the same. The idea of food made his stomach groan anew, but he tried to ignore it – it would be ages until he got anything to eat, as he'd have to serve at table and make sure the earl and his family had eaten their fill before he could help himself to what was left. Which might be a while if the Lady Isabelle got going. He turned to the wine, and he was just picking up a large jug of the stuff when Thomas appeared again. Somehow he managed to trip on nothing in particular, and he crashed into Martin's legs just as he was turning. Martin lost his balance, tried to save himself, and ended up pouring wine all down the front of his tunic.

The shock of the cool liquid made him jump, and he bellowed at the boy – who didn't have a drop on him, of course – both about his tunic and the waste of the wine. Thomas stuck his tongue out and Martin realised he'd done it on purpose. All the irritations of the morning got to him and he raised his fist, really meaning to teach the brat a lesson this time, but his arm was caught from behind him.

Furiously he turned, but he couldn't hit Adam, and why was he rolling his eyes and jerking his head like that? Oh.

The noble party were on their way in, and the Lady Ela was staring at him with even more venom than her son had done after the birching episode. Thomas skipped over to her and Martin admitted defeat. He stamped off to get changed – damn it, he'd have to put on that old tunic which was too small – and wished that he was somewhere else, out in the open, riding a horse very fast, away from all these *people*.

It was crowded at the high table, and Joanna squeezed up on the bench to allow Matilda and Rosamund to sit next to her at the end. Lady Isabelle was over towards the middle, and as she had her brother and future bridegroom close to her, and plenty of squires waiting at the table, she wouldn't need any more assistance. Joanna almost rubbed her hands at the thought of a nice peaceful meal, being able to concentrate on her own food, with a bit of chat with girls her own age – something she didn't get very often here at Conisbrough, and maybe, if she was honest, the chance to keep looking up to see what Martin was … oh. Where was he? She peered around, trying not to make it look too obvious, but there was Adam, there was Thomas, there was Eustace – who she supposed she'd be getting to know better once she'd joined Sir Gilbert's household – there were William Fitzwilliam's and Henry de Stuteville's squires, but there was no tall figure looming over them. For no particular reason that she could think of, she was assailed by worry. One member of the household was already dead, to say nothing of all that trouble a few weeks ago. What if? How would she – oh, there he was. He hurried in, trying to look unobtrusive, wearing a very ill-fitting tunic that she hadn't seen for a while, the one which had a rip in the elbow. She had meant to ask him if he would like her to mend it for him, but somehow she had never got round to it … Matilda was talking to her, and she hadn't heard a word.

'I beg your pardon?' She reddened.

If Matilda did know what was on her mind, she was far too discreet to say anything about it. 'Would you pass the venison?'

Belatedly Joanna realised that the dishes had been placed on the table, and that she was forgetting her manners. 'Of course, here.'

After the three of them had helped themselves, and after Thomas had splashed some wine in a cup for her, she dipped a piece of bread in the venison's rich spiced-wine sauce and chewed thoughtfully, leaving the other two to a discussion on embroidery techniques. She tried very hard to avoid looking towards the middle of the table. Come now, have some respect. He won't want to see you staring at him like a moonstruck child. Look away. Over there, down towards the rest of the hall.

Something was different from usual. What was it? The men were all there – a little more crowded than normal, but that wasn't it. The food was on the tables, the ale in cups, everyone ready to eat … but they weren't eating. One or two of them had spoons or knives at the ready, hovering, but everyone was looking round at everyone else, and there was an uneasy silence. Oh dear Lord. It was because Hamo had been poisoned. She dropped her bread in fright and looked round, about to tell the others to do the same. But everyone at the high table was eating happily, oblivious to the disquiet in the rest of the hall; evidently there was nothing wrong with their food. She picked up her bread again and continued her contemplation of the lower hall. Someone had cracked and started to eat, and now the rest were following suit. Once they all realised that no harm had come to any, the normal buzz of conversation resumed.

The contrast in colours in the hall was quite distinct. Up here, all was bright, the noble party in their Sunday reds and greens, and even some blue on the earl's sleeves, but down there it was brown and grey, with only the occasional dark russet standing out. There was one other who was noticeable, though – a monk, a Cistercian judging by his white habit. He was sitting towards the bottom of the hall, but she could see him quite clearly as he spoke with the man next to him. He certainly had a good appetite for a monk – he was shovelling the stew off his trencher with gusto. Mind you, so was Father Ignatius at the other end of the high table, so maybe that wasn't too unusual in a man of the cloth. Did they get much to eat in monasteries? She didn't know, never having been inside one, but most of them were from good families, weren't they? So they'd hardly let them starve. When you did see them out and about sometimes they certainly didn't have that gaunt ravenous look that one associated with labourers, but they didn't exactly look like beefy warriors either. Although this one did have something of a strange air about him. She was observing him from the side, of course: the high table went across the hall on the dais, but the two long boards for everyone else ran the length of the space. As he raised his head to drink, she was suddenly struck by a resemblance to someone, but she couldn't think who it might be or where she'd remembered it from. She looked again, but now he'd turned to talk to the man on the other side of him, and the moment was gone.

Deciding that she'd just imagined it, she turned her attention back to the meal in front of her, and the conversation at the table. Sir Roger, who was two places away from her on the other side of William Fitzwilliam – she wasn't sure how that had happened, who on earth would put Sir Roger, nice though he was but a poor knight, a place nearer to the earl than the earl's own brother-in-law? – was asking if anyone had heard anything about the death of the marshal. William

Fitzwilliam, aware of the slur of his positioning next to the ladies' companions, whether deliberate or not, had hardly spoken a word during the meal. He was eating fastidiously, careful not to get food lodged in his well-combed beard or down the front of his expensive tunic. As he heard the word 'murder' he stopped with the spoon halfway to his mouth.

'Murdered? Here? Who was?' he sounded only vaguely interested.

'My lord's marshal. They found him yesterday morning.'

'Oh, one of the servants.' He spoke dismissively and sucked the sauce from the spoon without getting any around his mouth. Sir Roger, who'd already tried to interest his other neighbour, the Lady Maud, in his topic, gave up and smiled at Joanna.

'Poor old Hamo. Poisoned here in his own office, and nobody cares. May his soul rest in peace anyway.'

Joanna was about to repeat the customary phrase but she was interrupted by an exclamation next to her. William Fitzwilliam, in the act of raising his bowl to his mouth to finish off the sauce, had spilled the lot all down the front of his tunic. Joanna forgot her own thoughts as she hastened to pick up a cloth and help him blot the stain before his clothing was ruined.

By the time she'd finished mopping up the sauce, the minstrel was taking his place in the hall ready to perform another instalment of his story. A hush descended and he began, accompanying himself on the vielle as he had done the previous evening. Joanna listened to it half-heartedly: was this really the best story to choose as the entertainment for a wedding? Surely there was something which involved love: she'd heard that there were all kinds of different poems going around the country, some of which had fair ladies in them, and brave knights seeking their hands. But then again, what did love have to do with marriage? And the few ladies at the high table were the only women in the room – in the castle, in fact – and nobody would think of asking them what they wanted to hear. So a tale of war it was. She wondered if the minstrel might know some of the songs about love, and if so, whether he could be brought into the great chamber to sing to them sometime while the men were out? She would ask when she got the time.

She didn't really want to listen now, but despite herself she began to be drawn in by the tale. The minstrel's voice was mesmerising, and she listened with growing horror as Roland and his friend Olivier were lured, unsuspecting, to the ambush which had been set for them. She imagined them: brave, handsome knights sitting tall in their saddles, riding obliviously towards their doom. She remembered Giles, her brother. How had he felt on the morning of his death? Granted, he'd been killed in a tournament accident, not in a battle, but still, he would have put on his armour and mounted his horse in the same cheerful way as the heroes of the poem, never realising that the day would be his last on God's earth. She hoped Roland and Olivier didn't have sisters waiting at home for news of them.

As the minstrel acted out a conversation between the two friends – amazing how he managed to put on such different voices for each character – one phrase caught her attention. *Rollant est proz e Olivier est sage*: Roland is brave and Olivier is wise. Matilda and Rosamund started whispering to each other about which quality they would prefer in a husband. The performance came to a dramatic end, with the French kneeling to receive God's blessing before the start of the battle, to riotous applause from the hall and a flourishing bow from the minstrel. The men started to file out from the lower tables: normally they wouldn't have stayed so long at a meal, but they'd all been enraptured, and the earl, in an expansive mood this Sunday, had made no move to dismiss them.

Those at the high table remained a little longer, finishing their flagons of wine. The other companions were still debating – Rosamund putting forward the opinion that bravery was what she wanted, and Matilda arguing for wisdom – and

Joanna turned to join them. Wealth or lands earned through bravery wouldn't last long if not supported by wisdom; but then, a man wouldn't get the prize of a rich wife or lands in the first place unless he was brave. Nobody would reward a coward. The question was still unresolved among them when Joanna noticed Isabelle making a move to leave. She hastened to assist, wondering if she would ever be given a husband, and what sort of qualities he would have.

—◦—

As Edwin walked through the village on his way to find the priest, he became aware of a commotion past the furthest houses. As it was the Lord's day the villagers shouldn't really be at work in the fields – most of them took the opportunity to work in their own gardens instead – but Father Ignatius knew they were only trying to do the best for their families, so he often turned a blind eye. A group of men was coming in from the north, but there was something not quite right about it. Firstly, it would be light for a long while yet so it was strange that they should be coming back from the fields; and secondly, there was a lot of angry gesticulating going on. Edwin hurried towards them.

At the centre of the group was a small family whom Edwin recognised as being from one of the village's more isolated outlying crofts, a few miles on the other side of the river near the Sprotborough road. The woman was heavily pregnant and stumbled along with a small child strapped to her back, and the man had a bloodied bandage about his head. He was carrying an older boy whose arm was clearly broken, hanging at an angle with a rough splint about it. He was pale and whimpering with the pain.

Edwin soon found himself surrounded by the angry mob. Everyone started shouting at him at once, demanding that something be done, and through the cries he made out that the family's home had been attacked by outlaws.

Looking round, he saw that his mother was nearby, as were many of the other women. She caught his eye and nodded, putting her arm around the exhausted woman and leading her away, still carrying the tot. Cecily was there too, and with her gentle guidance Osmund took the semi-conscious boy to carry him away to her house. Edwin told the injured man – John, yes, that was it – to come with him. There was nothing much the other men could do so he suggested they get back to whatever they had been doing.

This was serious, and he needed to tell Sir Geoffrey about it straight away – Father Ignatius would have to wait. It was bad enough that Brother William had been attacked on the road, but roads were often dangerous places. This raid on a family home was something else and needed to be dealt with.

As they strode up to the castle and asked one of the guards at the gate to find Sir Geoffrey for him, it struck Edwin anew how far he'd come in just a few short weeks. Would the Edwin of half a year, or even a season ago, have dared to march up and give orders in such a way? But now he knew that he was a man to whom Sir Geoffrey would listen, though he doubted he was about to do much for the knight's foul mood.

Edwin and John continued up to the inner gate and waited. It wasn't long before Sir Geoffrey arrived, his face still thunderous. He beckoned them into the gatehouse and, looking at John's bleeding head, bade them sit.

'So, what has happened?' He spoke in English, which Edwin had never heard him do before. In fact, thinking about it, he hadn't even known that the knight had any command of English at all.

John took off his hat and twisted it in his hands. 'I, sir, I mean – ' He swallowed and looked at Edwin.

Taking pity on the tongue-tied man, Edwin spoke, also in English. 'John's home and family were attacked by outlaws, Sir Geoffrey.'

The knight's face hardened even further. 'The same men who set upon Brother William on the road?'

Edwin shrugged. 'I can't say for sure, Sir Geoffrey, but it seems likely.' He turned to John. 'Can you tell us anything about them?'

John twisted his hat again. 'There was five of 'em, sir. And they was foreign.'

Sir Geoffrey looked at him sharply. 'Foreign? How so?'

John lost his voice again at the shock of being directly addressed by a knight. Eventually he managed to mumble, 'I don't know, sir. They was talking foreign.'

Edwin encouraged him to continue. 'So what happened?'

John gulped. 'I heard 'em outside in the garden. I went out with my cudgel and saw two of 'em – pulling up the leeks, they was. I shouted at 'em to leave, but while I was out there two more came round and went in the house, and another hit me from behind.' He stopped and swallowed again. 'I'm sorry sir, I must have blacked out for a moment, being hit on the head and all. I got up and went in the house, and they was all there. They'd knocked my wife and the littl'un on the floor, and one was standing over them with his sword.'

Sir Geoffrey looked up sharply. 'A sword? Hmm.' Edwin picked up on the knight's thoughts. The men that Brother William had fought off had had swords, and he hadn't thought much of it at the time. But of course it would be an unusual thing for any common man to have. Why hadn't he considered that earlier? But Sir Geoffrey was continuing. 'And your wife? She was not …' he struggled to think of the word in English. 'She was not attacked?'

'No sir. She be with child, thank the Lord, and near her time, so that must've stopped 'em. But she were crying, and they was twisting my lad's arm to tell 'em if there was bread and meat and any money. I heard … ' he paused and swallowed hard. 'I heard his arm snap, my lord, just as I came in the house.' He was pale, his face twisted in anguish. 'I was too late to stop 'em, my lord, but I rushed at 'em again. This time one of 'em hit me good and proper, and I don't know what happened after that. When I came to myself they was all gone, and so was all the bread and the pottage and what flour we had, and what was left of last year's oats. They took the young pig we was keeping to sell in the autumn, sir, and what will we eat now over the winter? And with the oats gone, how will we live until harvest time? How will I feed my family?'

Edwin's heart went out to the man. He looked at Sir Geoffrey, who was sitting with folded arms and a grim expression.

The knight spoke. 'We will deal with this. Conisbrough has been a peaceful place for most of my life, and I will not have this.' He looked at John. 'Rest a while in the village, find someone to look at you and your wife and son to see what can be done.' He turned to Edwin and switched to French, speaking more quickly and easily. 'Law and order is the bailiff's duty, but we haven't appointed a new one yet, and besides, this needs swords, not books and words. I will lead a party out myself and we will catch these malefactors and find out what is going on. See if you can find Martin for me. Tell him to meet me in the armoury, while I assemble some men.'

Somehow he was keeping a lid on his anger, but Edwin could see the rage bubbling underneath. He hoped he wouldn't be anywhere near when it finally boiled over.

Chapter Six

Martin hurried along to the armoury. When he arrived, there was a press of men outside being issued with weapons. Sir Geoffrey stood among the melee, issuing brief orders. He saw Martin approaching. 'Edwin has told you what's going on? Good. Find your gear – you can come with me. It will do you good.'

Martin could barely believe his luck. He shoved his way through the press and into the armoury. It was dark in there, and he tripped over a man who was bending to pick something off the floor. Apologising, he made his way over to the corner where his own equipment was. Once his eyes had adjusted a little more he could see it properly, and he started to lift it down. Damn it, he could do with Adam or Thomas here – he couldn't put it all on by himself. He grabbed the nearest man and bade him help, shrugging his way into his gambeson even as he spoke, the man helping to pull the thick, heavy garment down over his shoulders so that it hung properly to his knees. Martin felt a little immobile, and briefly considered not putting on the hauberk, but Sir Geoffrey would no doubt chide him if he wasn't wearing his mail, so he allowed himself to be helped into it. He smelled the metal surrounding him as it was lifted over his head and arms, and he wriggled around to make sure it all fell into the correct position. Lord, but it was heavy – even though it was far too short for him and barely reached to mid-thigh. He needed to practise wearing it more often.

He raised his arms above his head, and his assistant put a belt around his waist and pulled it as tight as he could. Martin felt himself almost jerked off his feet, but once he put his arms down again he could feel the difference – the tight belt took much of the weight of the hauberk. He shrugged his shoulders again and waved his arms to make sure he could move them freely. Good. He picked up the nearest shield and slung it round his neck by the long guige, pushing it around so it hung at his side. He peered at the pile of plain swords which were kept for use by the garrison – proper sharp ones, not the blunt things which the squires generally used for practice – and picked out one which looked a little longer than the others. He drew it from the scabbard and hefted it, feeling the balance. What little light came into the room reflected off the blade, and for a moment he imagined himself as the hero Roland with his precious sword Durendal. When he was a knight and got a sword of his own, maybe he'd give it a name, too.

The other man was staring at him. He sheathed the blade again and belted it around him, so the weight rested comfortably on his left hip.

And that was about it – much quicker than arming the earl. There was no point trying to put on a pair of chausses, as he knew from experience that none of them were long enough for him, and he wasn't entitled to a surcoat of his own, so he merely jammed the padded arming cap on to his head, picked up a helm and tucked it under his arm, and walked back outside, pushing his hands into his mail gloves as he did so and trying not to drop anything.

He could feel his heart thumping even through all the layers of padding and armour. He was going out on a real mission like a real knight. This was his chance – not only to show that he was strong, but also that he could be clever. He remembered the line he'd heard the minstrel speak at dinner – *Roland is brave and Olivier is wise*. Maybe he shouldn't be thinking about modelling himself on Roland: Martin had never heard the poem before, but no doubt it would turn out to be Olivier who was the hero of the piece. Roland would do something brave but stupid, and he'd need to be saved by his more intelligent friend. Well, from now on Martin would aim to be like Olivier, even if it wasn't in his true nature.

Most of the other men were ready and waiting, so once Martin and the last couple of stragglers emerged, they marched down to the stables. Within a short space of time they were all mounted, and Martin felt the excitement rise within him again. He felt proud as he pushed on his helm and took his place behind the knight, sword by his side and lance balanced upright in his right stirrup.

They rode out of the gate and through the village, the people there moving hastily out of their way and looking on with respect. One or two children even ran after them, cheering. Martin threw his shoulders back and puffed out his chest.

They left the village behind and took the winding road northwards and over the bridge, past the fields and towards the forest. Once they had passed the last cultivated area, the trees became thicker. As they trotted further into the woods they left most of the sunlight behind and only a few bright spears pierced the canopy and made dappled patches on the ground. Martin felt his mail beginning to weigh heavily, and his vision was impaired by the helm, which he also wasn't used to wearing for long periods. He really needed to practise more.

Sir Geoffrey had halted and was beckoning to them all. Martin reined in his horse and moved up to make room for another man to come up beside him.

Sir Geoffrey removed his helm. 'We're not far from where they were last seen, and they'll be on foot, so they can't be more than a few miles from here. We'll spread out in groups of three, each group containing a man with a hunting horn. As soon as you locate any of them, sound your horn and the rest of us will come. Try if you can to keep them alive, as I want to find out more about what's going on, but kill them if you have to rather than letting them escape.'

Martin wondered why his mail had suddenly become a little tighter, the helm a little closer around his face.

Around him the men were dividing into small groups. He didn't have a horn with him so he'd have to find someone who did. He fumbled as he tried to turn around and look for someone, and the tip of his lance caught in a branch. By the time he'd wrestled it free and regained his balance, most of the others were moving off. His horse seemed more difficult to control than it had been earlier.

Sir Geoffrey moved beside him. He had replaced his helm and was faceless, but the hand which he put on Martin's arm was reassuring. 'Never fear. It may seem harsh to you now, but don't forget, these men have been attacking our lord's people, and will cause him more trouble if we don't subdue them quickly. We can't have that, can we?'

Martin tried to nod, but the helm wouldn't allow such a manoeuvre. 'Yes, Sir Geoffrey.' He hoped the knight hadn't heard the slight shake in his voice.

'Good. Think of it as one more step on your path to knighthood, and you'll be fine. Now, ready your shield and we'll be off.' With an ease that Martin envied, Sir Geoffrey withdrew his arm and slipped it through the enarmes of his shield, so he was holding it braced, then flicked his reins back from his right hand to his left, all without overbalancing his lance.

The two of them were left in the glade with just one other man, a guard whom Martin thought was called Turold, who had a hunting horn hanging from his belt. Sir Geoffrey turned his horse. 'Come, then.'

It was hot work, for all the shade provided by the trees. After another hour or so, Martin was drenched in sweat, the gambeson now soaked and clammy beneath his mail. He had to concentrate hard to canter over the uneven ground, while making sure that his upright lance didn't catch in any more branches, and simultaneously trying to look out for the outlaws despite his limited vision. Every movement in the undergrowth made him jump. All this would have been slightly easier if Sir Geoffrey hadn't been setting *quite* such a pace.

Finally the knight stopped, removing his helm. Martin hastily did the same, relishing the coolness of the air on his face as the sweat poured off him. 'We'll rest the horses a few moments.' Sir Geoffrey took a wineskin from the saddle of his horse – why hadn't Martin thought of bringing one? He'd try to remember next time – and unstoppered it. After taking a swig he offered it to Martin. Martin drank gratefully, some of the liquid sloshing over his chin. It was watered down and refreshing; he felt revived. He looked around, but Turold was drinking from a skin of his own. He gave the wine back to Sir Geoffrey and remembered just in time not to wipe his mailed hand across his face.

Sir Geoffrey stowed the skin again, stretched, and laughed. 'Oh, it's good to get out from the castle walls properly. Reminds me of – '

He was cut off by the sound of a horn coming from a distance, over to the west. His demeanour changed in an instant. 'Come on!' He shoved his helm back on, set his spurs to his horse and was off.

Martin felt his heart hammering as he tried to keep up with Sir Geoffrey. How did such an old man react so fast? But there was no time to think of that now. He raced headlong after the knight, crashing out of the forest and on to the road.

Within a short time he could hear shouts, and he saw three of the castle men fighting in a ragged engagement against others on foot, straggling between the road and the edge of the forest. There looked to be six outlaws, some with swords and others with cudgels, and the castle men were hard-pressed even though they were mounted. As Martin neared them, one was knocked off his horse, and he fell to the ground with a thud, rolling to get away from the hooves and from the outlaw standing over him with a sword. He couldn't get up – he was going to be killed! The sword started its descent.

But it never reached the prone man as Sir Geoffrey thundered forward, lance at the ready, and spitted the assailant like a chicken. Martin tried not to retch as he saw the steel head of the lance burst forth from the man's back, fountaining blood everywhere. Sir Geoffrey merely dropped the lance, still embedded in the body, and drew his sword. Taking one look at the faceless armed knight, the nearest outlaw dropped his cudgel and grabbed at the reins of the riderless horse, swinging himself into the saddle even as it started to run, and then setting off at a gallop back towards the road. Before Martin could react, Turold was after him, fleet on his own mount.

Martin didn't know which way to go. He span his horse around, but knew he wouldn't be able to catch Turold now. Sir Geoffrey looked to have his own situation under control as he struck down at another outlaw, and then two more castle men appeared from the opposite direction. Outnumbered, three of the remaining outlaws dropped their weapons and raised their hands, but the fourth drew a dagger and hurled it at Sir Geoffrey. Martin shouted a warning, but the knight was ready and flicked it away with his shield as though it had been a fly. However, he and his men were momentarily distracted, and one of the outlaws took his chance and darted past, sprinting towards the woods.

Martin heard Sir Geoffrey bark his name, but he was already on his way, spurring his horse towards the man as he reached the edge of the woods and disappeared among the trees. Martin plunged into the shadow after him. His horse tensed as it went suddenly from light into dark, and started to pull up; Martin had to kick it on even as he tried to keep his eyes on the quarry, his own vision impaired by the helm. The man was panicking, running as fast as he could and making no attempt to hide. Martin urged his horse forward, but it was difficult on the uneven ground and with the trees so close together. A headlong gallop wasn't going to do any good. He slowed to a rhythmic canter and brought his lance down level into the couched position, ready to strike the man down.

He ducked under branches as he rode, watching the man all the while, at one with the drumming of his horse's hooves. So this was what all that quintain practice had been about! He had it now. He drew closer to the man, who panicked and slipped as he tried to look behind him, shouting something. Martin was catching him; he was only a lance length away. What was he going to do? He couldn't bear to drive the sharp steel into the running man's back. As he drew level with the man he swept his lance sideways and knocked him off his feet. But as he tried to halt and turn his mount to stand over the fallen man, he stopped looking where he was going. A low-hanging branch smacked him squarely in the chest and he was knocked flying off his horse, the world turning over, to land with a thump on the hard ground.

Everything stopped.

He was flat on his back, gasping, winded, unable to breathe. He started to panic, unable to get any air into his body. Two other castle men had followed and were now with him, dismounting as the outlaw regained his feet and scrabbled up the nearest tree.

There was shouting, but Martin couldn't hear the words through the padding of the helm which had kept his head in one piece. One of the men helped him to manoeuvre it off, and he slowly returned to himself as he felt the air on his face; the stars receded and he tried to inhale shallowly to ease the pain. At least he could breathe. Falling to the ground in heavy armour was a lot harder than doing it in a lightweight gambeson, that was for sure. He felt like he was made of lead. But as he was helped into a sitting position he realised that he hadn't actually broken anything – at least he didn't think so, as he was sure the pain would be a lot worse if he had. All that practice at getting knocked down had obviously sunk in, and he must have relaxed as he was supposed to. Thank the Lord he hadn't got his feet caught in the stirrups. And remarkably his horse hadn't bolted, either – it was standing a few yards away. One of his companions collected the reins.

The sound of steady hoofbeats came nearer, and Sir Geoffrey trotted into the glade. He reined in, removed his helm, and looked around. He cast a glance at Martin first of all, and Martin managed to raise a hand. The briefest smile passed the knight's lips, and he nodded without speaking as he turned to focus on the man in the tree.

'It will be better for you if you come down now.'

Sir Geoffrey had spoken in English, and the man merely scrambled further up.

Martin tried to force some words out, but he didn't have the breath. He inhaled deeply, wincing, and tried again. 'French,' he croaked. The knight turned. Martin tried not to wheeze. 'French, Sir Geoffrey. He was shouting in French.'

Sir Geoffrey glared up the tree, switched language, and roared. 'Come down now! If you don't, I will fetch archers to shoot you down, and dogs to rend your broken carcass. God's blood, I'll come up there myself and break your neck!'

Martin flinched, and the man in the tree looked like he might faint with fright. The branch he was holding trembled.

Martin thought Sir Geoffrey was going to go completely mad, but he regained some measure of self-control, much to Martin's relief. 'If you come down now you will be taken for trial.'

There was an agonising pause, and then the man started on his way down the tree. When he reached the ground, the guard who had been helping Martin stepped forward and grabbed him, twisting his arms behind his back. He marched him off in the direction of the road.

Sir Geoffrey stood over Martin and held out his hand. 'Good work. Now come, it would be better to get back to the castle before dark.'

Martin took his hand and was hauled upright. There wasn't a part of him which didn't hurt.

Sir Geoffrey thumped him on the back, which didn't help. 'Besides, you're going to be as stiff as a table in a few hours, and probably unable to move for a couple of days after that, so better to get home before it sets in.'

The other castle man held out the reins of his horse, and Martin grimaced at the thought of mounting. But Sir Geoffrey himself boosted him into the saddle and passed him his lance, so Martin concentrated on staying upright as they walked their horses back towards the road.

After Martin had run off to join the other men for the patrol, Edwin thought he'd try again to find Father Ignatius; it was late afternoon, which should mean he wasn't at a service in the church. He took a circuitous route around the village to avoid passing the door of William Steward's house, in case he insisted on coming too, and found the priest on his knees in the garden outside his home, weeding around his peas and beans. As he saw Edwin approach he stood and dusted off his habit. His face was red and sweat was dripping off him.

'*Benedicte*, my son. The Lord must have sent you to speak with me, to give me an excuse to sit for a while.' He shifted a log into the shade of the house's eaves, and settled his rather portly form on it, sighing. 'This weather is not made for such as me.' He tapped his stomach. 'I shouldn't really avail myself of our lord's table so often. More fasting would be good for my soul, but alas, I find the fine food a temptation which is hard to resist.' He took off his straw hat, revealing a very red-looking tonsured head, and used it to flap at a couple of flies which were circling him. He held the hat up in front of his face to shade his eyes. 'Well don't stand there, Edwin – you're making me look right up into the sun.'

Edwin dropped gratefully to the ground next to him. Father Ignatius was the only person in the village who wasn't bone-thin, which he supposed wasn't too bad in the winter, but it must be difficult for him in this weather. Still, he didn't have to swamp himself in padding and armour, or labour in the fields, so he probably didn't suffer much. Edwin himself had thought sometimes about becoming a cleric, but the likes of him wouldn't be allowed to be a priest or a proper monk: that took money and a good family.

He realised that Father Ignatius was waiting for him to say something. 'Sorry, Father, I was distracted for a moment. I was wondering if you could tell me anything about Hamo.'

The priest crossed himself. '*Requiescat in pace.*' He hesitated. 'What exactly do you want to know?'

Edwin crossed himself automatically, although it was Hamo's earthly existence he was concerned with at the moment, not his life in the hereafter. 'Well, to start with, do you know where he came from? Sir Geoffrey said Reigate, but I don't know where that is. Is it near here? Could I go there to find out more?'

The priest shook his head. 'No. It's many days' journey from here, down in the south of the country near one of my lord's other castles.'

'Oh.' That spoilt any chance of visiting Hamo's family home – he'd never get there and back. 'Do you know anything else about him? He must have been from a noble family?'

Father Ignatius blew out a long breath. 'Not noble, no. But knightly, certainly. I think his father was a retainer of the earl.'

'But they must have had land? He didn't inherit it?'

'N-oo. They will have had some kind of estate, otherwise our lord wouldn't have taken him into his service. But I don't know exactly where, or how big. But he wouldn't have inherited anything, or he probably wouldn't be the earl's household marshal. He had several brothers, I believe, although they're all dead now.'

Something wasn't right there. 'How do you know?'

'What?'

'How do you know his brothers are dead? Everything else you said was "I believe", or "I think", or "I don't know", but you were quite certain on that point.'

The priest shifted on his seat, his face even redder. 'I'm sure I didn't – I mean, I think – '

His confused reaction confirmed it. Edwin put up a hand. 'Father, please. There's something you're not telling me. I need to find out why he died, why someone might have killed him, and to do that I need all the help you can give.'

Another uncomfortable movement. 'You know very well I can't tell you anything the man told me under the seal of confession.'

'Well, no, but – '

The priest crossed himself. 'All I will say, my son, is that things are not always what they seem, and people do surprise you.' Then he sighed. 'You of all people should know that.'

The pain of the last few weeks was suddenly so vivid, so raw, that Edwin felt dizzy. He leaned forward to try and put his head down before he crumpled. Stars appeared before his eyes and he couldn't breathe.

He felt a hand on his arm, a voice coming from far away. 'Edwin? Edwin, I'm sorry. I shouldn't have said that – I wasn't thinking about how much it must have affected you.' The hand pulled him upright again, but he kept his eyes closed. 'Come now, say a prayer with me and with the Lord's grace you'll feel better.'

The familiar words of the paternoster did indeed calm him, and Edwin felt his head stop spinning. By the time he said

'Amen' he was nearly himself again, and he felt ashamed. But Father Ignatius didn't seem to mind – his face, still sweaty and red, held only concern. 'Thank you, Father.'

The priest smiled and patted him on the shoulder. 'I'm here to give you spiritual comfort, my son. Speaking of which, I think I see another duty beckoning.'

Edwin looked up and saw a man approaching, but as he tried to see who it was he looked directly into the sun and was blinded. The man was almost upon them before he saw it was Aelfrith, a freeman of not much more than his own age who lived on an outlying farm.

Aelfrith threw himself on his knees before the priest. 'Father, you have to come quickly. Mother is dying.'

Edwin knew from his mother and aunt that Aelfrith's mother pronounced herself to be 'dying' about three times a month, so he was sceptical, but Father Ignatius showed only compassion. He took Aelfrith's hands and urged him to rise. 'Come, my son, let me fetch a vial of holy water and we will walk together to comfort her.'

Edwin winced, for it was a full three miles to Aelfrith's farm, and Father Ignatius would surely melt like butter in the blazing heat of the afternoon, but he said nothing. Conisbrough was lucky to have a priest who did his duty to the poor folk as well as the noble ones. He watched as they disappeared around the corner of the house, and then stood up himself. He'd been a little too quick, for the dizziness came upon him again, and he put out an arm to the wall of the house for a moment to steady himself. Damn it, he still wasn't any closer to finding out more about Hamo. What had Father Ignatius meant when he said that things weren't always as they seemed? There was nothing hidden about Hamo – he was just a fussy little man whom nobody liked, albeit a man who had something of a gift for organisation.

Edwin sighed. How was he going to explain to the earl that he just couldn't do it this time? He would need to talk to the priest again, and soon, but he couldn't go chasing him down the road now, not when he was on a mission to visit the sick. He'd have to try and find out more from another source in the meantime – maybe William would know something? The Lord knew he didn't want a repeat of his uncle's earlier hysterics, but he was at something of a dead end, and other than the cook, William was probably the man who'd worked most closely with Hamo. With feelings of foreboding, he set off. At least he would be able to sit in the shade and get a drink from his aunt.

He wasn't far away from his uncle's house when he heard a woman screaming. He started to run, hurdling the low gate, sprinting across the garden and bursting through the open doorway before skidding to a breathless halt. Inside there was darkness, and his aunt standing there, looking at him in some surprise.

'Edwin? What is it?' Another soul-curdling shriek came from the direction of the bedchamber and Edwin pointed, unable to speak until he got his breath back.

Cecily rolled her eyes. 'Men!' She put a hand on his arm. 'It's just Joan, John's wife who came to the village today. The walk must have brought on her labour pains. She started an hour or so ago. From what she says it sounds a bit early, but not too much, so with the Lord's grace everything will be well.'

Another scream, followed by sobbing and panting. Edwin thought he could make out the words 'Holy Mother of God, help me', but it was difficult to tell.

Cecily patted his arm again, moved away and bent to open the kist which stood against the far wall. She looked calm, but she fumbled the lid and dropped it with a bang before picking it up properly again. 'Why don't you leave us to it? Godleva's taken the little one, and William had a boy help drag him over to Robin the carpenter's place earlier so he didn't have to listen to it. If you see him you can tell him not to come back until later.' Her voice wasn't as steady as usual. She stood and faced him, a clean cloth in her hands. 'And it might also be better if you take young John along with you.'

She pointed into the corner and Edwin noticed for the first time that the boy was curled up on a blanket in the corner of the room. Huge dark eyes stared out of his pale face, and he flinched as the sounds from the other room intensified again. His injured arm was freshly splinted and he couldn't move it, but he was pressing the other hand over one ear, and trying to cover the other by pushing his head down into his shoulder as another piteous cry sounded from the bedchamber.

Edwin moved forward with speed. 'Of course. Come on now – John, was it?' He tried to sound cheerful as he helped the boy to his feet, putting one arm around him and taking most of his weight as he led him out into the bright daylight. 'Your mother will be fine, I'm sure – women do these things all the time.' But Edwin had heard women crying out with birthing pangs plenty of times before, and they hadn't sounded anything like that. As they left the house, he was glad to see Agnes, the widow who kept house for Father Ignatius and who was also the village midwife, arriving. She would sort it all out. It would be fine.

Edwin staggered a little as the boy overbalanced on to him. They wouldn't be able to go far, but he had to get him away from those terrible screams. Perhaps the best thing they could do would be to go to the church and pray for the safety of the mother and the baby which would soon arrive before its time. He took a surer grip on young John's tunic and led him away.

Joanna tripped over the hem of her skirt as she ascended the stairs which led to the keep. Really, these garments weren't made for such activity. Still, discomfort was the price to be paid for elegance; this was one of her favourite gowns, with an embroidered hem and decorative buttons on the sleeves, second only to the one she would wear for Isabelle's wedding later in the week. Once she was inside the building she crouched to examine the hem to make sure she hadn't put her foot through it, but it seemed to be intact. Thank the Lord for that. Looking around her to check that nobody was watching, she carefully scooped up an armful of the fabric to hold it up out of the way of her feet and ankles as she started up the staircase which wound its way around the inside of the keep.

This part of the way was familiar; she went to the chapel every Sunday to hear Father Ignatius say Mass, so she knew her way there. As she drew near to it, she was surprised to hear a voice from inside the room. Surely nobody would be in there now, so many hours after the service? Neither the lord earl nor his sister were overly devout. Ah, but perhaps it was the new monk, whom she'd seen entering the keep earlier.

She hesitated as she neared the doorway, then stopped and peered round into the chapel. It wasn't the monk, nor yet the priest: it was William Fitzwilliam, on his knees before the altar, hands clasped, muttering fervently to himself. She couldn't make out any of his actual words, but he appeared in deep distress. What should she do? She couldn't stand here in silence, for she had an errand to run; but she didn't want to disturb him or to have him think that she had been spying on him in any way. She tiptoed past the doorway as quietly as she could and breathed a sigh of relief that he hadn't noticed her.

She'd never been past the chapel in the keep, for the rest of it was a very masculine domain: the earl's council chamber on this floor, and then his bedchamber on the floor above and the roof above that. But there was no way of getting lost: the door to the council chamber was just here, easily visible. She stopped, unsure of herself now. But Isabelle had sent her, so she had to go on; she let her skirts fall, made sure they were adjusted correctly so that her feet couldn't be seen, and knocked softly.

To be honest, she wouldn't have minded much if there had been no reply: she could have gone back to Isabelle and told her truthfully that she hadn't been admitted. But the low hum of voices stopped and the door opened to reveal Adam. Behind him, the earl looked slightly surprised to see her, but no worse than that, and he gestured to her to enter. She stepped into the room and curtseyed.

The earl looked to be in a good mood, sitting in a large chair next to a table strewn with pieces of parchment, with Sir Gilbert facing him, both with goblets of wine. Over to one side of the room, where the light from the single window fell, Brother William sat at a small writing desk, a quill in his hand and ink on his sleeve. He looked from her to the earl, and took the opportunity to put down his pen and flex his fingers. Now she could see him at much closer quarters than she had in the hall earlier she was struck again by his resemblance to someone, but she didn't have time to wonder who it was, as the earl was waiting for her to speak.

'I – ' She cleared her throat. 'I do beg your pardon for interrupting, my lord, but my Lady Isabelle sent me.'

'Yes, I thought that would be the case. And what does my sister send you for?'

Thank goodness he didn't look angry. 'Er, if you'll excuse me, my lord, she was wondering if Sir Gilbert will be joining her, as she said he'd said he was going to walk with her in the garden after dinner.' And what cheek of her to mention it – no wonder Isabelle had sent her instead of coming herself. One simply didn't order one's menfolk around like that, not when they had important matters to attend to. She looked at the floor.

But Sir Gilbert had given an exclamation and looked out of the window at the afternoon sun. 'No, you're right, Joanna, I did say that.'

The earl laughed. 'Then get yourself hence, man. We can discuss all this later – I have other matters I can go through with the good brother here, and you'd better attend to your bride. God knows it's made my life much easier having her so content.' He waved dismissal, and Sir Gilbert nodded his head and moved towards the door, waiting for Joanna to pass through it first. As they walked past the chapel entrance, Joanna risked a glance inside, but it was empty.

———————

Edwin didn't know how long he'd been in the church when he heard the sound of someone else entering. Young John had knelt with him a while but the pain and exhaustion had got too much for him, and he was asleep on the floor. Edwin felt sure there was no sin in this, after what the boy had been through, but he had an excuse half-ready in case the newcomer was Father Ignatius.

It wasn't: it was John the elder, who had a weary look as he came and lowered himself stiffly to his knees. He crossed himself and closed his eyes, lips moving in prayer. Edwin waited until he'd finished before speaking. 'Any news?'

John shook his head. 'I went to the cottage and the women said it were all coming along. But it don't sound right to me – not like the other times, anyway.'

Edwin said nothing. He hadn't thought it had sounded right either, but what did he know? He wasn't a married man, had never sat by and listened to his wife emitting piercing cries of agony and distress as she fought to bring another child into the world. What must it be like? How could anyone bear the pain? What if the woman screaming was … he couldn't bear even to think her name.

There was silence for a few moments before John nodded at the shrouded figure lying on a trestle near to the altar. 'Who's that?'

Edwin stood, privately glad of the excuse to straighten his aching knees. 'It's Hamo, the lord earl's marshal. He died last night.'

John drew in his breath as though he was about to say something, but then he didn't. Edwin turned to face him. 'What?'

John shrugged. 'Nothing, really. I were just thinking it were an unusual name.'

Edwin thought for a moment. 'I ... would you look at the body and see if he's someone you've seen before?' John nodded so Edwin shuffled up to the bier. He hesitated with his hand out before touching the cloth, then pulled it back.

The face was black and already swelling in the heat. A fly settled on one of the eyelids and Edwin flapped it away, feeling the gorge rising in his throat.

He looked enquiringly at John, who seemed unmoved. 'Yes, I seen him before. He's rode past a few times, sometimes on his own and sometimes with one of them lords.'

'Lord? What lord?'

John shrugged again, incurious about his betters. 'I don't know. A lord in fine clothes. I heard him say "Hamo" once or twice which is why I knew the name.'

Edwin covered the body up again. They would have to sort out the burial soon, for the corpse would soon putrefy in this heat. But what in the Lord's name could Hamo have been doing? 'You live out near the Sprotborough road, don't you?'

'Yes, west of it about half a mile, up a track. Why?'

Footsteps sounded from the doorway of the church. They both turned to see a black shape, the spectre of death outlined against the evening sun outside. Edwin shivered, and heard John catch his breath beside him. The figure moved forward and he could see that it was Cecily. She hadn't yet washed herself properly after attending to John's wife, and there were streaks of blood down both her arms and on her hands. Edwin stared at them, examining the paths they had tracked across her skin, in order to avoid having to look at her face, but he had to do it sometime. He looked up at the dulled eyes, at the deep sadness etched into her features.

Her words were aimed at John. 'I'm sorry.'

John buried his face in his hands.

Chapter Seven

Edwin left the church to give John some time alone with his grief. Outside, the glorious sunset mocked him as he slumped to the ground and tried to pray. Dear Lord, please take John's wife and his dead child into Your kingdom. They did nothing wrong; they were simply in the wrong place at the wrong time, as sometimes happens. Why do You let common folk be treated this way? Must it always be so?

He looked up as Cecily's shadow fell across him. She stood looking down at him for a moment, and then lowered herself to the floor. Edwin could see the tracks of the tears on her face, and he reached out to hold her hand, heedless of the dried blood on it. He'd seen plenty of that recently himself. She gripped hard, and sniffed as she tried to compose herself, breathing deeply.

'Do you know what the worst thing was?' Her voice was unsteady.

'Tell me.'

She took a shuddering breath. 'Not only did she die screaming, but she knew that her son was dead and that he hadn't been baptised.'

Edwin felt a cold chill despite the heat of the day. Not baptised? Dear Lord. The guilt crept up from his stomach, reaching for his throat. He'd seen Father Ignatius, had watched him go off to visit Aelfrith's mother. Why hadn't he said anything? Why hadn't he stopped him, chased after him, made him wait? Now the baby would be denied entrance to God's kingdom, would be left outside the gates for all eternity. And what about …?

Cecily saw what he was thinking. 'Joan, bless her, was shriven before it happened. As soon as her pains started around noon we called Father so she could confess, but I let him go – after all, these things normally take hours, even days. We had no reason to guess it would all happen so quickly.' She could hold back the tears no longer, and gave a long, gasping sob.

Edwin wasn't quite sure how to react. His mother's sister had always been there to offer him comfort when he needed it, had watched over him, and now she was looking to him. He did the only thing he could think of, which was to put his arm around her and wait until she had stopped crying.

The shaking of her shoulders grew gradually less, and he patted her awkwardly on the shoulder. 'Come now. Come, let's get up and walk, it'll be better than sitting here too long. And besides, a wash will do you good.' He helped her to her feet, and supported her as they moved towards the gate of the churchyard.

As they neared the road through the village, Edwin became aware of the sound of many hooves, and he turned to see Sir Geoffrey at the head of a party of men. Yes, they'd been out in search of the outlaws, hadn't they. Well, it looked like they'd found them. One of the men had a body lying across the horse in front of him, but there were, thank the Lord, no empty saddles, so the corpse wasn't one of the castle men. Behind the riders came seven or eight men on foot, their hands bound in front of them, tethered by long ropes held by several guards. As they passed, some of the villagers came out of their houses to see what was going on, and one or two of them spat at the bound outlaws.

'You bastards!' The voice was high with emotion, and Edwin wasn't quick enough to catch John as he hurtled past, throwing himself at the group of prisoners, knocking several of them to the ground as he screamed that he would kill them all. At once there was a melee of bodies and of shying horses, ropes becoming entangled around thrashing limbs. Edwin leapt forward to try and restrain John, who was struggling to draw the eating knife at his belt as he was borne down by the press of men. Eventually he managed to grab the enraged man, and together with one of the guards, who had by now dismounted, he pulled John's arms behind his back and held him still, panting.

Sir Geoffrey, still on his horse, watched as his men regained order, and then nosed his mount along to where Edwin was standing. He looked grim, and Edwin hastened to explain. 'He didn't mean to cause trouble, Sir Geoffrey, I'm sure he didn't. His wife has just died, and the baby too, so to see them coming past must have been too much. Please, Sir Geoffrey.'

The knight's face was stony, but Edwin thought he saw a glimmer of compassion as he looked down at John, weeping and now on his knees, moaning his wife's name. 'John, get up, you are forgiven. These men are outside the law, so even had you succeeded in wounding one there would have been no charges. Your actions are understandable, and I promise you they will face justice.' He turned his horse back towards the castle. 'Forward, men, and get them all inside the gate.' He looked back again. 'Edwin, see that John and his son ...' – Edwin turned to see that the boy had emerged from the church and was standing with Cecily – 'have somewhere to rest.'

Edwin's 'Yes, Sir Geoffrey' had hardly left his lips before the men were off again. The guard who had helped him restrain John gripped his shoulder in sympathy and remounted to follow the others. It suddenly struck Edwin that he hadn't seen Martin – surely he would have dismounted to help hold the distraught man? Where was he? He looked at the riders and spotted Martin among them, drooping in his metal hauberk. He was bare-headed and his face was completely white, eyes half-closed; he was swaying in the saddle. He seemed to be using all his strength just to stay on the horse, and he didn't even look at Edwin as his mount plodded up the hill behind the others.

Cecily and the boy stepped forward to John's kneeling form. She looked at Edwin. 'I don't know how to comfort him, but

I can take him home with me for now. Agnes has been laying out the bodies, and he'll want to see them. Thank the Lord Sir Geoffrey didn't rebuke him as well.'

Edwin felt his own voice coming from far away. 'I think Sir Geoffrey realised that when you've lost something, you want revenge.' Lord, but he was tired. He thought he'd go home and get some rest; he seemed to have no energy at the moment, and he was starting to ache all over. But he was to get no respite – as he started to put one leaden foot in front of the other he heard urgent footsteps pounding behind him, and a breathless voice. 'Edwin, Edwin!'

Edwin turned to see Dickon, the serving man he'd spoken to about Hamo, hurtling towards him. Dickon reached him, skidded to a halt and grabbed Edwin's arm. 'You have to come. You have to come right now.'

Joanna was enjoying the last of the evening sunshine on her face as she followed Isabelle and Sir Gilbert through the main gate, toying idly with the flower she'd picked. They had been out for a walk around the outside of the castle, where there was a sort of pleasure garden on the north side. It wasn't formally laid out like the one at her cousin's residence, where they had lived when Isabelle had been married to him, but at least out here they could talk in peace for a while, away from the cramped inner ward and the crowded outer one, and there was something of a meadow which ran down towards the river. She had ambled along behind them, ready in case she was wanted, but mainly keeping a discreet distance and daydreaming. Isabelle had been the beneficiary of a colossal stroke of fortune – imagine falling in love with the very person you were told to marry! How many women did that happen to? She didn't know, but not many, to be sure. All right, so some of them eventually achieved a kind of contentment, especially if they had a lot of children – well, a lot of sons, anyway – to look out for, but really, the kind of heart-singing, joyful love that poets sang about was either non-existent or aimed catastrophically at the wrong person.

Her thoughts turned to Martin and she sighed. She just couldn't see a way out of the situation they were in. Her heart leapt every time she saw him, and he remained in her mind's eye even when he wasn't around, but it was impossible. For a start, no squire was ever married, and it would be a good few years before he became a knight and was maybe awarded a manor of his own. Then there was the difference in station – although he was in the earl's household, his own family was not among the foremost in the realm, and hers was; admittedly, she was but a lowly distant cousin of the head of the family, but she bore the de Lacy name and she would be expected to form a suitable political union. She supposed she could get away with marrying someone with a lesser name if he happened to be very rich, but that wasn't likely to happen either. And quite apart from all this, her place was with Isabelle, and once she married Sir Gilbert they would all move to the south coast, and virtually the whole length of the realm would separate them. There might be the odd fleeting glance whenever the lord earl stayed at his castle at Lewes, but he didn't do that very often, and anyway, how would they ever get to talk to one another? She sighed again, more heavily this time, and realised she'd shredded the flower between her fingers. She threw it aside as they entered the inner ward.

Isabelle had heard her, and turned. 'Joanna, whatever is the matter with you today? If you start huffing any more than you already are then you'll – ' She was stopped by a gentle touch on her arm from her paramour. He smiled at Joanna in some sympathy, and her heart groaned again at the notion of having a strong, capable and tender man to look after her. Of course, Martin didn't have that assured grace and authority, but he was younger, he would grow into it, and he did have that deep voice, and the way the muscles in his forearms moved when he reached forward to pick something up from the table …

There was shouting going on. Mounted men were arriving in numbers in the outer ward, and three of them rode straight up through the inner gate. Sir Gilbert made sure his betrothed was safely out of the way, and then reached to pull Joanna from the path of any possible harm as well. As she stood she looked up at the riders. One was Sir Geoffrey, shoving his helm towards one of the guards who'd appeared in order to take his reins, and dismounting with the ease of a much younger man. One of the others was Martin, and she felt her heart beating a little faster. He was swaying in his saddle, and as she watched Sir Geoffrey and the other man move towards him to help, he fell sideways off the horse and crashed, unmoving, to the floor.

She heard Isabelle give a little scream beside her. The urge to throw herself forward was almost overwhelming, but she had to resist it, she must, or she would be ruined. She couldn't show favour like that. Sir Gilbert had moved swiftly, and he and Sir Geoffrey were kneeling next to the prone figure. He came back to them. 'He'll be fine, but he'll need some looking after for a while. They'll take him to Sir Geoffrey's chamber.'

Isabelle started to speak but then stopped and cast a long look at Joanna. Joanna knew she must look terrible, had felt the colour draining out of her cheeks, but she was rooted to the spot and couldn't open her mouth. And then, blessedly, miraculously, Isabelle was telling her to find cloths and water, herbs and poultices, and to go and tend the stricken squire as was her duty in the household. Could this really be happening? She stammered something which even she didn't understand, picked up her skirts and ran.

The heat hit Edwin like a wall as Dickon dragged him into the castle kitchen. It was oppressive, beating him back as sweat started to pour from him – and it was evening. Dear Lord, it must be like hell on earth when the cooking fires were roaring during the heat of the afternoon. Dickon spoke in his ear before melting away. 'You're the only one who can stop them.'

In the centre of the room, Richard Cook and William Steward were squaring up to one another, in the middle of a furious argument. William had his crutches under his arms and was leaning on the kitchen table as he bellowed, '... and poison, he said. *Poison!* Where can that have come from if not from here?'

Richard, huge, choleric, sweat dripping, loomed with his red face inches from William's. 'Don't you *dare* slander my name! He was in *your* office when he died, and ...'

Edwin looked around him. The kitchen staff, wearing only their braies and looking exhausted after their labours since daybreak, were clustered around the walls. Often a fight between two castle men would be an occasion for raucous cheering, with spectators encircling them and egging them on. But this was different; nobody moved. The men were white-faced, and the potential for real violence lay heavy in the stifling air. Edwin edged around so he could place himself between the argument and the row of shining knives laid out on the table.

The tipping point came. William's voice was getting hoarse, and it rose in pitch. 'I've never trusted you anyway, you foreigner, coming here and ...'

Richard's lungs reached full capacity, drowning him out. 'At least I can do my *job!* My lord brought me here because I'm the best – not some cripple who can't count! You only got yours out of *pity*.' He raised his hand and poked William in the chest, hard.

Edwin lunged. Fortunately he was quicker than William, who had to drop one crutch to free his hand, and he managed to throw himself between the two men before the fist connected. He pinioned William's arms and tried to drag him away, shouting to the men around to help as Richard took a step forward. But not one of them would dare touch their master; Edwin was on his own.

Richard hesitated and made no move to strike. Edwin spotted the moment of weakness and hissed in a low voice. 'Richard, for God's sake, can we move this away from all these men? Haven't you got a side room or something?' He stumbled. William was now concentrating more on trying to stay upright than on attacking Richard, and he was heavy.

'No, there isn't one.' Richard looked around him. 'All of you – out! Get some air. You can come back in to sleep when it's dark.' As the men started to shuffle out, he bent to pick up William's crutch, handing it back to him without looking in his face.

Edwin felt some of the weight lifted, though he still kept his arm round William to help him balance. 'Can we sit down?' He scanned the room but there were no chairs or stools – the kitchen men worked standing up at the fires or round the giant table. But against one wall was a low bench, currently holding baskets of trenchers, so he started to move towards that. Richard hefted the baskets out of the way and they all sat, Edwin placing himself between them.

Dear Lord, but it was *hot*. Edwin pulled at the neck of his tunic and wiped his sleeve across his forehead, realising too late that he'd been doing that a lot today and that his new tunic was getting filthy. His headache was coming back. If he'd thought quickly enough he could have left the other men in here while he took William and Richard outside, but it was too late now. He looked from one to the other, both silent. These men had always been figures of authority to him, but now they shuffled their feet and looked at the floor. It was up to him.

'Right. Listen. I don't believe either of you had anything to do with Hamo's murder. And I don't think you do either.'

There was silence.

'Neither of you liked Hamo, but neither of you would kill him. And certainly not by poison. But listen, *this* is not helping. Our lord has asked me to find out who did this, and it's difficult enough without you two starting a war.'

It was all too much. He had to stop or he was going to cry at the hopelessness and frustration of it all. He leaned back against the wall and let his head rest for a moment. Beside him, Richard grunted. 'All right. And the sooner you find out who did it, the sooner people can stop pointing fingers at us.'

William nodded. 'Agreed. But poison – you have to agree the kitchen is the most likely place for it to come from.'

Edwin looked at Richard in case he was about to get angry again, but he just waved his arm. 'So you say. But what about when the food is on its way here? And what about other poisons – medicines and the like?'

Edwin sat up again. 'I hadn't thought of that. But Hamo was eating his meal, not taking medicine for anything, when he died.'

William spoke again. 'What was he eating?'

Richard exhaled. 'I've been over that in my mind, but it was just what everyone else was having: mutton pie, vegetable pottage, and bread. All made in here and all brought out together, though I hear Hamo didn't sit down at the table with everyone else.'

Edwin broke in. 'That's right – I saw him at the door to the service area. He was checking everything was all right at the high table, what with the guests arriving early, and he must have put his on a tray in William's office and had it by himself later.'

Richard nodded. 'So someone must have poisoned it then. There were so many pies coming out of here, you could never have told which one was for whom. They just get passed out.'

William thumped a crutch on the floor. 'So you need to find out who might have gone in there after the meal and before he ate. That can't be too difficult, surely?'

Edwin's head was pounding again. 'You know what it's like at mealtimes. There were dozens of people milling around. It would be really difficult to pick out just one man who went in there.'

'Well, whoever he is, he'd better go and hang himself before you find him. I've seen what they do to poisoners.'

'What do they do?'

William opened his mouth to speak again, then shut it and patted Edwin on the shoulder. 'You probably don't want to know, lad.'

Edwin rubbed his sleeve on his face again. 'Anyway, we'd better get back down to the village before it's full dark. Come on.' He stood.

Richard and William, left on the bench, looked at each other directly for the first time. Richard stood and held out his hand. 'I'll help you as far as the gate.'

Edwin reckoned that was as near as they'd ever get to discussing what they'd said to each other earlier, but it was good enough. William took his hand, heaved himself up, positioned his crutches under his arms and dragged himself along, Richard beside him.

The cool air was new life to Edwin as they stepped out of the kitchen. He thanked the Lord for the slight breeze and hoped that his head would clear enough for him to be able to think properly once he got back to the cottage. There was no chance of sleep, but the quiet of the night might help him to rest a little.

The kitchen men who were standing or sitting around made their way back in, although one or two looked as though they might stay outside to sleep, and who could blame them? They reached the inner gate, and Edwin took Richard's place, ready to throw his arm around William's waist and grab a handful of his tunic to steady him if necessary. Then they made their slow and halting way towards the outer gate and the road to the village.

William was starting to flag long before they got there, and Edwin was very glad when they reached the cottage. Cecily came out to help, but William waved her away and dragged himself over the threshold.

As he watched, something occurred to Edwin. 'William?'

It was too much effort for William to turn round again, so he spoke over his shoulder. 'What is it?'

'You called Richard a foreigner. I thought he'd always been here?'

'Well, he's been here a good while – since you were born or thereabouts, I reckon. But he's from one of my lord's other lands, down south.' Leaning on his wife, he moved further inside the cottage, so his voice came out of the dark. 'Reigate, I think.'

As Edwin walked up to the castle in the bright light of dawn, his head felt like it might become detached from his body. The grogginess, from yet another sleepless night, was adding to the headache, which had now spread down his neck. He was struggling to put one foot in front of the other, never mind think straight. But he was still nowhere in terms of finding Hamo's killer, and he also wanted to find out if the outlaws had anything to do with it. He didn't dare approach Sir Geoffrey, but he thought Martin might be able to tell him more about their capture yesterday, as well as appreciating some company.

He reached Sir Geoffrey's chamber and walked in, questions already on his lips. But as he entered he saw Joanna sitting close by the side of the bed, her hand laid on Martin's forehead, and he nearly fell over his feet in his haste to get out of the room again, his face hot. Why hadn't he thought to knock? But Joanna had risen with speed and was calling him back.

'Edwin, come back. There's nothing – I mean, I was just checking his injuries to see if he needed a salve on his head. But it's fine, really. Please come back in.' She looked flustered and her cheeks were red. He followed her and approached the bed. There was only the one stool in the room, so he gestured to Joanna to sit on it again while he stood and looked down at Martin. The squire was very pale, and he looked as though he was in quite some pain.

'So, how do I look?'

Lying was a sin. But perhaps honesty could be watered down a bit? 'You don't look too bad at all. There's certainly nothing wrong with your face – you don't look nearly as terrible as Adam did that time when he got beaten up – and from what I can see of your feet sticking out the end of the bed, you've still got both legs. How do you feel?'

Martin grimaced. 'Like I'm on fire all over. And like I'm tied to a board. To start with I didn't think it was so bad – I even got back on the horse and rode back. But as we got nearer I could feel myself stiffening up, and by the time they'd got my armour off and put me here, I couldn't move. Sir Geoffrey said I'll be fine in a couple of days, but right now I'm starting to go black and purple all over and I don't think I could get out of this bed if it was on fire.'

Edwin nodded in sympathy. 'But you have no wounds anywhere, no cuts? Nothing's broken?'

Martin shook his head. 'No, thank the Lord.' Joanna crossed herself and Edwin gave a small prayer of thanks. Broken bones could cripple a man for life, and open wounds were even worse – many a man was killed by cuts which looked harmless to start with, for if they had the wrong humour in their blood then the wounds went bad and they died from the poison.

'So, what happened? How did you find the outlaws, and what were they doing? How did you capture them?'

Martin tried to raise himself, failed, and moved one hand stiffly as he gestured to Edwin to come closer. Edwin settled himself on the floor next to the bed, his legs crossed. Joanna was still on the stool, dipping a rag into a bowl of water and dabbing it on Martin's head. Martin looked up at her gratefully, and Edwin tried to ignore the awkward feeling he had at being here with the two of them. He listened as Martin outlined the events of the previous afternoon.

As the squire finished his tale Edwin shuddered at the thought of the man being torn to pieces by dogs. How could Sir Geoffrey threaten such a thing? How could he be so ruthless? He had never seemed that way, or at least not to Edwin – but perhaps that was what he was like when he was dealing with enemies. Edwin had seen enough knightly violence in the last few weeks to know that even the most pleasant-seeming men could be capable of atrocious violence under certain circumstances. But Sir Geoffrey? He wasn't sure he'd ever be able to look at him in the same way again. But then again, the outlaws were responsible for the death of Joan and her baby. His sympathy for the men wilted as he recalled the blood on Cecily's hands and the look in her eyes.

He realised that Martin had stopped talking. 'So, what will happen to them now?'

Martin tried to shrug, and then winced. 'My lord and Sir Geoffrey will try and find out why they're here and where they've come from, I guess, but there seems little doubt that they're the ones who have been causing all the trouble, so I guess there'll have to be hangings.'

There was silence.

It was Joanna who broke it. 'So, Edwin,' she said in a voice that was just a little too brittle, 'how have you been getting on? Have you found out who killed Hamo yet?'

It was Edwin's turn to shrug. 'I seem to be no closer than I was when I started. All I know is that he comes from somewhere miles and miles away, he used to have lots of brothers, and someone thinks he heard him say "William" as he was dying.'

Joanna paused with the rag in the air. 'William? Well, that's not much help. I can think of at least half a dozen Williams without even trying.'

Martin nodded. 'You can hardly find a family without a William in it somewhere.'

'I know.' Edwin was morose. How in the Lord's name was he going to find out any more?

'I'll tell you what, though.' Martin had spoken again and the other two looked enquiringly at him. 'I was angry that my lord wouldn't let me help you out as he needed me to stay with him, but I'm going to be no use to him for a few days anyway, so maybe I can help.' He flapped his hand. 'Oh, I don't mean I can run round and talk to people, but you can come here when you get the chance and tell me everything you've found so far. I know it helps you to get things straight in your own mind when you tell someone else.'

He was right, Edwin realised, although he'd never thought of it in exactly that way before. But yes, the chance to talk things through and to share the burden would be wonderful. The Lord knew he missed being able to sit with his father, and since he'd also lost … but better not to think of that, of him. That was over, dead and buried, and he needed to build himself a wall to stop his mind going there. He needed to think about something else. Think. Richard the cook came from Reigate. Did that have any bearing on anything? Might he have known Hamo before? And who in the Lord's name was 'William'?

There was a knock at the door and Adam poked his head round.

'Edwin, my lord earl wants to see you.'

Edwin's stomach gave a lurch as Adam led him from the room. He followed the squire over to the keep and up to the council chamber, a journey just long enough for his mind to create terrible scenarios. Had he done something wrong? Was he about to be castigated for something, those slate-grey eyes boring into him? He stood with his hands behind his back as Adam melted into the background, and tried to work out what sort of mood the earl was in. He wasn't throwing anything, which was a good start, but he didn't look exactly happy, either.

'Weaver, good.'

He really must ask Sir Geoffrey if he knew why his father had been called that. He'd never actually been a … but the earl was speaking.

'… and you'll realise how inconvenient this is for me.'

'Errm … Yes, my lord.'

'Adam works hard enough,' the earl threw half a smile over to the side of the room, and Edwin saw Adam straighten, looking as though someone had given him a bag of gold, 'but he can't cover for Martin as well as for that blasted boy. There just aren't enough squires around to serve everyone, and I won't have my sisters gossiping that they had to put up with less than perfect service here. You're the only other one I can think of who has manners fit to be anywhere near my family, and besides, you understand French properly. While my sisters are here and for a day or two until Martin recovers, Adam will stay with me and you will station yourself in the great chamber whenever they are in there to serve them and run any errands they want. Understood?'

'But – ' Edwin tried to stop himself but the word came out his mouth before he could prevent it. The earl stiffened and stopped his pacing to look at him. Dear Lord, he had started to contradict one of the most powerful men in the kingdom. How had he so far forgotten himself? The earl had his arms folded and his eyebrows raised. He'd have to say something now.

'S-sorry, my lord. I beg your pardon for interrupting. I j – ' his mouth was dry. 'I just wanted to ask what I should do about Hamo while I'm doing as you command?'

The earl grunted and waved one hand. The storm seemed to have been averted, thank the Lord. 'Hamo? Haven't you sorted that out yet? What do I pay you for?'

Even Edwin wasn't foolish enough to respond to that. The earl spoke again. 'Although that does remind me that I'll need a new marshal or we'll never get the household out of Conisbrough again.' He flicked his fingers at Adam, who sprang forward. 'Go and find Sir Geoffrey and bring him here.' Adam sped away, and Edwin felt a flicker of sympathy for the dead man. He certainly hadn't liked Hamo, but it was an ill thing that not one person seemed to be upset by his death.

The earl was continuing, almost to himself, as he walked through a shard of bright sunlight to look out of the narrow window-slit. 'God knows I've got enough to do when I'd rather be out hunting on such a fine day.' He turned again. 'Are you still here?'

He was half-amused rather than angry, but Edwin wasn't taking any chances. He bowed and backed towards the door until his heel touched it, and then went out and ran down the stairs as quickly as he could.

Chapter Eight

Edwin left the earl's council chamber and walked across the inner ward towards the great chamber, his dread increasing with every step. He stood outside the door for some while, wondering whether he was supposed to knock, or whether he should just open it and go in as quietly as possibly. In the end he compromised, knocked so quietly that nobody could have heard him anyway, opened the door a crack and peered round. The room was empty.

Puzzled, he went back outside, but he couldn't see anyone in the ward either. But there was noise coming from the great hall – of course, it was dinner time. He had so little appetite at the moment that he hadn't noticed. Oh well, they wouldn't want him until afterwards. He moved into the shade cast by the buildings and looked around.

A wet, retching noise sounded from quite near him and he jumped, thoughts of poisoning and death leaping into his mind. He looked further into the shaded corner where the wall of the great chamber met that of the hall, to see the minstrel vomiting out a stream of liquid. Oh dear Lord. He raced over and grabbed the man's arm. The minstrel gagged, spitting out more liquid and bending over double while Edwin looked on helplessly.

Eventually the coughing subsided and the minstrel looked up. He spoke in a strangled voice. 'What in God's name did you do that for?'

'Oh, thank the Lord you're all right! Er, what?'

'Grabbing me like that, you fool! You could have choked me!'

'But I thought you were choking already – that's why I ran over. I heard you being sick.'

The minstrel held up an empty cup. 'I was gargling, you halfwit. A hot infusion with honey in it, for my voice.'

Edwin wasn't sure whether he felt more relieved or stupid. 'I'm sorry. We've had a man die by poisoning recently and when I heard you making that noise and then saw you spitting it out, I thought ...'

'Yes, well, you were wrong.' The minstrel cleared his throat. 'Happily, it looks as though I will be all right to perform, no thanks to you. I have Roland's death to tell of, so I must be in perfect condition. It's one of the greatest scenes ever composed.'

'He dies? Oh ... I haven't been listening to all of it so far, but isn't he the hero? Isn't that going to be a bit of a sad way to end?'

The minstrel laughed. 'End? It's only halfway through. Don't you know anything? He dies, yes, but the mighty French army returns to crush the Saracens in revenge. The second battle is even better than the first one.' He moved towards the entrance to the hall, listening. 'It sounds like they're nearly ready for me, so stop pestering and let me prepare.' He picked up his musical instrument, which Edwin hadn't noticed lying on the ground, and stood by the door, ready to make his entrance.

Edwin went back up the steps and into the passage between the hall and the great chamber. It was a strangely shaped space, covering a corner and under the flight of stone stairs which led from the ward up to the wall-walk. If he waited here, he'd hear when the nobles were approaching, and he could slip in among the squires, hopefully without anyone noticing. He sat down with his back against the wall. Death. Blood. Fighting. Revenge. This was entertainment? He didn't think he'd ever understand these nobles.

He had no idea how long he'd been there when he heard the sound of people approaching from the great hall. The door opened – the one which led from the dais at the top end of the hall, so the nobles didn't have to go out the same door as everyone else – and the party swept through to the great chamber. Edwin joined the end of the group and went in. He looked surreptitiously at what everyone else was doing, and then took up a position at the very edge of the room, his legs as weak as grass in the wind, his trembling hands clamped behind his back, hoping that nobody would notice him. The Lady Isabelle settled herself in the centre of the room – the Lord knew what sort of response he'd get from her if he did anything wrong – together with the earl's other two sisters, their husbands, the two boys he'd seen arriving the other day, and Sir Roger and Sir Gilbert. To one side were Mistress Joanna and two other young ladies, who had taken up their sewing and were talking in low voices, and ranged around the walls were some other boys and young men, pages and squires. Eustace was one of them, and he'd given Edwin a slight if somewhat confused nod as he entered and took up his station.

Edwin had no idea what he was supposed to be doing. He stared at the nobles. What would they do if they wanted him to do something? What would be the signal? Did they actually ask, or were you supposed to just know?

He jumped as the tall thin man snapped his fingers at him. Edwin looked round in confusion. What did he want? The finger-snapping intensified and the man looked round in irritation. Edwin felt himself starting to panic. His eye was caught by a sudden movement across the room, and he looked to see Mistress Joanna gesturing to him out of the line of sight of the nobles. Once she saw he was looking, she mimed pouring something, and then pointed to a table near him. He saw on it a jug of wine and understood, thank the Lord. He picked it up and moved towards where the man – the earl's brother-in-law, but he didn't know which one – was sitting. There was an empty goblet near his elbow, so Edwin poured wine into it as carefully as he possibly could, and then stepped back to the safety of the wall, replacing the jug on its table. The nobleman didn't even look round at him, so he must have done it right. His hands were shaking so he put them behind his back again, picking nervously at his fingernails.

The men were discussing the episode from the Roland story which they had just heard. From what Edwin could gather, they'd all heard something completely different, and now he wished he'd gone back in to listen so he knew what they were talking about.

Sir Roger was arguing his point. 'But don't you see? Roland is inspired by our Lord God: he's fighting for the Christians against the pagans, so he dies a martyr.'

Sir Gilbert shook his head. 'I take leave to disagree with you, Roger – yes, he's fighting against the pagans, but he's fighting for his lord, doing as he was ordered. He's a vassal who obeys his king's commands to the end. *And* he was the victor in the field, because the pagans had fled.'

The tall thin man joined in. 'Yes, but what good did it do him? You say he was the victor, but he lost every single one of his men and left the Saracens alive so they could fight another day. What sort of service is it to one's lord to deprive him of twenty thousand of his men, and of Roland himself, for that matter?'

Sir Gilbert raised a finger. 'All right, Sir William, I concede your point. But what would you have him do? If your orders are to fight to the last man, how do you reconcile service to your lord with disobeying him to stay alive?'

Edwin made a mental note that the thin man must be William Fitzwilliam. He watched him shrug. 'To be honest, I'm not sure – fortunately I've never been in that position, so I don't know what I'd do if I were. But I do think that caution and prudence are the best courses of action on most occasions. That way you live to fight another day.'

Sir Gilbert sat back, a look of sadness on his face, and Edwin knew whom he was thinking of. A little thorn scratched his own heart as he remembered the merry smile and devil-may-care attitude. He put one hand on the dagger given to him by the knight who had saved his life.

The other brother-in-law, the one with the huge beard who must be Henry de Stuteville, was disagreeing with both of them. 'The point is, you should never get yourself in an impossible situation in the first place. A bit of forward planning from young Roland might have helped everyone.'

Sir Gilbert smiled despite himself. 'But you must agree, sir, that that wouldn't have made anything like such a good story!'

They all laughed. But Sir Roger, unsurprisingly, was still trying to push his own, more religious, view. It was common knowledge – even Edwin knew it, so it must be common – that Sir Roger had ambitions to go on crusade himself one day; it was easy to imagine him smiting the heathen with the divine light of righteousness on his face. Edwin caught some of what he was saying: 'But you haven't mentioned the crucial point, which is that as Roland dies, our Lord God accepts his glove in tribute, and sends His angels to bear Roland to Heaven. And *that* is because he's fighting for the Christians against the pagans, not because he's simply following orders …'

Edwin began to lose interest. As he hadn't heard the relevant bit of the poem, he didn't really understand all this. And besides, all the bits he had heard were either hugely gory, which he didn't find entertaining, or didn't make sense. Seriously, that Ganelon fellow – Roland's father, was it? But surely no father would be so at odds with his son – was, to everyone else listening, the villain of the piece. He was the traitor who was setting Roland up to be killed. But at the beginning of the poem he'd actually had a fair point: the pagan king was offering to hold Spain as Charlemagne's vassal and to become a Christian, which was what they actually wanted, surely? But all the men in the hall had erupted in boos, whistles and catcalls as soon as Ganelon had spoken in favour of accepting the offer. No, these nobles didn't want peace; they thirsted for blood, revenge, and the total annihilation of their enemies.

His mind was wandering. Mistress Joanna was trying to catch his attention again. She moved her head to indicate that he should move nearer to her, so he edged slowly around. At the same time she moved her stool slightly back from the other two young ladies, so that she was only a yard or two away from him as he stood. She shifted her position and brought her embroidery up nearer to her face, as though to see it better.

'What are you doing here?'

Edwin tried to whisper without moving his mouth too much. 'My lord sent me here until Martin is better. But I don't know who anyone is or what I'm supposed to be doing.'

She nodded almost imperceptibly. 'I'll try to help.'

While the nobles chatted in the middle of the room, Mistress Joanna continued to speak under her breath to him, explaining who they were, how they were related to each other, and what they might ask him to do. The girls who were sitting with her must have thought this all a little odd, but in a show of solidarity they too looked up from their sewing, and spoke a little more loudly to cover Joanna's voice.

Once Edwin was more aware of his surroundings he could relax a little. He breathed more steadily and looked with more interest at the earl's family. The lady he now knew was the Lady Ela was speaking about the wedding.

'But really, Isabelle, could you not persuade our brother to hold a proper wedding? Why, there's nobody here but family, and the event will be so small you'll barely notice it.'

Edwin gulped, for two entirely different reasons. Firstly, from what he knew of the Lady Isabelle, it was dangerous in the extreme to speak to her in such tones; and secondly, he'd thought the wedding was a very lavish affair indeed. Why, he himself had sat down and tallied up the vast quantities of food and drink required, and victuals were being sent for from across half the county. And that special wine had come in from France, for goodness' sake. But then again, these nobles were used to having such things done for them, without being aware of how much work went into it.

The Lady Isabelle was replying with nothing like the venom he would have expected.

'Ela, dear sister, you know William can't think of inviting all the lords of the kingdom when half of them are at war with each other. And besides, it all had to be arranged quickly, before he and Gilbert need to ride south. And anyway, Gilbert and I don't need a lavish feast – all we need is to be married in God's eyes.' She looked doe-eyed at her betrothed and put a hand on his arm. If Sir Gilbert was embarrassed by this show of affection he didn't show it; he put his own hand over hers, gave her a reassuring look and a pat, and continued the conversation he was having with Henry de Stuteville, which had moved on from Roland and was now about hunting.

But the Lady Ela wouldn't be satisfied. 'But Isabelle, the village church? I mean, not even to be married in the chapel here in the castle?'

At this, the Lady Maud, the other sister with the kind face, broke in. 'Oh Ela, really, have you so far forgotten your studies?'

Her sisters looked at her blankly. She laughed, the sound of a bell, and turned to her son. 'Pierre?'

He jumped up from where he had been playing merels with the other boy and stood to attention beside her. 'Yes Mama?'

'Whose feast is it in two days' time?'

'The feast of Saints Peter and Paul, Mama.'

She nodded, and patted him on the head. 'Good boy.' She picked a dried fruit out of the bowl to her left and gave it to him. 'You've been studying hard.' She dismissed him back to his game and turned back to her sisters, laughing again as she saw they still didn't understand. 'The church? In the village?'

Even Edwin knew what she was talking about by now, and realisation finally dawned on Lady Ela's face. 'Of course. The Church of Saints Peter and Paul. It will be auspicious to be married in their church on their feast day.'

It certainly would, thought Edwin. It was by far the most popular day for the villagers to be married, with Father Ignatius wedding a number of couples each time it came around. Not this year, though: none of the village folk would be permitted to sully the noble ceremony with weddings of their own. This year they'd have to settle for less important feast days.

The men's conversation on hunting became louder as their enthusiasm grew. Eventually some sort of consensus was reached that they should go out now.

Sir Gilbert turned to Lady Isabelle. 'Why don't you ladies come out with us? There isn't time to go after deer, so we'll just take the hawks out for a while until it's time for tonight's meal.'

Lady Isabelle looked at her sisters, who both nodded. 'Why, thank you – I think we will.' She turned to Mistress Joanna. 'Go and put out some riding clothes – I'll be there directly.'

The other ladies were also giving similar instructions to their companions, and various squires were sent out as well. Sir Gilbert sent Eustace off to see if the earl wanted to accompany them.

Henry de Stuteville bellowed to his squire. 'William! Find that hawking glove in my travelling pack. I haven't seen it since we've been here but it must be around.' He heaved himself out of the chair he'd been settled in and moved towards the door.

After some scurrying from the children and squires, a dignified hurry from the men and plenty of swishing skirts going past, there was silence in the room. Edwin was alone. Nobody had appeared to need him for anything, so he'd stayed where he was. Now he had the large, bright room to himself, surrounded by the detritus of the noble families. What should he do? They'd be gone for hours surely – until the evening meal, Sir Gilbert had said. Was he supposed to wait here? They couldn't expect him to, surely.

Gradually, he moved forward from his position by the wall. A stool had been overturned during the exodus so he righted it. He picked up a cushion from the floor and replaced it on a chair. It was silky and yielding to the touch. He picked it up again and squashed it between his hands. How did they make it so soft? It must have feathers or something in it, not the straw which filled the mattresses at home. He plumped it again and replaced it. He stood looking at the chair. It was so inviting: a soft cushion on the seat and another against the back. What must it feel like to sit in such comfort? He looked around the room. There was definitely nobody else there. Perhaps it wouldn't hurt if …?

He had taken one step closer to the chair when the door flew open. He leapt back, almost out of his skin, and swallowed down the sudden pounding in his throat. He was ready with all kinds of explanations, but thank the Lord it was Adam, who grinned and skipped over to a kist under the window.

'He's going!'

'What?' He couldn't be talking about the chair, could he?

Adam rummaged around in the kist and came up with a very sturdy but nevertheless fine-looking leather glove. 'Our lord is going out hawking with the others, so I can go too!' He smiled widely, and Edwin realised he didn't do that very often. Personally he couldn't think of anything much worse than getting on the back of a horse for fun, but it was the sort of thing nobles enjoyed.

'Oh, good.'

Adam shut the lid of the kist with a bang and moved towards the door.

'Wait!'

Adam turned. 'What is it?'

'Should I … I mean, shall I … I mean, do I have to wait here until they get back?'

Adam paused. 'I'm not sure, but I shouldn't think so. Our lord's whole family will be out until later, so they can't want you for anything in the meantime, can they? And even when they get back it will be time for the evening meal.' He started moving towards the door again. 'Are you supposed to be serving at table as well, by the way?'

Edwin reached out to the back of the chair for support, feeling his knees suddenly weaken. 'Me? Serve at … I hope not!'

Adam shrugged. 'Then you should be fine until after the meal. But maybe look out for us coming back and ask my lord then. Anyway, he'll be waiting. See you later!'

He skipped out the door and was gone. The seat looked even more inviting but he didn't dare collapse into it. Surely he wouldn't have to serve at the high table? Why, pages and squires spent years learning how to do that. He'd do it all wrong, make a laughing stock of himself in public. Everyone in the hall would look at him and say how inept he was.

His hands were shaking. He needed to calm his nerves and decide what he was going to do next. This was the opportunity to spend a couple of hours thinking about Hamo. He really needed to come up with an answer for the earl before the wedding, which was now only three days away.

To steady himself he began to tidy some of the things which had been left around the room. He collected the goblets and jugs and made sure they were all neatly on one of the side tables. He picked up the dish of dried fruits and placed it next to them. Edwin had never had a dried fruit before – well, apart from the little apples which they stored into the winter, but they were really common and didn't count. He peered into the dish. They were funny-looking things, all wizened like an old man, yet still plump and appetising. It wasn't stealing, was it? He ate the earl's food in the hall often. But these were different, these were for the nobles, they weren't for the likes of him … although surely nobody would notice just one going missing from a whole dish full. Promising himself he would mention it at his next confession, he selected an orangey-coloured thing about half the size of his thumb, and popped it in his mouth.

He was overcome by the sweetness. It was incredible. How could something so dried-up looking contain such a taste? And what was it anyway? It looked as though it might have been about the size of a small plum, but they weren't such a funny colour.

He realised that his hand was moving towards the dish again, so he pulled it back and decided he should remove himself from the temptation. To take more than one really would be dishonest. He would have liked to savour the fruit in his mouth for as long as he could, but once he was outside the room he might run into someone, so he swallowed it quickly. Still, the taste remained in his mouth all the way down the stairs.

As he descended he thought back to the scene in the room. Adam had been looking for a glove, and he'd left with just the one. Didn't you need a pair? But then Henry de Stuteville had asked his squire about his 'hawking glove' so maybe you did only need one. Henry de Stuteville was the brother-in-law with the big beard, not the tall thin one. He was married to the sister who was small and smiling, yes, the Lady Maud, that was it. And which squire was his? Oh yes, the one with the bent nose, William.

Which was another thing. Why were so many nobles called William? Didn't they have any imagination? It wasn't as if the king was called William, and his father before him hadn't been, either. Maybe there'd been some heroes in the past who went by that name, and the nobles decided to name their sons after them. Which brought him back to Hamo. Hamo, who, in his death throes, had said the name. But who could he have meant? If only he'd shouted 'Geoffrey' or 'Crispin' or some name that might have made life easier. But 'William'? Dear Lord. The earl, for a start, his wife's brother, at least one of the squires, William Steward, and no doubt half the garrison were called William.

He reached the outer ward and watched the noble party as they mounted. They made quite a picture in their bright clothes, and it wasn't often you saw so many ladies on horseback all together, each with their colourful skirt spread out over their horse. Behind them were some of the men whom Edwin recognised as working in the mews, the place where the hawks were kept. Each was holding his reins in his right hand, while perched on his gloved left hand – ah-ha – was a hooded bird. Presumably they would carry them out to wherever they were going, and then hand them over so the nobles could fly them at the prey. It was a decent enough way to get some meat, he supposed, though pretty time consuming, what with having to train the hawks and so on. He wondered why they didn't just make the kill and then fly away, rather than returning.

Oh well, it was nothing to do with him, anyway. He watched as the noble party rode out, then he ran his tongue round the inside of his mouth to seek out the last traces of the taste of the fruit, and followed on foot out of the gate.

Joanna felt the excitement rising within her as the party left the castle. She didn't ride very often, as it wasn't one of Isabelle's preferred pastimes; and when they travelled to one of the earl's other residences she generally sat pillion behind a groom or endured the jolting of a covered wagon. But now she felt the unaccustomed sensation of being in control as she sat astride her own mount – admittedly, a staid palfrey which Sir Gilbert had thoughtfully asked Eustace to find for her – and trotted behind the nobles. Once they had passed through the village and left the tilled fields behind, they increased their pace to a canter, and she welcomed the rush of air on her face on such a hot day.

They rode for a couple of miles westwards along the low road which ran parallel to the river, until they reached a green open space – in the winter it was marshy, but now it was a firm surface underfoot which sloped gently towards the reeds which lined the river. Here they reined in while the huntsmen dismounted, passed the birds over to the nobles and took their dogs over towards the riverbank.

Joanna didn't have a bird of her own, but she nudged her mount nearer to Isabelle to see if she could be of any assistance with the tiny merlin which was now perching on her mistress's decorative glove. Isabelle seemed to be fine, so Joanna took the opportunity to admire the much larger hawks which the men held. It was ironic, of course, that it was actually the female birds, the falcons, which were more sought after than the male tiercels, because they were bigger and more ferocious. A strange inversion of the natural order.

The earl was stroking the head of the bird which he held, while effortlessly controlling his mount with his legs and talking to Sir Gilbert at the same time. 'Lucky to be out this late in the year. My favourite hawk is already in moult, so I've had to bring this one – she's younger and not fully trained, but we'll see what she can do.' The bird, unhooded and slightly unkempt, looked lean and fierce as its eyes seemed to meet Joanna's, but then it was gone, soaring into the air to climb up above where the prey might be, circling along with two others sent by Sir Gilbert and William Fitzwilliam. The huntsmen were beating the reeds and crying out, and with a flurry a number of wild ducks flapped and took off.

The earl's falcon dropped like a stone out of the sky, diving at speed to kill an unsuspecting duck which fell to earth. Another falcon performed similarly, but the third hadn't struck so truly and engaged in a kind of shrieking combat before it finished its kill. The men cheered, the ladies applauded, and the dogs were sent to pick up the dead birds. The huntsmen took out their lures – pieces of meat with the wings of another dead bird attached, and swung them round to entice the falcons back. Joanna looked on as the earl took out his dagger, carved out the heart of the duck, and fed it to his falcon as a reward. The men offered him congratulations on his success, and then Sir Roger and Henry de Stuteville loosed their birds, and the hunt continued.

After the group of wild duck had been exhausted, the party moved a little further away from the river, towards a copse. Here a flock of songbirds were startled into the air, and the smaller birds held by the ladies were let fly. Isabelle squealed with delight as her merlin killed a number of larks, and Joanna applauded too – Isabelle was very fond of larks' tongues, and the thought of the delicacy to be served up later would surely keep her in a good mood.

As the afternoon wore on and the death toll mounted, the huntsmen tied the dead birds in pairs and slung them over poles, ready to carry them back to the castle. The day became a little cooler and the party stopped for a drink before turning back towards the castle. Most of them now rode at a more leisurely pace, but Sir Gilbert and Sir Roger, laughing and egging each other on in a boyish competition, raced off in front. Joanna looked at Isabelle, who was watching in delight, happier than she had ever been, or since Joanna had known her, anyway. Some way back from the path there was an old fallen tree; it had been there so long that a bushy undergrowth had sprouted around it. Sir Roger pointed and set his spurs to his mount, leaping effortlessly over the barrier. Laughing, Sir Gilbert set his horse to follow, but as it was about to jump some small animal – Joanna didn't see exactly what it was – scuttled out from the bush and startled it. The horse shied, missed its footing, hit its back leg hard on the fallen tree on the way over, and fell.

Isabelle shrieked as the earl swore and urged his own mount towards the tree. 'Gilbert! Are you – '

He stopped.

As the rest of the party caught up with him, Joanna could see that the horse had managed to get to its feet. Well, three of its feet, anyway: the back leg which had hit the tree dangled uselessly, broken, and the animal was trembling with shock.

And on the hard ground next to his horse, Sir Gilbert lay silent and still.

Chapter Nine

Edwin was entering the garden of his home when, to his surprise, Sir Geoffrey came out of the house.

They both stopped and stared for a moment before the knight recovered himself. 'Edwin. I just came to see how your mother was getting along now your father is gone. If she needed anything.'

He spoke in a level tone, but were his cheeks faintly red beneath his grey beard? Edwin was so taken aback by the sight of Sir Geoffrey, knight of the manor of Rochford, commander of the castle garrison, right hand of the earl, standing there among the beans, that he couldn't open his mouth.

Sir Geoffrey put a hand on his shoulder. 'I was going to look for you anyway. I wanted to talk to you about these outlaws. Come.'

Edwin allowed himself to be led up the garden path. His insides twisted slightly. 'You don't need me to … question them, do you?'

The knight shook his head. 'No. Once we had them in the cells and they knew there was no chance of escape, they talked readily and we didn't need to persuade them at all.'

Thank the Lord for that. He didn't think he'd have the stomach for trying to get confessions out of men who didn't want to give them. Once, when he was little, there had been a trial by ordeal in the village; his father had told him in no uncertain terms to stay away, but, curious, he'd crept among the legs of the crowd. The stench of burning flesh and the strangled noise emanating from the throat of the man trying not to scream as he carried the red-hot iron bar were branded into his memory. He shivered even now.

Sir Geoffrey was continuing. 'As we thought, they're French. They were fugitives from Lincoln – most of them fled south after the battle, but a few headed this way. Apparently they reckoned they'd have a better chance as the land wasn't razed and there weren't people lying in wait for them for revenge.'

At the name of the town Edwin felt a bit dizzy and stopped, bending over. By now they were by the village green, and fortunately Sir Geoffrey didn't notice – he'd already stepped away to hail Robin the carpenter, who was catching the rays of the evening sunlight to work on something on trestles outside his workshop. It was a coffin.

That didn't help. Edwin breathed deeply. The men who had caused terror and death in the area were normal men. They had done evil things, but they were ordinary villagers who had been called up by their lords to fight in a war they knew nothing about. Some of them might have wives and children back home. Their lords had been captured and would be ransomed – he'd heard it himself as he stood in the shadow of the great cathedral in Lincoln. But for these common men there would surely be no other penalty than death. They had been pulled from their homes, had killed and damaged, and now the people of Conisbrough would want revenge. And the wives and widows left in France would teach their children to hate, so that they too would want revenge in the years to come, and the wheel would turn once more.

Sir Geoffrey finished talking to the carpenter and returned. Edwin tried to look normal.

'It's nearly done – we should be able to bury Hamo tomorrow.'

That would be good. It was never wise to have bodies lying around too long in this weather. 'You won't send him back to his family?'

The knight shook his head. 'It's too far, and a dangerous journey through land still filled with Frenchmen. I won't waste another man's life conveying a corpse – we'll bury him here and send word to his family.'

Edwin looked around the village. It was peaceful in the late afternoon sunshine, children playing and squealing outside their homes, women moving in and out of their houses, some chatting to each other, the smell of woodsmoke and pottage as the supper cooked over the hearth, awaiting the return of the men who had laboured in the earl's fields since daybreak. It was as good a place as any to lie for your eternal rest.

Sir Geoffrey spoke. 'God knows there will be enough deaths and burials in the next few days.' Edwin looked at him questioningly. 'The woman and child tonight – the babe will have to go to its grave after dark, so Father Ignatius will bury its mother just before. And I've just told Robin to spread the word about the Frenchmen: now they've talked, we've no further use for them. We'll hang the lot at first light, and our lord wants the whole village out to watch, to show what happens to those who break his laws. But there will be no burial for them – they'll hang until they rot, as a lesson to others.'

He strode away, and Edwin tried to stay steady on his feet. Fortunately William Steward was hauling himself across the green, so Edwin went to speak with him, glad of the excuse to move.

They sat down on the edge of the platform of the pillory, and Edwin brought him up to date with the news of the day, such as it was. He tried to quell his panic at his lack of progress, and faltered into silence. As the sun started to set they watched the men returning from the fields.

The church bell began to toll, and gradually people emerged from their houses and made their way over. Edwin stood to follow them, heaving William to his feet and slowing his pace so his uncle could keep up.

He joined the end of the mournful procession as it wound round the outside of the church to a grave which had been dug close to the wattle fence marking the edge of the churchyard. Father Ignatius led the way, followed by John and three others carrying the parish coffin, then young John, with

Godleva just behind carrying the tot, and Cecily carrying a tiny bundle wrapped in linen; they were followed by more or less the entire village – a good turnout for a family most of them didn't know well, a show of solidarity.

Edwin watched as the woman's shrouded body was lifted out of the coffin and lowered into the ground. Young John was sniffing and rubbing his eyes, while his little sister howled in Godleva's arms. Their father stood with clenched fists as Father Ignatius said the prayers for the dead, and men shovelled earth into the grave. Then, as the sun dipped below the horizon and the last glow of the daylight bathed the scene, the priest led the way out of the gate and round to the outside of the graveyard, where a row of tiny mounds were lined up against the fence. There could be no burial in consecrated ground for an unbaptised infant, one still with the mark of original sin on it, but Father Ignatius was a merciful man, and he had always allowed such babes to lie as close to the churchyard as he could. As they stopped by the pitifully small hole in the ground, Edwin realised they were directly opposite the place where John's wife now lay, so that she and her child would be separated only by a few yards as they slept their eternal rest. Edwin closed his eyes and prayed as hard as he could that the child, innocent as it was, would not suffer the flames due to its unbaptised state. Surely the Lord could not be so cruel as to treat it the same as the godless and the heathens?

By now the crowd of villagers was drifting away – the burial of a baby was not an uncommon occurrence, and they had to rest before their labours started again on the morrow. Still, Edwin noticed that those of the villagers who had their children with them were holding them close. Finally, John and his family were led away by Godleva's father, and Edwin was left with his mother, his aunt and uncle, and Father Ignatius on his knees beside the grave. Cecily was upset, having watched the poor thing live and die within a few breaths, and his mother and William took her away.

Father Ignatius stood and brushed the earth from the knees of his habit. He sighed. 'Come, Edwin, come in and sit with me a while. I've buried many children in my time, but sometimes it's difficult to know why the Lord acts as He does.'

Edwin followed him through the darkness to the small house attached to the church. Once inside, Father Ignatius lit a rushlight and placed it on the table, where it spluttered unevenly, casting a small puddle of smelly light. He retrieved a flagon and two pottery cups, and poured a small amount of ale into each.

There was a melancholy silence for a few moments. Edwin felt he had to break it.

'How was Aelfrith's mother?'

Father Ignatius sipped his ale and exhaled slowly. 'She is well, thank the Lord. She needed comfort, but she will live to see another day.'

Edwin crossed himself and murmured thanks, but he wasn't surprised. Aelfrith's mother was well known, and the Father must have been aware that he'd have a long walk in the sun for nothing. But he looked more relaxed now that Edwin had changed the subject, so now might be a good time to try and continue the conversation they'd had earlier.

'So, Father, earlier when you were called away, we were speaking of Hamo.'

The priest coughed a little and put his cup down. 'Were we?'

'Yes, we were. And you were about to tell me of what he'd said to you.'

Father Ignatius made an uncomfortable movement on his stool. 'You know very well I can't tell you anything the man told me under the seal of confession.'

'I'm not asking you to. Sir Geoffrey said he had seen you talking together several times, and he can't have been in confession all the time.'

'Well ...'

Edwin could feel his temper being tested. He put his own cup down. 'Father. Do you remember the last time I had to ask you for information? A few weeks ago?'

Even in the dim and flickering light, Edwin could see the priest's face turning white. He crossed himself again and looked at Edwin, who tried to maintain his stern face. He still wasn't very good at this. Still, at least there was no option of having to resort to violent tactics with a man of God, like there might have been with the Frenchmen earlier. He continued to stare, and let the silence develop.

Eventually he had his reward. Father Ignatius looked down. 'All right. I don't think he meant anyone else to know, but as he mentioned it in conversation and not during the sacrament of confession, then I will tell you. He was considering taking holy orders.'

Edwin felt his mouth opening in shock.

Father Ignatius nodded. 'Yes. Hamo was going to become a monk.'

Joanna prayed with more fervour than usual as the meal was set before her. Dear Lord, what a lucky escape they'd had.

Isabelle had been in hysterics, unable to stop screaming. Joanna had tried in vain to comfort her as Sir Roger, who was nearest, flung himself from his horse and bent desperately over the prone man as the rest of the noble party dismounted and gathered round.

'He breathes!'

Joanna's relief was such that she staggered, even as she tried to hold Isabelle upright. Thank the Lord that Sir Gilbert had managed to fall sideways, away from the horse, otherwise he could have been crushed. Sir Roger, on his knees beside his friend, looked up at the earl. 'I think he's just knocked himself out, my lord. I can see no blood and his head doesn't seem to be dented. Perhaps we could arrange to carry him back to the castle?'

The earl jerked his head at the chief huntsman, who had been hovering in the background. 'See to it.' He turned to Isabelle and patted her on the shoulder. 'Come now, he'll be fine.' He seemed outwardly calm, but Joanna could see the worry in his eyes. She looked down before he might spot her staring at him, focusing instead on the dusty grass.

While the men were fashioning a makeshift stretcher from branches and cloaks, Sir Roger stood. He looked from Sir Gilbert to the stricken horse, now shaking all over and looking on the verge of collapse. After a glance at the earl he drew his hunting dagger with some reluctance. Joanna had the presence of mind to look away but she could still hear everything as he spoke softly and comfortingly to the animal before slitting its throat. The Lady Ela gave a cry as there was a choking noise and the carcass thumped to the ground, Sir Roger murmuring gently all the while, but her husband had little sympathy for her. 'They all go for dogs' meat in the end.' He turned away.

Joanna half-opened her eyes to see the blood spreading over the dry ground and Sir Roger, his sleeve splattered with red, wiping his dagger. The Lady Maud comforted her sister as Joanna supported Isabelle.

As they had made their careful way back, Sir Gilbert was already stirring, his eyes flicking from side to side. Joanna had looked around her as they entered the village, expecting their arrival with the injured man to cause a stir, but the streets were deserted: everyone seemed to be in the churchyard. So they wound their way up to the castle and the huntsmen carried him inside. Joanna prayed all the while, and the Lord listened: by the time Sir Gilbert had been laid in his bed in the guest quarters he was alert enough to recognise them and to ask what had happened to his horse. His attempts to get up were prevented by Isabelle, who, calmer now, told him firmly to stay put. He sank back on to the pillow, probably relieved if the unfocused look in his eyes was anything to go by.

And now they sat without him at the high table in the hall, less boisterous than they would usually be after such an outing. The talk was not of how many birds they'd killed, but of the near miss they'd had. Further up the table, William Fitzwilliam was shaking his head and saying that Sir Gilbert should have been more careful. The Lady Maud, serious for once, nodded in agreement. Henry de Stuteville, on her other side, leaned across. 'Yes, but it wouldn't have done you much harm if something had happened to him, would it?' He sat back and pushed a huge piece of spiced beef into his mouth, dribbling some of the sauce down his beard. Joanna gazed at William Fitzwilliam, who hadn't answered this comment, and wondered again at the scene she'd witnessed in the chapel. What had he been praying for? But she couldn't tell, and his face gave no sign.

Her attention was caught by Sir Roger, who was asking if she would like the beef dish herself. From the patient look on his face she guessed he'd probably said it two or three times already, so she thought she'd better pay attention to the meal. She wondered what the hall and the food would be like at Sir Gilbert's castle of Pevensey, which was where she and Isabelle would live after the wedding. Would it be as big as this? Surely not. Although Sir Gilbert was an important man he wasn't an earl and a cousin of the king, not like the lord earl who had vast estates and power. She was tired after the riding this afternoon, and, added to the lateness of tonight's dinner, she was starting to feel dozy. Her mind drifted.

As the meal drew on, the minstrel took his place again. His voice and his delivery were still as good as before, but this time Joanna hardly listened. After the emotion of Roland's death, the ensuing scene of battle and revenge held no attraction for her, although the men at the table were enjoying it. It was a shame Martin wasn't here – he'd probably have liked it. She had missed him serving at table, but she supposed she'd better get used to it.

A babble of sharp words erupted from nearer the centre of the table. William Fitzwilliam had obviously made some comment about the battle which was being narrated, and the Lady Ela was laughing at him. 'Oh, William, as if you could be one of those heroes! If you were there you'd be on the end of a Saracen lance by now! Either that or you'd be hanging around the edge because you were too cautious to join in.'

Joanna caught the sharp intake of breath from the other men. Surely even the mild-mannered, browbeaten William Fitzwilliam wasn't going to let that one pass by? But other than clench his fists under the table he did nothing; and after a brief pause, everyone turned their attention to the minstrel again.

<hr />

Edwin couldn't have heard that right. 'I beg your pardon?'

'I said, Hamo was going to become a monk.'

Edwin sat and gaped. He couldn't have thought of a more unlikely answer if he'd tried. The supercilious Hamo, fussy about every little thing, preening himself in his smart clothes, a monk? There must be some mistake.

Father Ignatius smiled. 'I see you are dumbstruck. But the Lord can inspire a vocation in the unlikeliest of places.'

Edwin still couldn't believe it. His mouth was still open, but no words came out. He tried again. 'Hamo? But he's ... he was ... so ... I don't know, I can't think of the word. But a monk? Really? I didn't think he was at all pious.'

Father Ignatius looked at him in some surprise. 'Edwin, Edwin. You're so childlike in your innocence, and you're mistaken on two counts. Firstly, Hamo was more godly than you give him credit for – what you saw was the outer man, but tell me, how well did you really know him? He wasn't fulfilled in his life here, but nobody except me knew it, as he had no friends in whom to confide.'

Edwin felt ashamed. He'd already noticed that nobody seemed to care that Hamo was dead, and it seemed nobody had cared that much when he was alive, either. And he, Edwin, was as much to blame as anyone: he'd only ever tried to avoid Hamo, so he wouldn't get shouted at or talked down to. How much better might things have been if he'd made an effort to find out more about him? But now it was too late. He vowed to himself that he would never make the same mistake again with anyone else.

Father Ignatius nodded to him, as though aware of his thoughts, and continued. 'And secondly, although it pains me to say it, rich men don't take the cloth because of an excess of piety – or at least, few of them do. No, they do it for power and influence. A younger son will never inherit his father's estates, so he has a choice – he can content himself with a few offcuts of land handed down, surviving by renting out his sword to others, or he can enter the Church and become a prior, abbot or bishop of huge influence. Some bishops are close advisors of the king, and even abbots can wield huge amounts of power. The abbey at Roche is not even close to being one of the largest in the kingdom, and yet it has lands and holdings in five counties. Imagine Hamo seeing himself in charge of all that.'

Now that made a lot more sense. Edwin could quite easily visualise Hamo in a white habit with a cross round his neck, fussing over the details of the tithes coming in from all over the place.

Another thought struck him as he looked at the priest in the flickering candlelight. 'You said a younger son won't inherit lands. Was Hamo a younger son? You mentioned brothers earlier – what do you really know about him?'

Father Ignatius shrugged. 'Only what he told me. As far as I'm aware, he was the youngest of four. He said that all of his brothers were dead: one was a monk and died some years ago; another had been dismissed from his eldest brother's service in some kind of disgrace and had subsequently been killed in a brawl. And finally the eldest brother died fairly recently – he had a letter about it just a few weeks ago. He'd been considering becoming a monk and asked me on several occasions how he might go about it and how much he would need as a donation.'

As Edwin considered this, the rushlight burned right down, gave a final splutter, and went out. He realised how dark it was.

He stood, groping for the edge of the table. 'Father, I'll leave you now. After all you've done today you'll need some sleep before the morning, and the Lord knows I've plenty to think about myself.'

He felt rather than saw the priest making the sign of the cross in the air. 'God bless you my son, and may He help you find out what happened to Hamo so he can rest in peace.'

Edwin moved cautiously towards the door. Once he'd opened it there was a bit more light, but not much – the moon was on the wane. Still, he was able to see across the green towards home. He lingered over his walk in the cool air, feeling no need to go in, as he knew he wouldn't sleep. Instead he returned to the edge of the pillory platform, where he'd sat earlier with William. It hadn't been used for its proper purpose for some while, so it was fairly clean, the wood unstained by the mud and filth which gleeful children – and some adults too – would throw at those unfortunates imprisoned there. He lifted himself on to it and sat, his feet dangling.

After some while he leaned back, breathed in the cool night air and looked up at the stars in the heavens. The village was silent – those who laboured all day slept soundly at night – and he was a little calmer. He thought about Hamo and his plans to become a monk. It was something he'd considered himself once or twice, but as his father's only son he'd had to put it aside, and besides, they probably wouldn't let him in anyway. No, his duty was to marry and have sons to continue the family line, to look after him and his mother in their old age, if they should reach it. Marriage … Alys's face appeared before him as clearly as if she were standing there, those blue eyes looking at his with what he imagined to be love, and he actually started to reach out his hand to take hers, before she disappeared back into the darkness.

The gibbet had been erected at the crossroads just west of the village, where the Thrybergh road met the one which led from Kilnhurst to Ravenfield. It was large, a frame made of thick, rough-cut beams which would be sturdy enough to take a lot of weight. Eight ropes were slung over the top, each ending in a noose which dangled limply in the morning air. A ladder leaned against one of the upright posts.

Although the day promised to be hot once more, it was early, barely past dawn, and still cool. Edwin shivered. He'd fallen into a doze on the pillory platform and woken in a panic just before dawn, wondering where he was and terrified, in his half-asleep state, of the pillory above him with its holes like two eyes and a gaping mouth. He'd staggered back home in time to find his mother just getting up, and he felt even less rested than he had before. His eyes were full of grit, and his head was dizzy as he stood with the other villagers, who had all been summoned to witness their lord's justice. Some of them looked apprehensive, children clutching at their parents' legs; others were belligerent, including John, who stood at the front of the group, feet planted apart, arms folded. Young John was next to him, standing firm despite his trembling legs, his young sister enfolded within the circle of his good arm.

Edwin had never seen an actual hanging before, although, like most people who'd ever travelled more than a mile or two, he had seen both fresh and long-dead corpses swinging from their nooses at crossroads, food for the crows. He'd certainly never seen such a large gibbet and couldn't help looking at the construction and trying to calculate whether it would be strong enough.

The crowd parted as the sound of hoofbeats approached. The earl rode at the front of a procession which included Sir Geoffrey, Sir Roger, Sir Gilbert – who still looked a little dazed after the accident Edwin heard he'd had yesterday – Henry de Stuteville and William Fitzwilliam. Their squires followed behind, also mounted, though not Martin, still presumably confined to his bed. Thomas trailed along behind them on his pony. Brother William, on his mule, brought up the rear. All the village men removed their hats as the party halted and drew up to one side of the gibbet. Behind the riders there arrived Father Ignatius, on foot, followed by the condemned men, hands bound behind them, each with a castle guard on either side. Some bore bruises; some stumbled, either in pain or in fear of what was to happen, needing the support of their captors; but two held their heads high as they marched, and another struggled against his captors, scrabbling his feet on the ground and throwing his weight back and to the side in a vain attempt to free himself. As they passed, some of the villagers looked away or crossed themselves, but others shouted or spat at the men, surging forward in anger. One of the prisoners stopped and doubled over as a well-aimed stone smacked into his forehead, slicing a cut above one eye; his guards hauled him upright again and pulled him onwards, blood streaming down his face. The man who had been struggling against his captors shouted something unintelligible and tried to throw himself into the crowd, but he was prevented by the soldiers, who wrestled him back and dragged him towards the gibbet. The potential for mob violence hung in the air, but the earl held up one hand, and the villagers quietened immediately.

All the prisoners were now standing under the crossbeam, looking up at the nooses or down to the ground. The earl nudged his horse forward and spoke, without the need to raise his voice.

'These men are enemies of our king and our realm.' He spoke in French, and paused while his statement was repeated in English by Brother William. 'They are outside the law and deserve no mercy.' Pause. Nods and murmurs from the crowd. 'They have caused damage and death to people under my care, and they will be punished accordingly.' Pause. Growls from the village men. 'Know, all of you, that I will protect you and that none shall break the law on my land without suffering the consequences.' More growls, louder this time. In what Edwin guessed was a pre-arranged move, Sir Roger urged his horse forward towards the earl. 'My lord, I beg of you to allow these men to be shriven before their deaths. Their lives are rightly forfeit, in vengeance, and the Lord shall judge them hereafter, but in allowing them to confess you demonstrate both justice and mercy.' He moved back.

Showing no surprise either at the request or at the formality of the words, the earl nodded and waved his hand at Father Ignatius, who turned to face the condemned and began to speak the prayer. *Deus, Pater misericordiarum* ...

Finally he got to *Et ego vos absolvo a peccatis vestris*, made the sign of the cross in the air over all the condemned men, and stepped back. Everyone looked at the earl, who nodded, and the guards of the first man, one of those who had been stumbling, stepped forward and placed the noose around his neck, jerking it tight. The man's face was completely white, eyes staring past the villagers into the hereafter. One of his arms hung at a strange angle, and Edwin suddenly recognised him as the man who'd been struck with Brother William's cudgel during the encounter on the road. With his last breath he said a few words in French, which drifted across the cool morning air. Edwin translated under his breath for the benefit of his mother and those close to him. 'He said may the Lord have mercy on his soul.' Surreptitiously his mother made the sign of the cross, but Edwin didn't dare in case the earl saw his movement and interpreted it as sympathy for the outlaw.

The two guards holding the rope then took the strain and started to haul, walking backwards and lifting the choking, kicking man into the air where he dangled, spinning around and jerking convulsively as the noose tightened around his throat. Once his feet were about three or four feet in the air they stopped pulling; another man climbed the ladder, and between them they tied the rope around the crossbeam. The two on the ground stood with their arms folded to watch the death throes; the other descended and moved the ladder along one place. And all the while the hanging man kicked and writhed.

Edwin hoped he wasn't going to be sick. He could hear that someone behind him was doing exactly that, but he couldn't turn round to see who it was, for his eyes were riveted to the horrific spectacle in front of him. He'd had no idea that it would take so *long* for someone to die by hanging, but the man was still alive, thrashing at the end of the rope, his face turning purple, mouth open in a silent scream. His eyes bulged further and further out of his head, and his tongue came out of his mouth like a blackened serpent. Then there was a stench as his bowels emptied themselves on the ground underneath him, and a sudden movement as the next man along in the line fainted and fell to the ground. His guards looked uncertainly at the earl.

The earl, unmoved by what he was witnessing, waved. 'Yes, yes, get on with it. We don't want to be here all day.' The guards placed the noose around the unconscious man's neck and hauled him up, tying the rope off as their fellows had done and watching the dead weight swing.

The third man said the same words as the first, which Edwin translated again, and then he too was heaved into the air, his body in spasms as it danced with death. The fourth man, a heavy-set individual of middle age, looked oddly composed, and as the noose was placed around his neck he looked straight at John and spoke several deliberate sentences.

Several people around Edwin were looking at him, and he tried not to attract the attention of any of the nobles as he spoke under his breath. 'He said he is sorry for what happened. He never wanted to come here, he was made to by his lord, he left his wife and family behind and he will never see them again. May the Lord watch over them.'

By the time Edwin had finished speaking the man was already dangling, and all eyes turned to the next in line. This was the man who had been struck by the stone, and the blood coursed freely down his face as his bound hands couldn't wipe it away. Man? No, a boy – not even Edwin's own age. His knees were giving way beneath him and as one of his guards held him up so the other could fit the noose, he soiled himself in terror. One or two of the hardier villager men guffawed, and for a reason he couldn't fathom, Edwin was sorrier for the boy for his public embarrassment than he was for his imminent death. The boy whispered a solitary word just before he was jerked off his feet, which was so recognisable Edwin didn't need to interpret it: 'Mother'.

The sixth man was the one who had been struggling against his bonds and his captors. He was still kicking at them and bellowing out defiant words. Edwin's blood turned cold as he listened, and the earl showed some emotion at last: he urged his horse forward a pace and shouted at his men. Three other soldiers held the man down as his head was forced into the noose; he was still roaring his defiance but it stopped suddenly as five guards together yanked at the rope and he shot into the air. Not wanting to displease their lord, the guards of the final two men in the line did their work at the same time, and soon all eight outlaws were swinging. The first three were already dead; the fourth followed a moment after. The defiant one, heavier than his fellows and having been jerked off his feet at some speed, seemed to die almost immediately, his head hanging at an angle. Edwin forced himself to look straight ahead as the final two kicked and thrashed their way into oblivion, their limbs growing still.

That just left the boy in the middle, who was still spasming weakly, blood dripping from him to mingle with the mess on the ground, tongue protruding, eyes bulging and his face, Edwin would swear, wet with tears. Beside him his mother sobbed and he put his arm around her. William Steward, upright still on his crutches, muttered under his breath that the smaller, younger ones always took the longest.

Edwin looked over at the earl, who was being spoken to by Sir Roger. Eventually the earl nodded, and two of the guards stepped forward to hold the boy's legs and pull down as hard as they could. The extra weight choked the final bit of life out of him and he was released from his struggle.

For a long moment nobody moved except for the dangling corpses, and then the earl and his companions started to move. Their horses, frightened by the scent of blood or maybe by the sight of the swinging bodies, were restless. The earl made a final announcement, his voice like stone. 'So perish all who disobey me, who break my laws and disturb the peace of my lands.' He nodded to the villagers as he turned his horse's head. 'You may go. Justice has been done.' He rode off, followed by his companions and their squires. Adam looked as sick as Edwin felt. Little Thomas seemed barely able to stay in his saddle, and for the first time Edwin felt sorry for the boy as his pony trailed further and further behind the large horses of the men as they headed back up the road.

The villagers started to drift off behind their lord, but Edwin stayed where he was. Now there was no danger of looking as though he was betraying anyone, he allowed himself a prayer for the souls of the executed men. As he finished, William started to move away, with a groan for his legs, stiffened from standing so long. He stopped and turned to Edwin. 'What did he say?'

Edwin tore his gaze away from the place of death. The sun was fully up, warmth spreading over the earth, and flies were already starting to buzz around the bodies. 'Who?'

William gestured. 'Him. The one who was shouting.'

'He said – ' Edwin stopped and swallowed. His voice was hoarse. 'He said he defies us, lords and all. His lord and his prince will invade again and succeed this time. England will be a smoking ruin and his brothers in arms will live to see the birds feasting on our corpses.' Several other villagers had stopped to listen, and they murmured among themselves. Edwin heard again the man's final words before the breath was choked out of him. 'He said the war isn't over yet.'

Chapter Ten

Martin tried to haul himself into a sitting position, failed, and collapsed back down on to the bed. He still ached all over and felt as though he were strapped to a board, but he'd made it slightly further up than he had last time. It was, of course, nice to have a bit of a rest for a change – not to mention the heavenly experience of having Joanna wipe his brow with a cool cloth – but he was starting to chafe at the inaction. She'd told them all about yesterday's hunt and dinner, and it sounded like he'd missed out on some good sport – apart from the accident to Sir Gilbert, of course, although thank the Lord he was fine now – and rumour had it there was going to be tilting or sparring practice today.

He hadn't seen the hanging, either, though he was less sorry about that. Edwin was sitting describing it to him, but between his obvious reluctance to go into detail while Joanna was in the room, and the sick look on his face, Martin couldn't make out much of what had gone on anyway, except that it had clearly been very unpleasant.

Edwin tailed off and they all looked at each other in silence for a few moments.

Martin had another go at sitting up. This time he was more successful, and with a bit of grunting and shuffling he was able to support himself against the wall and look at the room the right way up for the first time. Sir Geoffrey's chamber was furnished very sparsely – other than the bed and the two stools on which the others were sitting, there was a single wooden kist, and a cross-shaped pole, currently empty of its hauberk and helm. The knight wasn't one for decoration or material possessions, but even so, it wasn't much to show for a lifetime. Martin wondered, not for the first time, whether he'd end up like this, and whether Sir Geoffrey's own house in his manor of Rochford, which he visited for a few weeks once a year, was more lavishly furnished.

He looked from Joanna to Edwin. 'So, what other news?'

Edwin shrugged. 'We buried Hamo this morning, after we got back from … well, you know. And I still don't know who killed him.' He looked downcast, and Martin wished he could help a bit more. But Edwin needed cleverness, not brute force, and anyway he wasn't much good for brute force at the moment either. He sighed.

Joanna spoke in a brighter tone. 'Don't worry, Edwin. I'm sure something will come to you.'

Edwin gestured helplessly. 'To be honest, I'm not even sure why anyone would want to kill him. I mean, I know he was nasty – ' He stopped and seemed to be thinking of something. 'What I mean is … I know not everyone liked him and he didn't get on with everybody, but why would anyone want to kill him?'

Martin had been turning something over in his mind, slowly. 'Maybe they didn't.' The others were looking at him. He shifted slightly and winced. 'You said it was poison, didn't you? Well, that could've got into the food by accident, surely?'

Edwin was shaking his head. 'No. No, I don't think so. Why was he the only one who ate it? If it had got in the food by accident, surely plenty of other people would have suffered as well. And Richard Cook was certain that he ate the same as everyone else. No, it must have been done on purpose.'

'All right, so it might have been done on purpose. But by whom? Poison – that must be a woman, surely? No man would use something like that.'

Edwin made a noncommittal gesture. 'Maybe. William Steward was certainly more upset by the thought of being considered a poisoner than a murderer. But on the other hand, you could be a man who wasn't very good at fighting, or a man who wanted to keep it secret. After all, if you murdered someone by stabbing them or bashing them on the head, there's more chance of being found out.'

Joanna had been silent during the exchange, but now she spoke, leaning forward in excitement. 'You could both be right.'

Martin was confused. 'What?'

Joanna could barely remain seated. She looked so pretty when she was animated. 'About what you were saying before. Edwin could be right, and the food was poisoned on purpose. Otherwise, as he says, more people would have eaten it. But what if the poison wasn't meant for Hamo at all? What if it was someone else who was meant to die?'

Martin still didn't understand. 'But how could that happen? Why would you put poison in Hamo's food if you wanted to kill someone else?'

Joanna looked slightly less happy. 'I don't know. I haven't worked that part out yet. But it could have happened, couldn't it, Edwin?'

Martin looked round and realised that Edwin was staring at the floor. Or not so much at the floor as through it, the stare of a man who was searching for something in his mind. At last he looked up.

'My father – may the Lord have mercy on him – always said that in order to find something out, you should look not just at what happened, but at why. So, let's put to one side for a moment how it all happened, and think about why. Why would anyone want to kill Hamo? They wouldn't. Or, at least, we don't think so. So, why would anyone want to kill anyone?'

This was going a bit too fast for Martin. What did people kill for? 'War?' he hazarded. 'Money? Land?'

Joanna joined in. 'Hate?' She paused. 'No, wait – power.'

Edwin snapped his fingers. 'Yes. If you have power, you can get all the other things. So, who has power?'

They all looked at each other. The thought was almost too monstrous to say out loud. Martin stumbled over it. 'The earl?'

He was whispering. He cleared his throat. 'Someone wants to kill the earl?'

He thought he'd got it, but Edwin didn't look convinced. 'Hmm … maybe. But I need to think some more.' He got up. 'Anyway, I think I'm supposed to go back to the great chamber. The nobles all went for a ride after the hang– after this morning. But they'll be back soon, and I'm still supposed to be serving them while you're not there.' He smiled briefly. 'That's another reason for me to wish you a speedy recovery.'

Joanna also stood. 'I'll have to go too … my lady will want me when she returns.' As she turned, one of her hands came out towards him, but Martin didn't dare reach out and touch it. Instead he watched as Edwin held the door for her and she went out. Edwin followed her and closed the door behind him, leaving Martin to wait for the morning to pass as he stared at the wall.

———◆———

Edwin stood in the great chamber, waiting for the nobles to return. Joanna and the two other ladies' companions were in the room, sitting where the sun streamed in through one of the windows. Two of the windows in here had glass in, and it made the light break up into little jagged pieces on the floor. The dust rising from the rushes sparkled in the rays, and the occasional flea leapt ecstatically into the sunshine. Edwin wondered what time it was – about the middle of the morning, probably; it would be more or less time for dinner once the nobles returned. Thank the Lord he didn't have to wait at the table – he could simply melt into obscurity in the lower hall for a while, and nobody would expect him to have manners, or serve them anything.

The ladies were sewing and chatting, the bowl of dried fruit – which Edwin couldn't help noticing had less in it than it had the day before – to one side of them. He was the only other person in the room, and he studied them as they worked.

Mistress Joanna, of course, he was getting to know better every day. Matilda, the girl who was companion to the Lady Ela, was tall and willowy, with brown eyes and a languid movement. Her elegant long fingers were stitching gracefully. Rosamund, Lady Maud's companion, was shorter, paler and more vivacious, stabbing her needle energetically into some kind of brightly coloured embroidery. They were all completely different from … well, probably best not to think of her while she was so far away, but her blue eyes came to mind, and her smile. Not to mention her courage, determination and bravery in the face of danger and overwhelming terror. It was hard to imagine any of the ladies before him coping with life in a besieged city, while caring for several children.

The door opened and the Ladies Maud and Ela entered. Immediately Edwin felt much less relaxed, even though they weren't looking at him. Their companions fussed around them, settling them in chairs, fetching cushions and so on. They had hardly settled before the rest of the noble party came in, and the room was full of hustle. Edwin busied himself pouring goblets of wine at the side table, and passing them to the squires to hand over, so he wouldn't need to risk going too near any of the lords and ladies. As he filled the final one and turned to pass it over, he looked down and saw that little Peter was before him. He looked pale and his hands shook as he took the cup – fortunately Edwin hadn't filled it too full or it might have spilled everywhere. Well, thought Edwin, as he watched the boy walk with painstaking care over to Sir Roger, someone who's even more scared than me. He felt quite protective as he saw the boy hand over the goblet – Sir Roger smiled and murmured thanks to him, which was more than the other nobles had done – and scuttle back to the wall. He took up position very close to Edwin, their sleeves brushing. Edwin tried to send out supportive thoughts without actually moving, in case anyone should notice him.

There was a slightly sombre mood in the room, as well there might be after the events of the early morning. The ladies hadn't seen the hanging, obviously, but the men had, and it seemed even their hour's ride afterwards hadn't shaken the shadow of the gibbet from them. Edwin remembered how sick Thomas had looked, and glanced round to see how he was now. Odd, he wasn't there, even though the earl himself was in the room, with Adam hovering behind him. The two smaller boys were playing quietly in the corner – there would certainly have been more fuss and noise if Thomas had been there as well.

As if reading his thoughts, the Lady Ela cast her eyes round the chamber. 'Brother? Where is Thomas?'

The earl looked round, as if noticing for the first time that the boy wasn't there. He glanced at Adam, who shrugged apologetically. The earl pursed his mouth. 'Actually, I haven't seen him since we were at the executions.'

Lady Ela squawked. 'My precious boy! Lost in the forest!' She half-rose from her seat.

Her husband made a dismissive gesture. 'My dear, I'm sure he's just about some boyish prank. Try not to worry so.'

The earl looked more serious. 'This isn't the first time he's shirked his duties. William, you and I need to have a talk about that boy.'

William Fitzwilliam looked pained. He flicked an imaginary crumb off the front of his scarlet tunic and stroked his beard. 'Yes. It's time he – '

'William! How can you say such a thing!' Edwin thought the Lady Ela was addressing her husband, but in fact she had rounded on the earl with a tone that would have seen any normal person flogged. Edwin winced, and felt little Peter move even closer to him. 'He's too young to be keeping up with the men and all these great lumps of lads you have here. He's run off to rest, poor thing. You have to …'

The earl's knuckles turned white as he gripped the stalk of his goblet. He put it down with precise care before turning to his sister to reply. Edwin felt Peter's arm against his own, and he remembered the time he'd had to search for him throughout the castle grounds. There were many, many places in which a small boy could conceal himself, and if you included the estate, the village and the woods as well, Thomas could be very difficult to find.

The earl was saying something along the same lines, his voice controlled. He finished by telling his sister that the boy would no doubt come back when he was hungry, at which point he could expect to be chastised. The Lady Ela was becoming more indignant and Edwin worried that the scene in front of them was about to turn violent. He tried to remain calm. Peter had certainly never had the chance to turn up again when he was hungry – nobody would have thought to feed him, not before Sir Roger took him on, anyway.

Sir Roger and Sir Gilbert, away to Edwin's left, were looking at each other, trying to find a way to stop the conversation in its tracks. Sir Gilbert, exhibiting real courage, dared to interrupt his future brother and sister with soothing words.

'Come now, this may not be all it seems. The lad probably wandered away from the rest of us while we were out riding, following a deer or something, and he'll find his way back as soon as he realises he's late.'

The earl and the Lady Ela both paused in their argument and sat back. The Lady Isabelle threw herself into the conversation in support of her betrothed, remarking that she'd be very surprised if Thomas wasn't there at dinner.

'And speaking of which ...' Sir Roger had seen the man enter the chamber behind the earl, and he attracted his lord's attention. The earl turned and nodded to the servant to speak.

The man cleared his throat and announced that dinner was served. There was a flurry of skirts and fuss as everyone got up and went out; Edwin followed them through to the passageway, but he wasn't stupid enough to think he could go through to the top end of the hall. As they all paused and started to rearrange themselves in order of precedence he went out the door and into the ward towards the hall's lower door, entering to look for a seat. He was very glad to be down at one of the lower tables in the hall, away from the nobles. Of course, everyone else down there was already seated, waiting for those who would sit at the high table, so it was a bit crowded. Edwin squeezed himself on to a bench where there was a spare trencher. He looked towards the door to the servery, remembering that he'd seen Hamo standing there on the night he died. He recalled that Hamo had seemed rooted to the spot, looking at him as though he had seen something which shocked him. Now why had he done that? As he had done many times in the past days, Edwin turned over and over in his mind the reasons anyone could have wanted to murder Hamo. But he was less and less convinced – it now seemed to him that Hamo hadn't been the target, for it just didn't make sense. Nevertheless he was dead, and even if he had been killed by accident, he deserved justice. Edwin wasn't going to let anyone get away with this just because the victim wasn't important enough. He was still haunted by thoughts of …

The noble party finally entered and Edwin stood, along with everyone else in the hall, as they seated themselves at the high table. His eyes were immediately drawn not to the earl and his family, but to the line of squires behind them. Thomas was not there.

Chapter Eleven

Martin reckoned that dinner must be over in the great hall. There had been quiet for some while, but now there was noise and bustle, albeit muffled by the walls which surrounded him. He wished there was a window in the chamber so he could at least see outside to look at what was going on. But the grey expanse of stone to one side of him was the curtain wall of the inner ward, and no builder in charge of his wits would do something as foolish as putting a hole in it. Besides, it would only look out over the moat, which was stinking even more than usual in this weather. The other side of the room was made of wood and faced inwards, but there was still no way he could look out – the door was at the other end. It led to a covered but open passageway which ran around between the chambers and the courtyard, so that some light, air and sound leaked into the room, but that was about it. He didn't think he'd ever in his life spent so long without going outdoors, and the lack both of air and of ability to stretch his limbs was pressing on him, suffocating him. He was going to have to get out of here.

He managed to heave himself up into a sitting position. He pulled the blanket away from his legs – he hadn't really needed it in this heat, but he was only wearing a shirt and braies and it wouldn't be right if Joanna were to come in. He looked down at his legs. The fronts of them weren't too bad, but as he shifted himself and squinted behind him, he could just about see that the backs of his thighs were almost black. He guessed that his back would probably not look much better, either, judging by the stiffness in it. It felt as though someone had put a plank down the back of his shirt and then tied him to it. But he just had to get out of here. He manoeuvred himself so that his legs were over the side of the narrow bed, and slowly, carefully, he lowered his bare feet to the floor.

Someone came through the open door, and he nearly overbalanced as he started and clutched at the blanket, but it was just Adam, carrying a platter of food. He looked surprised – probably at seeing me the right way up, thought Martin – and shoved the platter on to the low stool before coming over to stand before him.

'Are you supposed to be getting up?' He sounded a bit harried.

Martin grunted. 'I don't care whether I'm supposed to or not – I can't stay in this bed a moment longer. Help me up.'

He held out one of his hands for Adam to pull on, and used the other to push himself off the bed. A moment's dizziness hit him as he stood upright, and he felt a strange draining sensation in his legs. He leaned on Adam's shoulder for balance until the room stopped moving.

'Good. Now, stay by me while I try walking.'

Movement was fairly difficult, but it wasn't as impossible as it had seemed yesterday. As he hobbled slowly back and forth, his legs began to feel like part of him again; and his appetite was returning. He tried to pick the food up off the stool but he couldn't bend at all and had to grab at Adam to stop himself falling over like a small child.

He stood up again, carefully. 'I tell you what – you pass me the food, and I'll stand and eat it while you get my clothes and tell me what's going on.'

Adam nodded and handed him the meal. 'I'm sorry it's not on a proper trencher – I thought that would go soggy and fall apart while I was on my way here so I just put it in a dish.'

Martin didn't really care, though it was odd to be eating out of a serving platter. He wolfed down the beef and what tasted like some duck as Adam found his hose, tunic, belt and boots and put them on the bed, talking all the while. He was just running his finger round the edge of the dish in order to lick the last dregs of the sauce when he caught the last thing Adam had said.

'Missing?'

Adam nodded. 'Yes, he's been gone since this morning when we all had a ride in the woods after the hanging. Lady Ela is shouting at everyone, Sir Geoffrey thinks he's done it on purpose, and our lord is furious.'

Well, that sealed it then. He couldn't leave Adam on his own if the lord earl was going to lose his temper. He squeezed the boy's shoulder. 'Come on – help me get dressed and I'll come back out with you.'

He was rewarded by a very relieved smile. Adam had to crouch to help him put his feet into each hose and then roll them up far enough so that Martin could reach to grab the lace at the top and tie it on to the drawstring at the waist of his braies. The tunic wasn't too bad as he could get it over his head without having to move too much, but he gave up when it came to the boots – too small, as his boots always seemed to be – and let Adam deal with them. He was good at it; all that practice serving the earl and his previous master, no doubt. Finally Martin buckled his belt, and, feeling like a man again instead of an invalid, he walked stiffly towards the door, glad to leave the sickbed behind.

Sir Geoffrey was striding about the inner ward talking to various men as Martin made his way carefully down the stairs at the end of the passageway. The knight turned as one of the men pointed, and greeted Martin.

'So you're up and about, eh?'

'Yes, Sir Geoffrey. Adam told me about Thomas and I'd like to help.'

The knight snorted. 'You wait until I get my hands on that boy. He'll remember it until the day he dies. But yes, let's get him found before the Lady Ela's screeches raise the roof.' He looked Martin up and down. 'Most of us are off into the woods – Adam, go and mount up – but I don't think much of your chances of staying on a horse.' Adam scurried off. 'You'd better take some men and search round the outer ward. There are dozens of places there a boy could be hiding.'

Martin refused to allow himself to look relieved, but he had to admit to himself that he'd been wondering how in the Lord's name he'd be able to ride. He nodded and started to turn away. Sir Geoffrey looked as though he would move off, too, but he stopped and grasped Martin's arm. 'It's good to see you, lad. You had me worried for a while back in the woods, but you're a strong boy.' The old eyes, lined with the years, looked into his own. 'A strong man, I should say. Welcome back.'

With a final squeeze of his arm, Sir Geoffrey moved away. Martin stood looking after him, pain forgotten, floating in the air.

Hours later the afternoon sun was blazing in the sky. Martin had been through every nook and cranny in the outer ward and there was no sign of Thomas. None of the men there had seen the boy; he'd even stopped the imposing figure of Crispin the smith from his work to ask. Now he stood outside the entrance to the kennels and stretched. He ached all over, but the movement was slowly coming back. He nodded to his men to go and get themselves a drink, and they saluted and moved away while he stood looking around him. Another hot sweaty rider came in through the gate, empty-handed, shaking his head. Where in the Lord's name was that boy? Martin had started off being angry that Thomas was causing everyone so much trouble, but now he was starting to get worried that something had actually happened to him. What if he were lying injured in the woods somewhere? What if …?

He turned as the sound of multiple horses came from the gate. Sir Geoffrey rode in, followed by another man who was leading a pony on a rein. There was no mistaking the small mount with its distinctive forehead blaze, but the saddle was empty.

***

Edwin sat in the embrasure up on the curtain wall, trying to think. He had joined in the search of the ward, but when it had proved fruitless he'd decided that he was likely to be more useful thinking while others looked. He had last seen Thomas that morning, after the hang– after the events at the crossroads. To start with Thomas had looked elated and Edwin had been shocked at his callousness. But afterwards, he had looked frightened and sick, as well he might after witnessing the executions. Most of the other children, and indeed some of the adults, had been the same. But wait, Edwin hadn't looked at him straight afterwards – he'd been too busy keeping his own stomach inside himself. No, he hadn't looked up until after the earl's final words. What had he said? Something about punishing the malefactors. Yes, and then, as he had turned away, 'So perish all who disobey me.' And it was *then* that Thomas had turned green.

Dear Lord, was Thomas frightened that he was going to be hanged for something? If so, did he have anything in particular that he was guilty of? He was the earl's nephew, he wouldn't be punished for stealing food or any such petty crime, it must have been something more serious … oh my Lord. Could he have had anything to do with Hamo's death? But surely that wasn't possible. The two of them had had a few run-ins, but that wasn't surprising given their respective temperaments, and surely such a small child could not be capable of such evil?

He sat back against the wall. As it happened, that might solve one of his problems, as it pretty much put William Steward in the clear. If there was a less likely scenario than William poisoning Hamo (rather than, say, beating him to death), it was him getting Thomas to poison Hamo for him – William loathed Thomas even more than Hamo did. But that wasn't exactly proof, and if, when he laid his thoughts before the earl, the earl decided that William had murdered Hamo, then he too would be swinging from a gibbet unless Edwin could prove otherwise.

But why might Thomas do such a thing, and who else might be involved? He couldn't go and tell all this to Sir Geoffrey until he'd straightened it all in his mind. At that moment he looked down and saw the knight clattering through the cobbled area by the gate, with the riderless pony behind him. Edwin felt a jolt. This was serious. Had Thomas, in a panic, run away from the earl's men after the hangings and then fallen from his horse? He can't have been attacked by any more outlaws or they would have taken the pony, so it must have been an accident. But what if someone else had assailed him? What if Thomas, rather than being the guilty party, had seen something which incriminated someone else, and that someone had taken steps to ensure he wouldn't talk? A chill ran through Edwin despite the heat of the day, as he remembered another page, another little boy who now lay silent and still in his grave. He had to stop this evil before anyone else died.

But there was another possibility. What if Thomas were the accomplice of the guilty party, and that man had simply hidden him away safely somewhere? That would make it someone who cared about him, for otherwise the boy might be seen as disposable. Someone who had influence over the boy, who wanted to keep him safe …

It was all going round and round in his mind as he made his way down the steps, so much so that he stumbled as he reached the bottom. His head felt like it was splitting apart again so he stood in the shade for a moment before stepping out into the blinding light of the inner ward. He found Sir Geoffrey in the armoury, being divested of his mail and the gambeson underneath, sopping wet as the soldier dropped it on the floor. He waited until the man had left and Sir Geoffrey had taken a large swig from a wineskin.

The knight nodded to him, still a little breathless. 'Well?'

'I think I've got an idea.'

The knight wiped the back of his hand across his mouth. 'Good. Tell me.'

'Well, I think Thomas has disappeared because he knows something.'

'You mean someone has done away with him?'

Edwin shook his head. 'No. I think … what I mean is …' how could he say this about a member of the earl's family? 'I think William Fitzwilliam might have murdered Hamo.'

'*What?*'

'Well, a lot of things seem to point that way – John said he'd seen them meeting each other sometimes; Hamo called out "William" when he died; and he doesn't seem to be very upset that his son has disappeared. Thomas looked greensick after he heard my lord saying "perish all who disobey me"; I think he was imagining his father, or even himself, swinging from a gibbet. When William realised that Thomas had seen him doing something and might tell our lord, he took him away and hid him somewhere.'

Sir Geoffrey stroked his damp beard. 'Well, it's possible. But you will need to have something better than that before we can go to the lord earl with accusations against his goodbrother.'

Edwin nodded. 'Oh, yes, I don't want to tell our lord yet. For one thing, I still don't know *why* William Fitzwilliam might have wanted to kill Hamo, and until I know that I won't be satisfied that he actually did it. Something still isn't right. No, what I'm suggesting is that we watch him carefully to see if he gives himself away at all. Surely if he does know where Thomas is then he will go to him eventually.'

'All right. We will keep this between ourselves for now, but we will keep him under our watch to see what he does. In the meantime, you see if you can find out more.'

'Yes, Sir Geoffrey.'

The knight stretched. 'In the meantime I am going to change my shirt. At my age, if I sit around wet like this, I'll either get the summer ague or my bones will grow too stiff to move.' He half smiled. 'The perils of age, lad.' As he passed he gripped Edwin's shoulder briefly. 'You'll get there one day, but not for many years, thank the Lord.'

Edwin watched him go, and then went out into the brightness of the ward. He could smell the evening meal being prepared, and sniffed the air.

If anything, it was even hotter in the great hall than it had been the evening before. No fires were lit, of course, but the place was packed with sweaty men sitting shoulder to shoulder, causing a wet fug in the air, and their smell was drowning out the scent of the pottage. Edwin had managed to bag himself a place on a bench which was near the door, so an occasional waft of air came his way, for which he was grateful. He could feel the sweat under his arms, and his shirt and tunic sticking to his back. From his place he had a good view of the door to the service area, and he watched the men scuttling in and out with their heavy loads of dishes, glad at least that he didn't have to work in the kitchen in this weather.

He recalled that on the night he died, Hamo had stood in that very entrance. He had spoken to the serving men as they went back and forth, and then he had stopped and stared at Edwin, his eyes so wide and his face so pale that he might have seen the very devil himself. Edwin shuddered and crossed himself at the thought.

'Did you want me for something?'

'What?' Edwin came back to himself to realise that the man opposite him, a visitor he didn't recognise, was addressing him. 'Oh, no, sorry.'

'Well, stop staring at me like that then.' The man returned to his meal.

Edwin was about to explain that he hadn't been staring at the man but rather beyond him, but he swallowed the words before he could say them. Of course! How could he have been so stupid?

He looked around. Yes, there he was. Edwin got up with some difficulty, apologising to the man on his left as he kicked him trying to get his legs back over the bench, hurried round the bottom end of his table and over to the lower end of the other one which ran parallel down the hall. He tapped on a shoulder. 'Can I talk to you for a few moments? Outside?'

Joanna tried to ignore everything going on around her as she ate her meal. It wasn't often that she could tell herself she was happy. Not only had she spent some precious moments alone with Martin over the last couple of days, not only had she spoken to him and Edwin about something of wider significance than embroidery, but her future suddenly looked better as well. A few stolen moments were one thing, but her future, at least for the time being, was in serving Isabelle, and upon Isabelle and her whims her happiness naturally depended. And Isabelle had *actually noticed* that she would like to go and look after Martin, and had *actually suggested* that she do it. Could this be the same lady she had been serving all these years? The one who generally treated her as a possession, as though she were as unfeeling as a tapestry on the wall, or as useful as a comb to be picked up when she needed and discarded again afterwards? Truly, love could work miracles. She gave a small prayer of thanks as she sipped her wine.

But she couldn't shut it all out for long. The afternoon had been terrible, with all the nobles – other than Isabelle, who was too overjoyed at Sir Gilbert's escape and too excited about her wedding drawing ever nearer – arguing and sniping at each other and inevitably taking it out on their squires and companions. The Lady Ela had been hysterical when she'd heard about Thomas's pony being brought in, and she'd shrieked at her husband and at the lord earl, who at least had the option of saying he had matters to attend to, and leaving the room.

William Fitzwilliam had no such escape route, and he'd had to sit and listen to his wife's frenzied outbursts, sitting stoically and trying to ignore her. Joanna simply couldn't read him at all. Was he upset about his son's disappearance? Was that what he'd been praying about in the chapel? But no, that had been before Thomas had vanished, and before the hangings.

Somebody else was watching William Fitzwilliam closely, she realised: Sir Geoffrey, who was placed next to him at the table. Come to think of it, he'd been – unusually for him – in the great chamber since he returned from his latest search for the boy, and he'd positioned himself near to the earl's goodbrother then, as well. Joanna looked at the knight with more interest, noting the way he held his eating knife almost like a weapon. He was eating little and drinking less, his grey-bearded face stony as always. He'd been at Conisbrough since long before she arrived and to her was as much a fixture as the keep, but she had never really spoken to him – well, she had no need to, did she, for they lived in different worlds although they shared the same walls – and she admitted to herself that she was just a little bit scared of him.

As she watched, Sir Geoffrey cast a glance behind him. Joanna followed his gaze and noticed the man-at-arms standing in the shadows towards the back of the dais. She didn't know his name, but she recognised him immediately – the one with the barrel chest and the neck almost thicker than his head, whose favourite trick was to pick up two of his fellows at once, one in each hand. Now that *was* unusual. Why would he be here while they were eating?

The remnants of her daydreams dissolved, and she lost her appetite. She poked her spoon into the sauce on her trencher as she looked across the table. Matilda was tearful, having been pinched by the Lady Ela for some minor infraction, and nursing the bruises on her arms. Rosamund was quiet, overawed by the currents of ill-feeling around her as she had been all day. Past Sir Geoffrey and William Fitzwilliam sat the Lady Ela herself, her face blotchy as she listened to the minstrel, who had rather unluckily got to a bit of the poem where the great Charlemagne was wailing out his grief for his lost nephew. The earl, in the centre with Isabelle and Sir Gilbert on either side, stared straight ahead of him as he chewed, paying only the barest minimum of courtesy to them. Past him, Henry de Stuteville and the Lady Maud were sober, although she was attempting some little good humour with her son and nephew. And at the far end of the board, Sir Roger and Father Ignatius were debating something in low tones, trying not to cause a disturbance.

Joanna put her spoon down. She was annoyed – either with herself or with others, she didn't know – that she couldn't hold on to her happy thoughts. In between the gloomy faces at the table, the menace of the man behind them, the subdued air in the rest of the hall, and the despair in the voice of the minstrel, who for once she wished would shut up, they were outnumbered. She wondered when the meal would ever end.

———

Brother William looked surprised at Edwin's summons, but he obligingly wiped his knife and spoon, stowed them away, and rose.

Edwin led him out of the hall and into the ward. Where would they not be overheard? Most men would be in the hall eating, but others would still be about their duties. He settled on his favourite embrasure up on the curtain wall – their voices would float away up in the air, and he'd be able to see anyone approaching along the wall-walk – and led the way up the steps. Although the sun was waning, the stones had stored the heat of the day and were still uncomfortably hot. He asked the rather bemused brother to sit, and then joined him.

'So, Edwin, why have you dragged me away from my fine meal?' There was an edge to the voice, and Edwin remembered again the scene he'd witnessed in the woods. Monk he might be, but Brother William was a dangerous man. He began to feel that bringing him on his own to a precarious position high off the ground might not actually have been a very good idea.

'On the – ' He stopped and cleared his throat. 'On the night Hamo died, I saw him in the great hall. He was standing by the service door, and he was staring at me as though he had seen a spirit. All this time I've been wondering why he should have looked at me so, but now I've realised that it wasn't me he was looking at – it was you. That was the day you arrived. Did he know you?'

Brother William flexed his arms and Edwin instinctively flinched. But the monk was merely stretching. 'Ah, it is good to be out of the hall. Fear not, Edwin, for I shan't harm you. I wasn't going to say anything: after all, Hamo is dead, God rest his soul, what good would it do? But if it helps you to find out who killed him, then I will tell you our family history.'

Edwin jerked his head up, and the monk nodded.

'Yes, family, for he was my brother.' Brother William sighed, and paused to look out over the moat, the outer ward and the golden fields of corn beyond. 'Settle yourself, for this may take a while.' He folded his hands inside the sleeves of his habit.

'I am – or I was – the third of four brothers. Our father was adamant that one of his sons should go into the Church: I think he wanted to atone for something he'd done earlier in his life, and giving the Church one of his children, together with a hefty donation, was his way of doing it. My eldest brother Fulk agreed with him entirely, as well he might, given that it would never be him who had to renounce the world and take up the habit. He swore to uphold my father's wishes.

'To start with there was no problem – my second brother Roger was more than happy to take the cowl, and he did so, and rose to be the abbot at Faversham. I was always one for fighting and training, so I became a knight and was part of my brother's household. Hamo was the youngest and he always knew there'd be nothing for him, so he made a career for himself in another way by serving my lord earl. We were all happy until about five years ago, when my brother Roger died. Fulk received word of it in a letter, and almost immediately he told me I'd have to leave the household and take the cowl, as he'd sworn to our dead father that one of us would always be in the Church, sacrificing his worldly life in order to pray for our father's sins. As you might imagine, I refused – I was happy being a knight and I was pretty good at it. I didn't have any lands of my own, but I was a good brother to Fulk and a loyal member of his household.

'All of that counted for naught, though, against our late father's wishes, so Fulk threw me out and said he'd have nothing further to do with me. He had some influence with others, and he went about saying that I'd always sworn I'd enter the Church and that I'd reneged on my oath and was no man of honour. So of course I couldn't find a place in anyone else's household either. I had no patronage, and the Lord knows you can't get anywhere in life without that. I thought I'd give it a try, though – if God wanted me to stay out in the world he'd find a way to support me. But He didn't, and I ended up living almost like a peasant. The only way I could have sunk lower would have been to become some kind of robber knight, using my abilities and my weapons – for I still had those – to steal and survive that way. But I couldn't in all conscience take to preying upon innocents, so I decided the Lord was telling me to follow my family's wishes and join a monastery. So I swallowed my pride and went back to Fulk to tell him I'd changed my mind. Once he knew he had his way then all else was forgotten – he came up with a donation which enabled me to take a good place. The only small piece of control I had left was that Fulk wanted me to become a Benedictine, so I defied him and joined the Cistercian order instead. I started at Boxley and then moved to Roche about a year ago.

'Abbot Reginald, may the Lord bless his soul, could see I was a reluctant brother, so he made excuses for me to be out of the abbey from time to time – I was a useful man for him to have around as a travelling companion when he needed to go anywhere, or if there were tithes or money which needed protecting. I knew that Hamo had joined the service of my lord earl, and knowing he was so close, I had half-formed a plan anyway that I might try to ask him if he might take my place. To be honest I can't even begin to imagine that he'd say yes, but I was desperate enough to try anything. God knows Fulk wouldn't be bothered which one of us was a monk as long as someone was. So when Abbot Reginald said that a clerk was needed to join the household, everything seemed to fit together. But of course now it's too late.'

Edwin stared. 'But … forgive me, it probably isn't my place to tell you, but your brother Fulk is dead.'

Brother William sat up straight. 'Fulk? How do you know?'

'I heard it from Father Ignatius. Hamo had a letter giving him the news, and he told the good Father.'

He waited to allow Brother William time to receive the news in his heart. The monk crossed himself, closed his eyes and muttered a prayer to himself. When he opened his eyes, Edwin continued. 'There's something else – Hamo thought you were dead as well. Apparently Fulk had told him you'd left his service and then been killed in a brawl. No wonder he looked as though he'd seen a spirit that night.'

This time there was silence, silence which stretched out into the sky.

Eventually Brother William spoke. 'Well, there you are then. No household to go back to. Fulk's sons will believe I'm dead and gone as well, so no point turning up there asking to be taken back. The eldest boy will no doubt have the same trouble again, for he has several brothers of his own. No …' he sighed again, 'a monk's life for me then. Do you know, I've spent so long railing against my habit that I hadn't noticed at all that I'd got used to it. Well, not the endless services or the lack of worldly goods, but it does seem fine to be a part of something, to have "brothers" who are closer to me than my blood kin. I'll stay in the order, or at least for now, as long as I can remain in the service of my lord the earl, and we shall see what happens. Maybe a suitable household position will come up with someone. The Lord may well have plans for me yet. But if the time comes when the choice is between leaving the order or cloistering myself in the abbey again, I will take the wide world as it is, and starve in it if I must, rather than going back and suffocating.'

Edwin hesitated to say it, but he felt he had to. 'There's one more thing you should know.'

'What's that?'

'There's no easy way to tell you, but … Hamo was thinking of becoming a monk.'

There was a pause and then Brother William threw back his head and roared with laughter, continuing until he shook and his face ran with tears. 'Oh, God mocks me and the Lady Fortune spits in my face once more.' He stopped laughing, suddenly, and drew his sleeve across his eyes. 'Still, what makes us men is the ability to take what we are dealt and make something of it, I suppose. Now, if you will excuse me, I think I will leave you. I've lost my appetite for food, but I believe I need to pray.'

Edwin watched him make his way along the wall-walk and down the steps, looking after him until long after he had disappeared from sight.

Chapter Twelve

Try as he might, Edwin just couldn't get to sleep. He turned himself over and over on his straw palliasse while his head buzzed like a hive. It was far too hot, which wasn't helping: even with no blanket and the fire dampened down it was stifling. But he couldn't bring himself to open the cottage door and leave it gaping into the darkness. He tried to lie still, but the sound of small creatures in the thatch above him was echoed by the thoughts scratching around in his head. Why would William Fitzwilliam want to murder Hamo?

He dozed a little and imagined that Hamo was calling to him, crying out in his agony. Help me, screamed the spectre. I'm burning. I have poison inside me and it's burning me up from the inside.

Poison. Edwin was awake again. Poison was an indiscriminate weapon – it could have been meant for anyone. So don't keep thinking of who could have done what and when; think of why. It's all about power, Joanna had said. So who has power? The earl, of course. But nobody would want to kill him – that would throw all their lives into chaos and danger. Edwin turned over again, feeling a flea jump from the palliasse on to his neck. If the earl died … he jolted fully awake and sat up, slapping his neck to kill the flea. If the earl died, someone else would take the title, and the power. Until now, that man would be William Fitzwilliam. After the wedding, that man would be Sir Gilbert – he was marrying the earl's eldest sister. What if William had meant to poison Sir Gilbert, and had ended up killing Hamo by mischance?

Edwin rose and cautiously opened the window shutter. The village was in darkness and all was quiet except for the sound of a baby wailing further down the street. Yes, it was logical that the displaced heir might want to murder the new heir, to retain his position – and that of his sons, including the one he might have used to help him. And it also followed that he would want to make it look like some kind of accident – he would never inherit otherwise. But poison? In a large household further swollen by all those guests? How could he possibly hope to kill just one man? And how could Hamo have got in the way?

He went to lie down again, but the open window bothered him: shadows flitted outside, and in his half-awake state he imagined dark horrors sliding in. He got up and closed the shutter again before returning to his palliasse to lie restless once more. He had to sort this out, or the earl would be very displeased. Martin was now up and about, so Edwin wouldn't be needed in the great hall any more, thank the Lord, so he'd have more time to think. But just sitting around all day tying his head in knots wouldn't help.

Edwin got up again, went over to the bucket in the corner of the room, and splashed some water on to his aching forehead. The bucket was nearly empty – his mother would have to take it to the well in the morning, for the water butts in the garden were dry too. Thank the Lord that the well in the village had never been known to go dry, not even in the hot summers which the older inhabitants remembered from years long past. But that didn't help the fields, which were parched. On the morrow, the whole village, under the reeve's direction, were going out to the north field to carry water from the river to the wheat and rye crops; it was a day for working in their own fields rather than the earl's. Edwin thought he might go with them, at least for an hour or two – it would be hard physical labour, but not much concentration would be required, so he would be able to think while he was doing it. And maybe a day's toil would mean he would actually be able to *sleep* tomorrow night.

As the sun rose, he met everyone else out on the green. The men were joined by most of the women and any children old enough to walk and carry a bucket, for the business of stopping the fatal drooping of the crops was crucial to everyone if the village was to avoid hard times and starvation next year. It was going to be another scorching day, so Edwin took the precaution of tying a piece of linen around his neck to protect it from the sun, as his head was already thumping after his sleepless night and he didn't want to make it any worse. His mother held out a full aleskin and he tied it to his belt; it would be thirsty work. He hefted his bucket – it was heavy enough empty, the Lord only knew how the little ones would manage – and attempted a smile for his mother and aunt. William Steward hovered in the background, his face like thunder at being left behind with the old and infirm.

They all set off, walking until they reached the bank of the river. The water was lower than Edwin had ever seen it, but there was still plenty to be had; he joined the others making their way over the dry, cracked bank and then through the wetter mud, and dipped his bucket into the flowing river. It immediately became almost too heavy to lift, and he struggled back up the bank and over to the edge of his own strip to pour the water carefully on the earth around the nearest wheat and rye. If he could save it, the mixed crop would give him the maslin for the winter's bread.

After he'd done this a few more times he stopped to look around him. Everyone was doing the same, but surely there must be a better way? He stopped to survey the field. There were twelve strips in this part, each starting near the riverbank and running up a slight incline for a furlong or so – whoever had laid out the system in the distant past had sensibly decided not to have the strips running parallel to the river, lest one or two villagers gain the advantage of the water – and each strip had a furrow separating it from the next, wide enough for a man to walk down without disturbing the crops. He looked around at all the men, women and children going back and forth from the river with their buckets, and an idea came to him. There were, let's see, fifty-six people there ... he watched a young child fall over with a full bucket, spilling the precious water everywhere and being smacked on the back of the head by her father, and revised that down to fifty, ignoring the smallest half a dozen children. If they all stood about five yards apart, they would stretch from the river to the top of the field, and could pass buckets along the line. After they had watered the top of each strip, everyone could move a pace closer and they could water that part of each strip, and so on. The smallest children could ferry the empty buckets back from the top of the field to the river. But how to persuade people? Despite his exalted position in the earl's household he wasn't the bailiff, the reeve or even the hayward, so he had no right to direct the work of the men. He spotted the reeve, heading back to the river with an empty bucket, and drew him to one side, murmuring in his ear.

Before the sun was much higher in the sky Edwin stood as part of a long line which ran from Wulfric, boots and hose off and braies rolled up, standing knee-deep in the river, to the reeve himself at the top. All he had to do was move a few paces to his right to collect a bucket from Cecily, then carry it a few paces to his left to hand it to his mother. It was less backbreaking for all concerned, the reeve was happy as everyone thought it had been his idea, and the villagers were smiling, one or two even having the breath to sing as they worked. Edwin revelled in the monotony of his task, secure in the knowledge that he was part of a group, and not some strange individual who didn't fit anywhere. He sighed. He hadn't done much of the thinking he'd promised himself, and time was growing short. What would happen to him if he couldn't present the earl with the answers he wanted? Would he be dismissed? Would he be happier leaving the earl's personal service and going back to this? Would the earl let him if he asked? Maybe that would be better for everyone. But as his arms grew tired, he knew this was not for him. Although it was nice to be working with his body for a change, that was what it was – a change. Deep in his heart he knew he would go mad if he could not stretch his mind every day, and not for the first time in his life he wondered what it was about him that made him so different from the other villagers, and why the Lord had chosen to make him so.

The day grew nearer to noon; to add to his aching arms and back, his mind hurt from thinking itself round in circles. Had William Fitzwilliam tried to murder Sir Gilbert by getting Thomas to put poison in something, which had then killed Hamo? In which case, why hadn't he tried again once his scheme had failed? There was the accident with the horse, of course, but the way Mistress Joanna had told the tale, it was just that – an accident. So maybe Hamo *had* been the intended target. But why would William Fitzwilliam want to kill him, if indeed he was the culprit? Had Edwin got this all wrong?

He stopped to wipe his brow and watched the children scampering to and fro after delivering buckets to Wulfric. Hadn't there been more of them earlier? Indeed, someone else had noticed one of the children was missing – a father towards the top of the bucket chain was calling out, worried, though he didn't leave his place in the line. Others started to look around them and call out, and it wasn't long before a boy of about five appeared from a clump of reeds on the riverbank. He ran to his father, who picked him up, hugged him, put him down, clouted him on the back of the head, and sent him on his way up to the top to collect another bucket.

As the sun reached its high point the reeve called for a rest, and the grateful villagers congregated on the riverbank. A solitary tree offered some little shade, and the two pregnant women among them sat down next to the trunk, fanning their faces and rubbing their backs. Bread was produced, supplemented for some by onions or hard cheese, and everyone gave their attention to eating. After his brief meal and a few draughts from his aleskin, Edwin stood – he had to go back to the castle. But he'd stood up too suddenly, and the pulsing in his head caused him to feel dizzy. He went down to the water's edge, soaked his neckcloth in water, wiped his face and then put it back round his neck. It would be dry again by the time he got back, but he could get some water from the well. He bade his mother and Cecily goodbye and gave a brief wave to the others. There was some grumbling among the men about shirking his share, but the reeve, knowing they'd be able to accomplish twice as much thanks to Edwin's idea, walked with him some few yards and murmured that he'd make sure his strip was watered along with the others. Then they'd move another quarter of a mile along the river to the next field and be able to do the same again before night fell.

Edwin made his way back along the scorching path towards the village, squinting in the blinding brightness, his head still pounding. He staggered. There seemed to be flashes of light around him. When he reached the shade of a couple of trees he stopped, took the aleskin from his belt and gulped down the rest of the contents. It tasted different from how it tasted straight from the barrel, of course, but it was refreshing nonetheless. He didn't know how nobles could drink wine all the time – the great chamber had smelled of it when he was there, and frankly he'd found it had made his head swim.

He paused in the act of stoppering the skin again, trying to force himself to think straight. Wine. Poison was an indiscriminate weapon, so how would a murderer ensure that he only killed his chosen target? He'd put it in something which only certain people were going to drink. And a special barrel of wine had been ordered for the bridal couple. He had to go and tell Sir Geoffrey about this.

He started back on his way, but the headache turned to dizziness, and the dizziness to nausea. He stopped by the edge of the road to vomit, then staggered on. The flashing lights continued, splintering the world around him. Somehow he reached the village, but it was deserted, the very old, the very young and those about to give birth dozing, and everyone else out in the fields or at their daily work in the castle. He reeled. By the time he reached the church he couldn't see his way at all. The light was so bright that the ground was moving, and there were strange dark spots appearing before his eyes. He went into the graveyard. Why was he here? Wasn't there something important he was supposed to be doing? But the sun had tipped over from its high point and one end of the church offered some shade. Oh, the relief of being out of the light. The stone was quite cool. No, he really had to go and see someone about something, didn't he? He'd just rest here a few moments, and then he'd remember what it was.

He fell to his knees, then lay down on the welcoming ground, and passed out.

'Edwin. Edwin, wake up!'

Through the thumping of his head, a voice was speaking from far away. He tried to reply but only managed to groan, a groan which turned into a whimper as he moved his head.

'Edwin, talk to me, lad, I can't tell whether you're alive or dead.'

Very cautiously, Edwin opened one of his eyes a little way. He wasn't blinded. He was in a patch of shade, and William Steward was leaning over him, one hand gripping his shoulder and shaking him. Edwin licked his dry lips. 'I'm alive, uncle. I'm alive.' He opened both eyes. The patch of shade was now quite large. 'How long have I been here?'

William shrugged. 'I don't know. I came to find Father Ignatius and I found you lying here. It's late in the afternoon.'

'What? It was only noon when I – ' Edwin tried to raise himself but the world started spinning again and he subsided.

'You're all right, lad, probably just too much sun. It happens sometimes.'

Edwin felt ashamed of himself. Everyone else, children and pregnant women included, had been working out in the heat all day; he'd managed a few hours and then fainted. What a weakling.

'Listen, let's try getting you sat up, and then I'll fetch you something to drink. You'll be fine after that.' William, sitting awkwardly himself with his crutches thrown beside him, managed to get one of his arms around Edwin and heaved him up like a sack of turnips until he was in a sitting position. Edwin leaned his back against the wall of the church and waited for everything to stop spinning. William began the laborious process of dragging himself upright; Edwin knew it would be pointless offering to help, partly as he couldn't stand up himself, and partly as he didn't think he could bear William shouting at him to say he wasn't a helpless babe. So he said nothing.

Eventually William stood. 'See? That leg's getting better – it won't be long until I can go back to work.'

And thank the Lord for that, thought Edwin, though he still didn't speak.

'Right, stay there and don't move until I get back. Then once you've rested and drunk, you can get on with whatever you're supposed to be doing.' He began to haul himself away.

Yes, thought Edwin, I can get on with whatever I'm supposed to be doing, but what was that? I was on my way back from the field, and I was going to the castle, wasn't I? But why? Oh, how my head aches. But at least things are starting to look a bit straighter now, it must be wearing off. But I won't try getting up just yet.

He looked out over the graveyard. It looked peaceful from here, for there were no new graves within his line of sight – just older ones, mounds of grass of different sizes undulating gently up to the fence, the odd wooden cross leaning, and occasional wildflowers striking their bright notes against the parched grass. Strange how such a gentle covering could mask the seething corruption underneath; all those bodies rotting away and filled with worms and maggots. Appearances could be so deceptive. But it was just their bodies: their immortal souls were making their journey through purgatory to the bliss of heaven. The loss of his father suddenly hit Edwin again and he felt like weeping, although no tears fell from his eyes.

Time passed. It would take William some time to find both a drink and someone to carry it for him. Edwin stared into the distance for what seemed a long while before he noticed a movement at the other end of the churchyard. It was Peter, kneeling where his family were buried. His little shoulders were shaking. Edwin didn't like to interfere, but he couldn't stand to see such misery without trying to help. He was feeling more like himself now, anyway. He got up, very slowly, and picked his way through the mounds to where the boy was.

Peter looked up in some alarm when the shadow fell over him, but even as he half-rose to flee, he saw who it was and sank back down. He lowered his head and scrubbed at his eyes with the sleeve of his tunic. 'I wasn't crying.'

Edwin sat carefully beside him, far enough away so that the boy wouldn't feel threatened. The dizziness had receded, thank the Lord. 'Of course you weren't.' He leaned back, unsure of what to say, and exhausted.

Peter sniffed loudly and drew his arm across his face again. The tunic had once been fine, but Edwin thought that it probably wouldn't last too long if it was treated like that all the time.

'Your father was a good man.'

Edwin was surprised, having never known Peter start a conversation before. He sighed. 'Yes, he was.'

'Mine wasn't.'

Edwin struggled to remember Peter the elder. He had a vague recollection of a man with a limp and rotten teeth whom he'd never really spoken to. 'Why do you say that?'

Peter shrugged. 'I don't know. He used to beat us, even my baby brother when he cried,' he gestured towards a tiny mound to his left, 'and especially when he'd had ale. But … '

There was silence for a moment. 'But what?' The boy's head had gone down again. 'You can tell me.'

It came out in a wail. 'But I miss him! And my brother and sister, and m-m-my mother!' His voice rose as he burst into tears and flung himself at Edwin.

Edwin couldn't help it – he put his arms around the small figure and held him as he sobbed uncontrollably, rocking him back and forth and making comforting noises until the tears subsided. Was this what it was like to have a child of your own? He felt almost unbearably protective of the boy. Here he was, feeling sorry for himself because of his headache, and missing his father, but he was a man grown and could stand in his own shoes. Besides, he still had his mother and his friends – Peter had lost everything, and he was still a child. And until Sir Roger had shown the compassion to intervene, nobody had cared.

Edwin shifted his weight, his arms still about the boy. How best to comfort him? 'Peter. Tell me something you remember about your father that you liked.'

Peter stopped and looked up, his eyes puffy but showing interest. 'Something I remember?'

'Yes. There must be something that you used to enjoy, or something he did which you liked.'

There was a pause while Peter thought about it, wiping his sleeve absent-mindedly across his face again. 'When he was happy, he would throw me in the air, and I would be flying.' For the first time there was the hint of a smile. 'And he always made sure that when there was something to eat, that we all had some and not just him.'

Edwin was encouraged. 'What else?'

Peter thought for a moment, tears forgotten. 'Even when there wasn't much to eat, he tried to get us something. Sometimes we would go to the wood to look for mushrooms or nuts, and he showed me how to trap wild birds. Or sometimes we went to the mill at night time to see if there was any flour left over we could pick up.'

'You stole?'

Peter looked uncomfortable. 'Yes. But only leftovers and only because we were hungry. He made sure we didn't starve. He was my Pa and he wouldn't make me do anything bad.'

Edwin nodded. 'No father would, who really loved his son.' He wondered if his own father would ever have taken to thievery if his family was really in need. What was more important, keeping God's law or doing everything you could to keep your loved ones from the grave? Not that it had helped Peter's family in the end – they had all died off in an epidemic of the coughing sickness a few winters ago.

'I have to go.' Peter disentangled himself and stood up. 'I must get back to my lord.' He puffed out his little chest. 'He *needs* me.'

Edwin smiled. 'Yes, yes he does. And I'm sure you're a good helper to him.' He watched as the boy looked down at the graves, bent to pat the earth on the smallest one, then straightened and walked out of the graveyard. Edwin remained where he was, considering the subject of families. Something was buzzing at the back of his mind, but it wasn't his earlier dizziness – it was a nagging thought, although he couldn't think what it was or why it was important. He looked again at the graves. He'd never had any brothers or sisters, so he couldn't imagine what it was like to share his parents with anyone. He'd always had his father to himself, and he'd never appreciated what a privilege that was. His father had taught him everything, from honesty and goodness to thatching and daubing, to the duties of a bailiff. He was always ...

Ah, that was it. He'd said it himself. *No father who truly loved his son would make him do something bad.* Father hadn't. Peter the elder hadn't. Even Ganelon hadn't, for he was Roland's stepfather, not his father. And of course William Fitzwilliam hadn't. He might be a sour man, a weak man, but he had his pride, and he wouldn't persuade Thomas to poison anyone's food. The significance of the scene by the river that morning flooded back to him. The man there had been worried for his son's safety, but he hadn't left his place in the line as he still had his duty to do. And so did William Fitzwilliam: of course, he was worried about Thomas, but he was a man, a nobleman, and he couldn't show weakness before his peers and his lord. He'd tried to hide it behind a mask of insouciance. In reality he had no idea where Thomas was, which meant it hadn't been he who had hidden the boy or scared him off. And he would always act with caution, which didn't fit with the idea of murdering someone under the earl's own roof.

Which meant that they didn't need to keep him under close watch, and that Edwin was back at the beginning of his labours again. The weaving had unravelled, and now he must start afresh with a new pattern.

He sat unmoving. There was no particular need to go anywhere, and a new idea was starting to form in his mind. He wasn't quite back at the start. It was still possible, nay, likely, that Thomas had done the poisoning or had had something to do with it. But if his disappearance was protecting someone, and if it wasn't his father, then who was it?

'Edwin!' The shout broke the thread of his thought. It was William, dragging himself laboriously into the graveyard on his crutches. He was followed by Agnes, the priest's housekeeper, carrying a pitcher. 'Edwin, thank the Lord, you look like you've come back to the living.' William gestured to Agnes and she set the pitcher down. She put one wrinkled hand on Edwin's forehead and looked him in the eye for a moment, before murmuring to him. 'No, not just the sun – did you get dizzy and see strange lights?' Edwin nodded. 'Do not worry, youngling, it will pass. Drink plenty and try to stay out of bright light for the rest of the day. Then get your mother to make you a feverfew infusion tonight before you sleep, and all will be well tomorrow.'

Edwin nodded his thanks and she stood and moved away. He picked up the pitcher and tasted – small beer, a refreshing brew which wouldn't dull his mind too much. There was much to do. He drank deeply, dribbling some as he gulped, then lowered the vessel and wiped the back of his hand across his mouth.

William looked on approvingly. 'Good lad. Your colour's coming back. Come.' He held out one hand, and Edwin took it, careful not to pull on it too hard as he hauled himself up, in case they both overbalanced. William clapped him on the back. 'Now. What do you need to do?'

Edwin managed half a smile. He still didn't have the pattern complete, but he was starting to see it in his mind. 'Thank you, uncle. I need to go to the castle, as I have some news for Sir Geoffrey and the earl.'

William nodded. 'I'll come with you.' He held up one hand. 'Don't worry, I won't get in your way or start a fight with Richard. But I need to show them that I'm recovering, before they put someone else in my place.'

As they made their laborious way up to the castle, Edwin had time to straighten things in his mind. Nobody had wanted to poison Hamo – that had just been an accident. The real target was Sir Gilbert, who was about to marry the earl's eldest sister and who would therefore be the heir to the title. He would, as Mistress Joanna had known, have the power. And so who would want him out of the way? The people he had dispossessed, of course. William Fitzwilliam was married to the next sister, and so had been the most likely candidate, but he was not an ambitious man, and he wouldn't have encouraged his son to do something so vile. So that left one other – Henry de Stuteville. And what better way to assure himself of the earldom than to murder the heir and have the next in line suspected of the killing? His nephews adored him, and he would have had no problem getting Thomas to do something which he'd probably described as a prank. He'd given something to Thomas and told him to put it in the special wine for the bridal couple – probably telling him it would give them an amusing case of the runs on their wedding night or something. But Thomas hadn't realised he'd been given deadly poison. And Hamo had ordered the wine to be placed in the office, not in the kitchen; and as he'd eaten his solitary meal he hadn't been able to resist tasting some of it, with fatal consequences.

Presumably, had Henry de Stuteville succeeded in killing Sir Gilbert, he would have shown himself a loyal supporter of the earl so that he would be the ideal person to succeed him. Edwin had it all worked out now, and as he struggled to help the cursing William through the gate to the outer ward – the walk from village to castle was longer than it looked, and William might have been overambitious about his recovery – he knew he could explain it all to the earl. First, though, he'd have to make sure that the poisoned wine was somewhere safe. But there was no particular hurry – it was for the wedding, wasn't it, so Sir Gilbert and Lady Isabelle wouldn't be looking to drink any of it until tomorrow. Still, he'd better slip through the hall to the serving room while the meal was taking place in order to check it was still there.

By the time they reached the inner gatehouse William was really struggling and had slowed to such an extent that he was hardly moving. Edwin chafed at the delay, and it was with relief that he left William with the porter on duty to rest, while he made his way to the hall.

The evening meal was in full swing and Martin was busy. With so many people at the high table there wasn't much room for manoeuvre, and he was continually elbowing the other squires and trying not to trip over. The nobles had almost finished with the savoury dishes – all fish today, of course – and he started to take the bowls off the table and replace them on the sideboard. His own stomach groaned at the sight of all the fine food, and he stuffed a small slice of eel pie into his mouth while nobody was looking, just to keep him going until he was allowed to eat properly.

But before that could happen, there was the business of the toast to the bridal couple to be made on the eve of their wedding; a special barrel of wine had been ordered specifically for this occasion. Martin carefully broached the top of the barrel. Funny, it was looser than it should have been, good thing it hadn't all spilled on the way here. The aroma of the wine floated up into his nostrils as he removed the lid, and he inhaled the rich, unfamiliar scent. Truly this was an exotic drink, like nothing he'd ever smelled before. He dipped a jug into the smooth, dark, ruby liquid, and filled the two ornate goblets which Adam had placed on the sideboard. He was sorely tempted to have just a little sip, just to try out the enticing drink, but he couldn't. It was one thing to sneak a bit of pie while nobody was paying attention, but this was the special stuff for the bridal couple, and they alone must drink it.

The goblets were full, so he and Adam carried them to the table and placed them in front of the Lady Isabelle and Sir Gilbert. The other nobles were served with cups of a different wine so all was ready for the toast. Then Martin moved back to watch as the earl stood, followed by everyone in the hall. His stomach was growling so much that he barely listened as his lord made a short speech extolling the beauty and virtue of his sister and the bravery and prowess of her betrothed. Anyway, once the toast was over he would be able to eat something.

Martin watched as Sir Gilbert and Lady Isabelle raised the goblets to their lips.

Chapter Thirteen

Edwin wondered why it was so quiet when he entered the great hall. All the men in there were standing in silence, looking at the dais where the high table stood. To start with he couldn't see what was going on – he'd always wished he was taller – but when he moved round a bit he could see the earl standing with his goblet raised, speaking of the bridal couple. Edwin wouldn't interrupt that: he'd find the earl and Sir Geoffrey afterwards and explain about tomorrow's w– wait a moment. The earl was toasting the bridal couple. All the nobles had cups of wine. Sir Gilbert and the Lady Isabelle had ornate goblets in their hands. A small barrel stood on the side table. Sir Gilbert was about to drink. He was raising the goblet to his lips. Dear Lord.

'Stop!'

Every head in the hall turned his way, and Edwin realised that the voice he'd heard shrieking was his own. Sir Gilbert had, thank God, paused, the goblet hovering near his mouth with the wine mercifully untasted. But the earl's face was thunder as he looked down the hall.

Edwin gulped, but he had to go on. He took a few steps towards the dais. 'Sir Gilbert, please don't drink the wine. It's poisoned.'

Immediately there was uproar. Everyone seemed to be shouting. One or other of the ladies at the high table gave a shriek. Sir Geoffrey leapt up, his stool crashing to the ground behind him, and strode round the table to stand by the earl. He had no sword, but stood with a knife in his hand as though to repel any attack on his lord. All the nobles put their cups down, and then Martin and Adam started collecting them and putting them out of harm's way on the side table. Edwin could see which were the ones the bridal couple had held, as they were distinguishable by their handles. The earl himself, after a brief start of surprise, held his own cup out to be collected, then folded his arms and turned that frightening stare on Edwin.

'This had better be good.'

Edwin felt his face burning. He shifted uncomfortably, but that gaze was pinning him to the floor. 'My lord, I think Hamo died after he tasted the wine that was delivered for the wedding. Someone poisoned it, meaning to kill Sir Gilbert, and Hamo …'

At the mention of his name, Sir Gilbert, who had been standing protectively next to the Lady Isabelle, also strode round the table. He reached Edwin and gripped his shoulder. 'Edwin. Be very careful about what you're saying. Are you sure?'

Edwin nodded, still without taking his eyes off the earl. 'Yes. Once you're married you would be my lord's heir, and someone wanted to stop that. To start with I wondered how he thought he could do it with poison, but if this wine was just for the bridal couple, then – '

The earl had moved closer to him. 'You said "he". Who?'

Edwin could hardly manage to open his mouth. His voice came out in a squeak. 'My lord, perhaps we could go somewhere more private?'

A shake of the head. 'Speak. Speak now, before these witnesses.'

Edwin could feel himself fading, the hall seeming further away. He licked his lips. 'My lord, I …' Dear Lord, he was about to accuse the earl's own brother-in-law of murder. But Sir Gilbert was still holding his shoulder, holding it with the sword arm which had saved his life and the life of the woman he loved, just a few weeks ago. He heaved a shuddering breath. 'My lord, I believe it was Sir Henry de Stuteville.'

A gasp sounded from those men at the near end of the lower tables, but it was drowned out by the bellow of rage from Sir Henry, who stormed round the table and grabbed the front of Edwin's tunic in one huge fist. His bushy beard scratched Edwin's face as he propelled him backwards. Edwin felt himself at the centre of chaos, trying to stay on his feet, someone behind him holding him up as he was shoved, and several other men attempting to pull Sir Henry off him. There was a struggle before they eventually succeeded and he could breathe again. The man behind him turned out to be Sir Roger, who placed a calming hand on his arm. Sir Henry shrugged himself free of the restraining hands of Sir Geoffrey and Sir Gilbert and turned in fury to the earl, who had not moved.

He opened his mouth to speak, but was cut off by the earl raising his hand. 'Stop. I will hear you, but I will not have this riot under my roof.' He looked at Sir Geoffrey. 'Clear the hall.'

Sir Geoffrey gestured to several of his sergeants, who started to shepherd men away from the tables. Most of them moved unwillingly, grabbing food to take with them and turning to witness the spectacle until the last moment as they went out the door, but eventually the lower part of the hall was empty and unnaturally silent, the detritus of the meal scattered everywhere. Those on the dais stood immobile.

The earl looked at the high table. 'You too, ladies. This is no place for you.'

Edwin watched them as they scuttled away. The Lady Maud looked as though she would protest, but one look from the earl silenced her before she could start, and the Lady Isabelle pulled her away. Edwin could feel his heart throbbing in his throat. He had to explain things. Once the earl knew all the facts, surely he would understand? But he had turned away from Edwin, towards his goodbrother.

'Henry, now you have gathered yourself, perhaps you would like to speak.'

Henry de Stuteville looked at Edwin as though he were something unpleasant on the sole of his boot. 'My lord, surely you don't expect me to demean myself by responding to the mad ravings of this peasant?' The earl said nothing, but regarded him steadily. Sir Henry smoothed his beard. 'Very well. If I must put it into words, I did not poison this wine, and I did not attempt to kill Sir Gilbert. Is that satisfactory?'

The earl nodded and turned to Edwin. 'It must have taken quite some nerve to stand up and make this accusation. I assume you think you can prove it?'

Edwin tried to control the trembling in his limbs. 'Well …'

Sir Henry laughed derisively. 'You see? My lord, surely you give no credence to the wild allegations of such a person?' He looked around, surprised that the other men there had not rushed to his defence. Then he smiled. 'Will it settle the matter if I drink this wine? Will that prove my innocence?' He strode over to the side table, lifted one of the double-handled goblets and gulped down the contents so fast that a trickle of the wine escaped and ran down his beard and the side of his neck like blood. Edwin started forward in horror, and noted that Sir Geoffrey and Sir Roger both made similar, albeit smaller, movements – so they'd believed him. But Henry de Stuteville was standing proud, the empty goblet in his right hand, his left wiping across his mouth. He tossed the cup dismissively to one side and folded his arms. 'You see? I live.' He smiled at the earl, but the look he turned on Edwin was one which held such malice that Edwin could feel it in the innermost part of his being.

The earl turned back to him, those eyes looking right through him now. 'I am … disappointed.' Edwin felt stabbed. 'Go now, and I will deal with you in due course.'

Edwin stumbled off the dais, all support gone, all eyes on him as he took the longest walk of his life down the empty hall. He could feel the stares of the nobles, and his back burned. Once outside he was surrounded by men wanting to know what had happened, but he pushed blindly past them and did not stop until he reached his cottage. He barred the door, fell on to his palliasse, and, despite the heat of the evening, pulled a blanket over his head, curling under it like a babe and shuddering with an emotion he couldn't even name.

⸻⸱⸻

Martin tried to stand as still as possible. Thank the Lord his stiffness was wearing off now so he didn't feel the need to shuffle around to a more comfortable position, which might have drawn attention to himself. For the air in the room was like dry tinder, and it would only take one spark to set it all ablaze.

He felt sorry for Edwin. All along he hadn't seemed happy with the task laid upon him, and obviously the pressure had got too much for him – he'd been forced to make a guess which had turned out to be wrong. And there would be no coming back from it: he was disgraced in the eyes of the earl and would surely never work for him again. The earl himself was absolutely furious at the public embarrassment and, since they'd all retired to the great chamber, he'd spent his time stalking about, alternately swearing and apologising to Henry de Stuteville. Martin had the feeling that it was only the presence of the ladies that was keeping the earl from flinging cups around and breaking things.

Meanwhile the Lord Henry was (understandably, Martin supposed) livid about the insult to his honour and was demanding drastic punishment for Edwin. Martin trembled at some of his more violent suggestions. But both Sir Geoffrey, who was unusually in the chamber, unwilling to move away from the earl, and Sir Gilbert had tried to calm the situation with a view to saving Edwin's life and limbs. And, thank the Lord, Sir Henry's insistence on retribution was having the opposite effect on the earl to the one intended – he didn't like people making demands to his face, so he was veering away from any specific promises of punishment. Martin began to breathe a little more easily.

Eventually everyone stopped striding about and sat down to wine, quieter conversation, and, in the case of Sir Roger and Sir Gilbert, chess. Martin listened to the sound of the pieces being moved as the talk swirled around. Click. The consensus in the noble party now seemed to be that Hamo had died by accident after ingesting something which didn't agree with him. Click. Edwin had been wrong all along about it being poison. Click. 'Check.' After all, it had been four days now and nobody else had died – if there was poison in the castle supplies, they reasoned, someone else would have been affected. Click. 'Checkmate.'

Martin took the risk of looking up from his feet and gazing around him. Sir Roger was wryly acknowledging that his game had been poor, while Sir Gilbert smiled. Most of the nobles were nodding sagely at the lack of evidence of poisoning, but over to one side, his face illuminated by a torch on the wall, Sir Geoffrey was looking down and shaking his head.

An argument was breaking out on the other side of the room. Martin tried to swivel his eyes to see what was going on without moving his head. It was the Lady Ela, haranguing the lord earl again. Martin was glad he hadn't turned round.

'William, you need to do more to find Thomas! The poor boy is still out there somewhere, lost and lonely, and you don't seem to care!'

The earl bunched his fist, and Martin gulped. But his voice remained level. 'Sister, as I have said – *repeatedly* – we are searching for the wretch, not that he deserves it. He's on foot, so he can't be far away. And when we find him, if he's alive, he'll wish he weren't by the time I've finished with him, I can tell you. And if he's dead, frankly you should rejoice at losing such a troublesome and useless boy so early in life, before he can do any real damage.' He raised his hand to forestall her as she opened her mouth to speak, and looked instead at William Fitzwilliam. 'You'll need to do a great deal better with your other son if you want him to be worthy of any inheritance later.'

William Fitzwilliam nodded without speaking, but the Lady Ela shrieked. 'Him! Why, he's never – '

She was cut off abruptly as her husband took three steps towards her, brought his arm back, and slapped her across the face as hard as he could. The smack of his hand on her flesh echoed round the room, which fell silent.

Martin risked a fuller glance, still trying to remain immobile. The Lady Ela was leaning back in her chair, her hand to her face, white, staring up in disbelief at William Fitzwilliam, who was shaking with rage. 'Be *quiet!*' He leaned over her, his face close to hers. 'I will not take this disrespect any longer! God knows I've put up with you long enough, flaunting your higher birth at me, but I will be the master in my own household, damn it, and you will *learn!*' She flinched further away. 'Dear Lord, I've even been praying for the strength to deal with you and that cursed boy, wondering why I've let you cosset him so much. Just look how he's turned out, bringing shame on me, and all because of *your* foolishness. No more, I tell you!'

Everyone else was observing the scene while pretending to look away. Joanna and the other girls buried their faces in their sewing. The Lady Ela cast a glance at the earl.

William Fitzwilliam followed her gaze, stood up straight and made a small bow. 'Begging your pardon, my lord, under your roof.'

The earl merely flicked his fingers, a cold glance passing over the lady without engaging. 'Something you should have done a long time ago, evidently. She's your wife and it's up to you to control her, my sister or no.'

William Fitzwilliam straightened his tunic and smoothed his beard before turning back to his wife. 'Now, you will go to your chamber and stay there until tomorrow, and we will have no more whining about the boy. And from now on you will remain silent and obey me as a wife should.'

The Lady Ela stood and gave a stiff curtsey to her husband and to the earl before turning and leaving the room without speaking. She was still white, except for the scarlet mark of his hand on her face. Her companion – Martin couldn't remember her name – also stood and bobbed a hasty curtsey herself before following her mistress out the door. Martin felt sorry for her, having to walk the whole length of the room like that with everyone looking on in silence. For silent it was. There were, what, over a dozen people in the room, but you could hear a flea jumping in the rushes and a dog yawning over by the fireplace.

The earl broke the quiet, slapping the arm of his chair. 'Good. Adam, wine.'

The spell was broken. Martin realised he'd been holding his breath. The room went back to normal as the nobles began to chat again and the wine circulated. The earl turned to the Lady Maud, sitting nearest him and with a strange look on her face. He patted her hand. 'Ah, Maud, the last and least of my sisters, but the one who has always given me least trouble.' She smiled at him. 'Although,' he joked, 'I have high hopes of Isabelle from now on!'

Sir Gilbert ventured a small laugh, and Henry de Stuteville made some comment or other about making sure he started off right, to avoid trouble later. All was well, all was jocular.

Martin wondered why he felt so shocked. After all, every man from the king to the lowliest serf had the right to chastise his wife, and most did so physically. He thought back to when he'd been little and the earl had been married, and couldn't recall any specific instances such as the one he'd just witnessed, but then again, she'd done as she was told, hadn't she? So she hadn't brought anything on herself like the Lady Ela had. A man couldn't put up with disrespect like that, and certainly not in front of his peers and his overlord. William Fitzwilliam certainly looked happier, or at least more relieved, and the other men were congratulating him in their words and gestures.

Slowly the room began to empty as the nobles headed off to their beds ahead of the wedding tomorrow. The earl and Sir Gilbert were last out, waiting until Joanna and the Lady Isabelle had disappeared off into the curtained area at the end of the room. Various squires trailed out, and Martin moved to follow, but was stopped by Sir Geoffrey's hand on his arm.

The knight kept his voice low. 'Something is still not right.'

Martin was confused. 'The Lady Ela …?'

Sir Geoffrey shook his head. 'No. No, that's not important. I mean Edwin, and what he said.'

Martin's mind gave a jerk. Lord, he'd almost forgotten about that! It already seemed long ago. 'But he was wrong, wasn't he?'

'Yes. But wrong in what? Certainly that wine wasn't poisoned. But Edwin wouldn't be so far mistaken as to invent that whole tale he told. Some part of it may well be right, and what if it's the part about somebody trying to kill Sir Gilbert? And I am not convinced of this idea that Hamo died by accident. If Edwin thinks it was poison then I am inclined to believe him.'

Martin wasn't quite sure what he was meant to say. 'So you think there's still danger?'

Sir Geoffrey glanced towards the bedchamber and gestured to him to keep his voice down. 'Yes. I don't know what or who, but this game is not yet played out. Edwin is gone, so it will be up to us. Keep your eyes and your ears open,' he dropped to a whisper, 'and trust nobody.'

The sun shone through the windows of the great chamber as Joanna combed Isabelle's hair. For her wedding day she would wear it loose and flowing around her shoulders and back, so Joanna wanted to make sure it looked as beautiful as possible. Isabelle was already wearing her wedding gown; the earl had spent a fortune on a length of blue silk, and the colour was fabulous, mesmerising. It was set off by a necklace and a gold headband inlaid with jewels which would hold the hair in place in the absence of a wimple.

As she drew the ivory comb through Isabelle's hair, Joanna reflected on the events of the previous evening. She'd been shepherded out of the hall along with the other ladies, and so had not seen the end of the scene on the dais, but Martin had told her of Edwin's humiliation and expulsion from the hall. She felt sorry for him – she didn't know him all that well, but he seemed a nice, gentle sort of man, and both Martin and Sir Geoffrey respected him, which was a recommendation in itself. The rest of the evening in the great chamber had been awful, and she'd been glad to escape once Isabelle had decided to retire.

'Joanna, I think that's enough now.'

Joanna came to herself with a start. She'd been combing Isabelle's hair over and over again, and it glistened in the sunlight. 'Oh, sorry, my lady.' She replaced the comb on the dressing table, carefully, for it would be a difficult item to replace if it broke, and fitted the gold circlet on Isabelle's head, smoothing back a few stray hairs.

Isabelle stood. 'Well, how do I look?'

'You look beautiful, my lady. Truly.' And she did – not so much from the fine gown and jewellery, although these were magnificent, but rather because she looked happy. The habitual expression of petulance and disappointment which she had worn ever since Joanna had known her were gone, and she was transformed. After all these years of snipping and sniping, spitefulness and tantrums, Joanna found that she could be glad for Isabelle and her good fortune. She smiled.

Isabelle was looking her up and down. 'You look very presentable, too. But maybe ...' She rummaged in the box of jewels on the table and picked out a necklace studded with green stones. 'Here. Robert gave it to me when we were married, so it comes from your family.'

Joanna reached out to take it and place it round her own neck. Isabelle's first husband, Robert de Lacy, had been her cousin, though she hadn't known him very well. 'Thank you, my lady – I'll be honoured to wear it, and I'll take good care of it until this evening.'

Isabelle smiled and put a hand on her shoulder. 'You can keep it. Today is a day of new beginnings, so it's fitting you should have something new.' Joanna was overwhelmed and tried to speak, but Isabelle put a finger to her lips. 'Shush now, or I'll be in no fit state to be seen.' She squared her shoulders and smoothed her hair. 'Now. Let us go out and see what our new life brings us.'

Joanna followed her past the curtain and out into the great chamber, where the earl was waiting, drumming his fingers on the arm of a chair. He stood as they entered, magnificent in a tunic shot through with gold which matched the rings on his fingers, and nodded his approval. 'Good. Shall we?' He offered his arm.

As he and Isabelle swept towards the door, being held open by Adam, Joanna noticed Martin for the first time. He was looking at her with such admiration in his eyes that she couldn't mistake it. Her heart lifted. Maybe she did look well in her new gown and necklace. She cast a glance to make sure Isabelle was out of sight, and curtseyed to him, laughing. 'Shall we?'

Carefully, Martin held out his own arm; and from the chair to the door, before they might be seen in public, she held it as she floated behind her mistress, imagining that one day she might have a wedding of her own.

Outside the rest of the party were assembled, and the earl led Isabelle to the white palfrey which was waiting with flowers braided into its mane and tail. As she was in her new gown, and as the palfrey would be led at a sedate walking pace, Isabelle sat sideways in the saddle, her skirts spread out over the horse's rump. Although the church was only a matter of a few hundred yards away and the wedding would be small, some ceremony was necessary for an earl's sister, so the party rode out through the gate accompanied by soldiers marching on either side, with many of the rest of the household walking behind, wearing their Sunday clothes. This time Joanna didn't have her own horse, and alas, it was Martin who was leading Isabelle's, so she sat pillion behind Sir Roger, spreading her own skirts out and holding his belt. Despite last night's events, the party was merry as it made its way to the village, even Henry de Stuteville patting his ample frame and saying he was looking forward to the feast later. The only exception was the Lady Ela, her face bruised as she sat behind her husband without speaking.

The village was nearly empty – Joanna assumed their work wouldn't stop for the wedding – but there were a few old men and women, a couple of younger women who were very heavy with child, and a few small children. Most were staring at Isabelle, as well they might, for the sight of a woman's long hair in public was rare, as was a gown of that astounding colour. Joanna also spotted William, the castle steward, holding himself up on a pair of crutches; he pulled off his cap and bowed his head as they went past. Most of the riders were too busy with their own conversations to notice him, but Sir Geoffrey acknowledged him with a nod. Thank the Lord Edwin didn't seem to be anywhere, or there might have been violence despite the happy occasion.

They stopped outside the church, where Father Ignatius was waiting, and dismounted. Sir Roger helped her down from the horse, his hands on her waist, and Joanna noticed Martin scowling in the background. She shook out her skirts and stepped forward to help Isabelle do the same, making a few last adjustments to straighten her necklace and smooth her hair. Then the earl, Isabelle and Sir Gilbert stepped forward to stand in front of the church door.

The ceremony itself was simple. The earl announced in a loud voice that he gave his sister to Sir Gilbert, and then he named the dowry payment; Sir Gilbert in turn declared which of his lands would be hers to hold as a dower and which would be hers to keep if he died before her. Joanna listened to the list, having no idea where any of the places were, but wondering if she might see them one day. But then, if she did, it would be as part of her new life, the life which didn't have Martin in it. She wished she knew what to feel. Every moment of the day she seemed to be veering back and forth between excitement at the possibility of new horizons and the crushing sadness and panic at the thought of leaving the place which had been her home these past years.

The priest asked if anyone knew a reason why the two should not be married, which was thankfully met with silence. The bride and groom made their vows – he to guard and cherish her, she to honour and obey him – and plighted their troth. Sir Gilbert put a ring on Isabelle's finger, and Father Ignatius pronounced them man and wife. Then they all went into the church for the nuptial Mass.

When they emerged, the villagers were still there, chatting to the household staff who had remained outside, some of whom were their friends and relatives anyway. They all raised a cheer, and Sir Gilbert, disentangling his hand from Isabelle's for a moment, reached to the purse at his belt. He smiled broadly and to their delight flung a handful of pennies into the air, which they scrabbled for, shouting out their thanks. Joanna spotted one figure not moving: it was the little boy who was Sir Roger's servant, whose name she couldn't at present remember. He had looked as though he might join in, but was too proud to crawl with the other children without his lord's approval. Unfortunately Sir Roger wasn't looking that way, as he was watching the shower of coins; but Sir Gilbert saw him, and with precision he placed a penny on his thumb and flicked it straight at him, to be caught neatly. The boy had a smile which was nearly bigger than his face, and Joanna nodded to herself at the thought of Isabelle's future.

Then it was back to the castle for dinner. Joanna didn't have a large experience of weddings, but she had thought that this would be the main feast and that they'd probably be in there all day. But in fact it appeared that this was to be a normal meal, as the men had decided to celebrate the occasion with tilting and sparring during the afternoon, so they didn't want to be too full of food or too drunk. The main celebration would therefore be in the evening.

But still, the meal was good and the company jovial, and there was applause when the minstrel took his place for the final time to conclude his epic tale. Joanna concentrated on the dishes in front of her during the gory final battle and its aftermath, wondering at the cheers and whistles when the traitor Ganelon was torn apart by wild horses. But one part of the narrative caught her attention: a lady called Aude, who was Olivier's sister and betrothed to Roland, didn't appear in the story except at the end to hear about what happened and then to die of grief. Joanna almost snorted to herself – women didn't simply die of grief when things like that happened, however much they might want to. And she should know.

She sat in silence for a while, dipping a piece of manchet loaf into the sauce on her trencher and chewing it absent-mindedly. She was at a crossroads in her own life, one even bigger than when her own brother had died. Was she to be like Aude, pathetic and anonymous? No. She would not die of grief at the thought of being separated from Martin. Instead she would go forth into the world, to the other end of the realm, with Isabelle, and would see where life took her. If she was meant to be with Martin then the Lord would arrange that in some way which He knew best. She put the bread down firmly and clenched her fist under the table. She would be brave. She would be a woman of the world.

As the meal wore on, she wondered if she could get away from the table without anyone seeing her tears.

Chapter Fourteen

Martin was excited. As the earl and his guests left the table, he piled some food on a trencher and stuffed it in his mouth as fast as he could. There was to be sparring, and he was to take part along with the other squires. Thank the Lord his stiffness was wearing off – he still felt tender and bruised, but at least he could move. He looked around at the others, trying to assess whether any of them would be difficult opponents. His eye passed over the couple of little pages, past the adolescent who was Henry de Stuteville's second squire, and over to William, the senior in that household, who looked pretty tough and who'd obviously broken his nose in a past encounter. The only other one who might give him any trouble was Eustace, Sir Gilbert's squire, who was quiet but efficient in everything he did, which would presumably mean he paid proper attention to his training.

He finished eating and hurried to the armoury to collect his gear before heading out to the tiltyard, a little slowly due to the weight of the armour slung over both shoulders. Adam had gone with the earl to attend him until he was ready to come down too. At the tiltyard Sir Geoffrey was organising some training bouts in a roped-off area: most of the castle guards who weren't on duty were there, along with a number of Sir Gilbert's men and some from the other households, and the castellan had set some of them up in pairs to spar, while the others cheered them on. Martin watched for a while as he waited for the earl and his guests to arrive, which they did at a leisurely pace some time afterwards. They'd changed out of their wedding clothes, even the earl.

The nobles stationed themselves around the rope and watched their men spar, making some small wagers with each other on the outcomes. Meanwhile, at the earl's nod, Sir Geoffrey set up some separate bouts between the squires. First up were Adam and Henry de Stuteville's second squire, who were about the same age. They put on padded gambesons and fought with the familiar wooden swords which Martin himself had often used when he was younger. He had now moved on to using metal weapons of the same size and weight as real ones but with blunted edges, such as those the other men were using. Still, he well remembered the pain that even the wooden weapons could inflict, and he winced in sympathy as Adam received a solid thwack to his right elbow which he would feel even through the padding. He dropped his sword for a moment, the blow having numbed his fingers, but after a polite enquiry from the other, he grimaced, picked it up again and indicated that he was ready to continue. Martin heard a grunt of approval from Sir Geoffrey beside him, keeping an eye on his charge even while concentrating on everything else.

Martin turned his attention back to the men-at-arms who were sparring with blunted weapons, to see if he could pick up any tips from their greater experience. He might be strong, but, as Sir Geoffrey always said, it was no use relying on strength alone if the other man was cleverer or more skilled than yourself, so it would be good to take the opportunity to learn in the hope that he might one day be of some use to his lord. One of Sir Gilbert's men in particular caught his eye. A man of average size or just more, he was moving more quickly than many of the others despite the weight of his mail, and, unusually, he seemed to be using the point of his sword almost as much as the edge. The blade seemed to flicker as he brought it back and forth, confusing his opponent as he landed a number of blows. However, as Martin noted, the strikes may have been great in number but they weren't overly hard and perhaps might not have been incapacitating even with a sharp weapon. Still, he resolved to experiment with the technique himself when he next had the chance. That would show cleverness.

Adam and the other squire had finished their bout, and now Eustace and William were gearing up. Damn – if they were to fight each other then that would leave nobody for Martin to face, and he might miss out. He watched them for a while: he'd been right that Eustace was competent and that William was quite tough, but he rapidly came to the conclusion that neither of them was a match for him, and he regretted that he wasn't going to get the chance to show off a win to the earl.

He looked at the earl, who was conversing with Sir Gilbert while they watched the boys. Eventually Eustace emerged the winner and Sir Gilbert patted him on the back as he divested himself of his gambeson and took a drink. Then he spoke to the earl again; they nodded to each other and the earl beckoned to Martin and told him to go and fetch his armour. As he raced off – followed by Eustace, who was panting, as well he might be – he could hardly believe it. He was about to see the earl himself engage in a bout with Sir Gilbert! What a privilege to be able to see not one but two of the nobles of the kingdom displaying their skills. The two squires grinned at each other as their ways parted inside the inner ward.

Within a short space of time Martin returned laden with the earl's equipment. There was a collective sigh of expectation as all the men in the tiltyard realised what was about to happen, and a hush descended as the two nobles were armed.

Martin laid everything out on the ground and turned to help his lord. He stood ready as the earl buckled a belt around his waist, and then assisted him to don his chausses – mail leggings which were held up by being tied to the belt with leather thongs. Next he held up the heavy quilted gambeson while the earl inserted his head and arms, and then he pulled it down firmly to ensure that it was fitted correctly about the shoulders ready for the hauberk. Then it was on with the padded coif so that the links of the mail hood wouldn't get caught in the earl's hair; Martin stooped to tie the strings under the earl's chin. The hauberk came next, the mail made up of thousands of riveted links and immensely heavy. Martin ensured that the garment didn't get caught on anything and fell smoothly down to the earl's knees before helping him on with the mittens which hung from the end of the sleeves and making sure the hood wasn't obscuring his face. Then the earl raised his arms while Martin buckled a much sturdier belt around his waist, pulling it as tight as he could to help support some of the weight of the armour so it wasn't all hanging from his shoulders. This was followed by the great helm which covered the whole of his face, and then the shield on his left arm. Finally Martin held out the great sword in its scabbard, but the earl gestured that he wouldn't belt it round him. Instead he merely drew it smoothly, the polished blade glinting in the sunlight, and stood ready for his opponent. Martin saw that Eustace had been marginally slower in arming Sir Gilbert, but in a few moments he too was ready.

This bout was more formal than the others had been. The crowd moved back to give them plenty of room, men wary of the sharp weapons, and the earl and Sir Gilbert bowed to each other before taking their guard. They were fairly evenly matched in size, the earl being perhaps an inch shorter than his opponent, but stockier. They circled for a few moments, each trying to manoeuvre the other so that the sun was in his eyes, but each too canny to fall for this old trick. Then without warning the earl struck. Martin had seen him train before, of course, and was expecting it, but even so his lord's movement was almost too fast for the eye to see. However, Sir Gilbert caught the blow easily on his shield and deflected it down, before flicking his own blade out. The earl was ready for the riposte and the two of them moved apart again.

As the match continued, Martin realised exactly how much work he would have to do if he were ever to reach the standard of the two men in front of him. Of course, they weren't really trying to kill each other, but they were otherwise in earnest: their concentration was intense, their movements tight and controlled, and their reactions phenomenally fast. The men around watched entranced, and Martin noticed Sir Geoffrey beside him nodding appreciatively at each clash. As time went on, Martin knew he would have been getting tired by the weight of all the armour, but the nobles didn't seem to flag: the benefits of having trained in the armour daily from a young age. Martin hardened his resolve that from now on he would make sure he wore full armour even to train with blunt weapons, otherwise he'd never get used to it.

The combatants were still engaging, and, as Martin watched, Sir Gilbert attempted a thrust which turned into a well-disguised uppercut. A collective groan went up from the earl's men who were watching, but he was not fooled and reacted with skill. Instead of deflecting the blow away with his shield he caught it neatly with the blade of his own sword, twisted and flicked it just enough to render his opponent slightly off balance, and then used his own shield to ram forward. Sir Gilbert's head went back and he was forced to take an involuntary step backwards: and then the earl had him, sword point levelled at his throat where the tipping back of the helm had exposed the mail.

Amid applause from the men, the earl stepped back; Sir Gilbert lowered his sword and acknowledged defeat with a bow before both men removed their helms and shook hands. Both smiled broadly and complimented each other, and Martin hastened forward to take the sword, shield and helm from his lord before he should have to drop them. Now *that* was demonstrating cleverness instead of strength. This is what he would need to work on.

As he took the earl's sword and sheathed it carefully, he started to feel a little morose. Everywhere he went he was surrounded by clever men. How in the Lord's name was he supposed to live up to their standards?

Sir Roger was nearby, and he came to talk to Martin. 'Why the long face?'

Martin mumbled something about strength and cleverness, which he wasn't sure the knight had understood. 'You know, like Roland,' he added.

Sir Roger looked perplexed. 'Sorry?'

'You know; "Roland is brave but Olivier is wise". The minstrel said that in the poem the other day. I missed a big bit after that, but I bet it was Roland who got them into all the trouble which happened, while clever Olivier sorted it out.'

As he looked miserably at the floor, Sir Roger burst out laughing. 'Oh no, you've missed the point completely. It's *Roland* who's the hero, Roland who the poem's named after. He might not be clever, but he was loyal, brave and strong, and he was true to himself right up until the end.'

Martin stared.

Meanwhile, Sir Gilbert had been speaking to the earl about Martin, noting in a jovial voice that he was a fine-looking fellow and surely he shouldn't be the only one not permitted to engage in some training? 'Perhaps he'd like to share a bout with my squire?' Eustace, who was collecting his lord's weapons and who was still sweating from his previous bout and from running to fetch the armour, stepped forward resolutely, but looked a bit apprehensive as Martin straightened from talking to Sir Roger, unfurling his full height.

'No, no, that will never do.' The earl's voice was firm. 'Your lad is to be congratulated on his eagerness, but he's much younger and it wouldn't be fair to subject him to such a mismatch. Martin may spar by all means, but we shall have to find another opponent.' He looked round enquiringly. Several men shuffled as though they might volunteer, but before they could do so, Sir Roger was stepping forward, clapping Martin on the back as he went past. He made his bow to the earl.

'Please allow me, my lord. After all, I used to defeat him years ago when he was smaller – surely he should have the chance to repay the favour now?'

The earl, all smiles, agreed. 'A fine idea, Roger. And if he is to fight a knight then he may as well do it properly – the experience will do him good.' At first Martin didn't know what he meant, but then he realised that the earl was pointing towards a full set of armour and, lying ominously next to it, a sharp sword.

Before he knew it, Sir Roger had agreed and was being helped into a spare gambeson. Martin looked stupidly at the armour on the ground without moving until Adam came over and nudged him. 'Here, I'll help.' Soon Martin was almost ready, weighed down by mail, and Adam was placing the helm on his head. Immediately the noise around him dulled as the helm pressed the padded coif closer over his ears, and the bright sunshine disappeared all around to be replaced by the narrow field of vision afforded by the eye-slits. He could hear little but his own breathing, close inside the helm. He held the sharp sword as though it were alive, which in some way he supposed it was. His fear was partly that he might be injured – the sight of Sir Roger's glinting blade was enough to instil nervousness, even though he trusted him – but also that he might accidentally hurt the other. What in the Lord's name would he do if he inadvertently managed to cripple one of the earl's knights?

But there was no more time to think, as Sir Roger was bowing. Unused to being offered such courtesy Martin attempted a clumsy bow of his own before taking his guard, bracing his shield arm and bringing his sword up to the ready position.

He felt huge and lumbering next to the knight, who managed to look lithe even wearing layers of padding and armour. And Sir Roger was certainly quicker than he was, already circling and looking for an opening.

Now think, think. Come on, it's only a training bout, you've done this hundreds of times before. Martin felt a strange sensation coming over him. He had been put in an unfamiliar and potentially embarrassing, not to mention dangerous, situation, and was being watched by crowds of men and his lord, but all of that melted away. He was conscious only of the man in front of him, and of his own body smoothly handling the weapons. A different part of his mind seemed to take over, and he was ready. He raised his own sword and lunged.

At first he tried to be clever, as he'd always wanted to be. He tried using the point of the sword as he'd seen the other man do earlier, tried to be subtle like the earl. But Sir Roger was cleverer, and quicker. Martin was losing ground. He let himself be defensive for a few moments while he tried to think. This wasn't going to work – he needed another plan. Sir Roger was staring at him from behind the eye-slits of his helmet. *Roland is the hero – he stayed true to himself.* Oh, who was he trying to hoodwink with all these attempts to be clever? He was bigger, taller, stronger, and he should use the attributes the Lord had given him. Starting now.

The bout continued, and even as he concentrated just on defending himself, Martin more than held his own, although he was unaware of the cheers and appreciative comments which were being passed. He was growing in confidence, realising that fighting in this way was what he had been born to do. He parried Sir Roger's attacks easily and then went on the offensive a little more, managing to land a few blows of his own on his opponent's shield. As he went on and realised that he was not yet on the ground and defeated, his confidence grew even further. Now was the time. Shifting his weight, he struck with his shield first, extending his arm and using his strength and longer reach to ram into the smaller man and force him back. Then he brought his sword round in a wide arc, able to make the obvious and undisguised movement knowing that the other wouldn't be able to get his shield back into position properly while he was off balance. He struck with the sword as hard as he could, every ounce of power in his body braced behind the blow. The blade crashed into the shield, and Sir Roger, already staggering, was thrown bodily across the grass and landed flat on his back several feet away. Martin roared, not sure whether he'd done so out loud or whether the exultation was contained within him.

Cheers erupted around him which he could hear even through the helm and the padding, and belatedly his senses returned to him and he realised what he'd done. Oh dear Lord. He threw down the sword and shook the shield from his arm, wrenched off the helm and knelt down by his opponent, asking frantically if he was all right. Sir Roger sat up and divested himself of his own helm. Looking slightly stunned, he spoke. 'I'm fine, I'm fine, please, don't worry about it.' He grimaced as he moved his left shoulder, but rose easily enough once he'd put the shield down. He stood. Martin realised just what an embarrassment he'd inflicted on his superior and hung his head, but Sir Roger was as gracious as ever. He stepped forward and raised Martin's arm, turning him towards the men so they could salute the victor. Then he turned to the watching earl. 'My lord, I think the future of your household is in good hands with this young man. Please allow me to congratulate you both.'

There were more cheers, but the earl said nothing, nodding to Sir Roger before looking at Martin with such a frank appraisal that he had to drop his head and look away. And then it happened: the earl, his lord, stepped forward and shook his hand, saying that he'd done well. He, Martin, being congratulated in front of all these people! He was dazed, not knowing where to look, but fortunately the earl and Sir Gilbert turned to move off, and then others were drifting away and the entertainment was over. Sir Roger also withdrew and Martin was left with Sir Geoffrey and Adam.

The younger boy helped him out of the mail and the by-now incredibly sweaty gambeson, and Martin welcomed the fresh air through his shirt as he started to gather everything to take back to the castle. Sir Geoffrey had as yet said nothing, but once the area was clear and the squires were both laden, he too offered his thoughts. 'An interesting lesson. I've been telling you for years that skill is the most important thing, but it would seem that brute strength has its place as well.' Martin had no time to consider this properly before the knight was continuing brusquely. 'Come now, boys – most of this will need checking and cleaning before it's put away again.' But behind the offhand manner there was admiration, and the nod and look he gave to Martin would stay with him until the end of his days.

'Edwin, get up.'

Edwin groaned and pulled the blanket further over his head. It was early evening and he hadn't been out of the house all day. He couldn't. Everyone would look at him, point at him, talk about him. He, Edwin, the great failure, the man who thought he was right, who thought he was as good as his father. He'd wandered around the cottage for a while, and then retreated to his palliasse in the corner.

'Edwin. You do as you're told right now!'

He moved the blanket away from his face. His mother was standing over him, her hands on her hips. 'Oh, *what*?'

She folded her arms and said nothing. He tried to stare her out, but that never worked. 'Sorry, Mother. It's not your fault.'

She sighed and lowered herself to the floor to sit beside him. He sat up to offer her some room on the palliasse. 'No, and it's not yours either. It was too difficult a task for the lord earl to give you.'

Edwin put his head on her shoulder and burst into tears. She put her arms round him and stroked his head, making soothing noises as she had done when he was little. Eventually the storm subsided and he was able to sit up, scrubbing his sleeve over his eyes. 'Father would be so ashamed of me.'

She used the corner of her apron to wipe his face. 'Perhaps. But not for the reason you might think.'

He stopped, arm halfway across his face. 'What?'

'Your father would never condemn you for being wrong. Everybody makes mistakes. But he wouldn't like you giving up.' She put a hand on his arm. 'Do you honestly think that the lord earl's new goodbrother is in danger?'

'To be honest, I'm not sure what to think any more. But on balance, yes.'

'Then what is that compared to your own discomfort? Yes, you feel humiliated, but is that an excuse to lie here and brood when you might be better served putting right your mistake?'

Edwin finished wiping his face and nodded. 'All right. That's what Father would have done, so that's what I'll do.'

Suddenly she was crying as well. He exclaimed and made as if to put his arms around her, but she waved him away. 'I'm all right, I'm all right. It's just … both of us have to stop doing this. I miss him with all my heart, and so do you, but he's gone. We have to look forward, not back over our shoulders.' She dried her eyes and stood. 'Come now. Get up, go out and see if you can still be of assistance to our lord earl.'

Edwin stood up as well, embraced her, and walked out of the door.

He needed to *think*. Since that episode yesterday his head had been much clearer, but he still couldn't see his way through the tangle. Maybe it was time to cut through all the knots and start again. Henry de Stuteville had not poisoned the wine. That much was true, as he knew to his bitter cost. But Hamo *had* died by poison, of that he was certain – so if

Henry de Stuteville hadn't done it, who had? Should he go back to suspecting William Fitzwilliam? And why had William been seen speaking to Hamo?

He looked up, surprised to find himself in the graveyard. Oh, Father, I need you now more than I've ever needed you, but I have to stop doing this, stop coming here and acting as though you are still alive, still ready to help me. I have to stand in my own shoes now.

Edwin tried to empty his mind as he looked down at the grave, to force everything out of his head. He breathed deeply, feeling the air filling his chest and then exhaling to push out the darkness within, the corruption, the mass of confusion. Concentrate only on the grass before you, and nothing else. God's sweet air in, and the demons out. At length he could feel a kernel of calm inside him, and he exhaled one last time. He crouched and put one hand on the warm earth. The rock of his life. But the rock of his *past* life. 'Goodbye, Father.'

As he left the graveyard he saw a small group leaving the village: John and his two children – and Godleva. Godleva's mother and Cecily were bidding them farewell, and Edwin moved to speak to them. 'What's going on?'

Godleva's mother spoke proudly. 'My daughter's got married.'

Edwin was taken aback. 'What?'

Cecily replied. 'This afternoon, after the Lady Isabelle's wedding. Didn't your mother tell you?'

'Er, no. But ...' Edwin gestured to the graveyard, where John's first wife had been lying for less than one day.

Godleva's mother took on a defensive tone. 'Well, the man can hardly keep his own house while he's working in the fields, and the little girl isn't more than three – a few years off being able to take care of the place. He needs a wife, and where else is he going to get one? He won't be back here until the Michaelmas fair, probably.' She looked belligerently at Edwin, and he felt obliged to say something.

'Well ... congratulations. I hope she'll be happy.'

He received a snort in reply. 'Happy? Maybe she will and maybe she won't, but she won't starve – he's got a nice place out there near the Sprotborough road.'

Edwin looked after the departing group. John was carrying a pack – Sir Geoffrey had seen to it that some dried meat from the castle kitchen and a couple of bags of oats and beans had been supplied as recompense for the loss of his pig, for it wasn't in the best interests of the earl's estate to let a good working man starve – and he had one arm about the shoulders of his son, whose arm was still bound but who had lost the deathly pallor he had arrived with. Cecily expected him to make a good recovery, thank God, for a one-armed man wouldn't be much use in the fields in the years to come. John was calling to Godleva to keep up as she toted both the little girl, strapped to her hip, and the small bundle which constituted her dowry and possessions.

Edwin wasn't quite sure how he felt. He'd certainly been uncomfortable when Godleva had made advances to him, but perversely his pride felt dented that she had dropped him so quickly and transferred her attentions to another. But John had been able to offer what he wasn't ready for: an immediate marriage and a home of her own.

A home near the Sprotborough road.

He ran after them, shouting for them to stop. They turned in surprise as he barrelled up to them, Godleva smiling as though he'd come to speak to her. He ignored her and addressed John. 'You live near the Sprotborough road.' John nodded. 'But you didn't actually say it was him, did you? You just said a lord.'

John looked confused. 'What you talkin' about, boy?'

Edwin started again. 'You said you'd seen Hamo talking to a lord. And because you live out that way, I assumed you meant William Fitzwilliam. But you didn't mention his name, did you?'

'I told you, I don't know what he were called. Just a lord.'

'What did he look like, this lord? Tall and very thin? Neat little beard?'

John shook his head. 'Nay. A big man, not thin. And a great bushy beard.'

Edwin's mind was racing. John was still looking at him. 'Is that all you needed? We've a way to go before dark.'

Edwin came back to himself. 'Oh, yes, of course. Thank you.' He looked at Godleva. 'And … good luck.'

He watched the new family set off on the long road to their holding. They would have a hard life there, especially in the winter, but they would be together.

In the meantime, he had some more thinking to do. Henry de Stuteville had been seen talking to Hamo. He needed to go up to the castle.

As he neared the great hall his pace slowed. He'd been let through both the outer and inner gate without a problem, so maybe word of his disgrace hadn't spread too far yet, or at least not enough to see him arrested. But his courage failed him and he stopped outside the door. Everyone in there would have seen what happened last night, and they'd all start whispering about him. What would F – , but no, he wasn't going to think like that any more. He was his own man. He would go in, however difficult it was.

Edwin could feel his face become hot as he entered the hall. Everyone was looking at him, faces turning as he trudged past, shoulders hunched. He changed his mind and was about to turn and leave, but a white-robed arm reached out to stop him.

It was Brother William. 'Come now, come. There's no need to run away. The Lord visits humiliation on us sometimes, and we have to face it like men. Come, and sit.'

Edwin didn't really want to, but Brother William's arm was strong, so he lifted his legs over the bench and sat down.

Fortunately not too many people had noticed him, as the kitchen servants were now bringing in the sweet dishes for the nobles and the spiced wine to go with them. The greatest spectacle was a huge marchpane in the shape of the castle keep, which was carried in by two men who heaved it up on to the centre of the high table. As it went past, Edwin could see that it even had little shields around it, presumably made of sugar paste or something edible, coloured with the coats of arms of the earl and his guests. It was a masterpiece, and the ladies on the dais clapped their hands in appreciation.

Brother William pushed some stew towards him. 'Now, eat something. It'll do you good.'

Edwin didn't think he'd be able to force any of it down, but he took his spoon out of his belt pouch and pushed the food around. Brother William, who was tucking in heartily, nudged him. 'Come on, it's very good – not as nice as that gigantic marchpane on the high table, maybe, but tasty. And better for your soul, as well. Just look at that thing up there – with the cost of the sugar on that, you could feed a poor family for weeks.'

The spoon stopped moving. Edwin stared at his bowl. He wasn't seated in the same place he had been on the evening when Hamo had died, but he could still picture the scene. Hamo had stood and stared at him and at Brother William; he hadn't eaten as he would do so later once everyone else was fed. And while he stood, Thomas had slipped out behind him, his mouth full of stolen sugar. Thomas, who had run away in terror after realising the consequences of using poison. But he hadn't poisoned the wine.

Edwin looked up to the high table. Slices of marchpane had been carved and were being served to the nobles. The earl was there, his sisters and brothers-in-law, Sir Gilbert, Sir Geoffrey, Sir Roger, Mistress Joanna and the other lady companions. He couldn't do it. After what had happened yesterday, he absolutely could not stand up and make his accusations again, only this time about the sugar. He couldn't. He would never, ever live it down. He'd have to leave Conisbrough. The earl would kill him, and if he didn't, the humiliation would.

He looked again at the guests. They all now had trenchers in front of them with slices of marchpane on. They were looking at the earl to wait for him to start eating first. All those faces. The earl, who had taken him from his ordinary life and made him into more than he'd ever thought to be. The Lady Isabelle, torn between looking eagerly at the marchpane and lovingly at her bridegroom. Sir Gilbert himself, who had been with Edwin at Lincoln, saved his life and brought him home. Sir Roger, who had been his friend and introduced him as an equal to knights. Joanna and the other ladies, innocents all, who might die for nothing. And Sir Geoffrey. Sir Geoffrey, the knight who had been his father's best friend, who had watched from afar as he himself had learned to walk and to serve his lord. Sir Geoffrey, who didn't like sweet foods but who would eat it anyway out of politeness to the bride and groom, and so as not to shame the lord whose family he'd served all his life.

It was all so unreal. His legs would hardly hold him up, but Edwin felt himself rising from the bench and walking to the middle of the hall. Would his voice even function? Everyone was looking at him again. Dear Lord, he prayed. Give me strength. He took a deep breath as he saw the earl pick up the slice that would kill him.

'Stop!'

Chapter Fifteen

Only once had Edwin seen his lord so furious. It would take him a long time to get over that memory. And this time it was directed at him.

The earl shoved his chair backwards, knocking his trencher to the floor as he pushed away from the table, and strode round to the front of the dais. Edwin wanted to flee but there was no chance; he was too close. Henry de Stuteville was also standing, fists clenched.

Edwin's first thought was that the earl was going to hit him, but of course he wouldn't sully himself doing such a thing in front of his guests. Instead he impaled Edwin with the look which had sent men to the gallows.

He had to say something, but it was all reminding him too much of last night. Henry de Stuteville was looming towards him. 'My lord, if this is another of this peasant's futile attempts to – '

But he was cut short by a dreadful whining scream. Even the earl jumped, and they all turned to look back at the dais, whence the noise emanated. A dog had seen its chance and headed for the earl's dropped trencher; it had been eating the marchpane but was now throwing itself around in a dreadful agony.

'Put it down!' The voice was Sir Geoffrey's, taking charge of the situation and barking an order at the nobles, heedless of rank. The Lady Isabelle was sitting almost stupefied with her marchpane halfway to her mouth, but Sir Gilbert knocked it out of her hand, looking up and down the table to see that everyone was doing the same.

And so it was that both the knights were concentrating on the noble party, and neither of them saw what Edwin saw:

Henry de Stuteville, watching the earl watching the final thrashing of the dog's death throes, drawing a knife from his sleeve and lunging at the earl's unprotected back.

Edwin wanted to move, wanted to shout, but he was stunned, rooted, his feet somehow mired in the rushes and made of lead. He could see the blade, he could see his lord half-turning but off balance and unable to get out of the way, he could see the earl's eyes opening wide at the sight before him, he could see the open mouths of the men trapped behind the table as they realised what was happening and that they were powerless to help.

But suddenly Henry de Stuteville was hurled backwards, the arm holding the knife mercifully thrown up and away from the earl. He crashed down in a heap with his assailant on top of him. While everyone else had been watching the dog, Martin had not taken his eyes off the earl, and he had thrown himself forward to tackle de Stuteville to the ground.

They were thrashing around on the floor, the knife still in de Stuteville's hand, and Edwin belatedly realised that he should do something to help. He took a step towards them, but already the men from the lower tables were swarming up and he got knocked over in the rush. He fell into a mass of bodies and felt a sting to the side of his face before a hand grabbed the back of his tunic and yanked him out of the melee.

Fighting had broken out in the lower hall as well, as de Stuteville's men were jumped on and held back by others. The struggle on the dais had reached its conclusion; Henry de Stuteville was hauled to his feet, his arms twisted behind him by four men, his knife in Sir Gilbert's hand. Sir Geoffrey was helping Martin up. Edwin looked anxiously at him – as, he noted, did Mistress Joanna at the end of the table, her hand held to her mouth in horror – but although the sleeve of his tunic hung torn and loose, he didn't look like he was bleeding. Thank the Lord.

The earl, who had stood aloof from the brawl, looked around him at the carnage of his sister's wedding feast. He turned to Edwin. If he'd looked angry before, then now … but praise God and all the saints in His heaven, the fury was not for him. The earl merely took one step towards him and asked, 'How did you know?' But as Edwin opened his mouth to reply, he was cut off with a gesture. 'Never mind that now. It will keep. See to your face and report to me later.'

His face? Edwin put a hand to his cheek and was surprised to see the sticky redness on his fingers. Somebody was still holding his tunic and he saw that it was Brother William. The monk smiled. 'I told you you'd get yourself in trouble throwing yourself into a rescue like that. But don't worry, it's only a scratch – you won't even have a scar to show for your pains.' The voice was jocular, but Edwin felt the grip on him tighten. He should go, but he was drawn to the scene before him, the family split asunder. Something still wasn't quite finished, but he knew it would come to him in a moment.

The earl strode forward to within inches of his would-be murderer. He was shaking with the effort of controlling his fury, and Edwin knew that the rage wouldn't be held in check for much longer. De Stuteville struggled and heaved in his captors' grasp, but he couldn't move. Instead he spat on the floor and swore.

'Oh Henry, you *idiot!*'

Along with everyone else, Edwin looked round to see the Lady Maud, face contorted, shrieking at her husband. 'You fool! That poison was our only chance! And now look what you've – '

Edwin nodded to himself as uproar broke out again.

Edwin stood in the earl's council chamber. It was dark and cool; even the hot midsummer sunshine couldn't penetrate the thick walls of the keep, so they had no residual warmth now it was dark. The room was lit by more candles than his mother would use in a year, and proper wax ones too, so that they cast a more even light without spluttering and making everyone's face jump about. He'd been with Sir Geoffrey after the meal as he'd questioned Henry de Stuteville; initially he had been worried that they might have to use force, but it had been easier than he expected – the formerly larger-than-life lord had deflated, and he confessed everything.

'So,' Edwin concluded, 'to start with I thought he wanted to kill Sir Gilbert, so he wouldn't be my lord's heir, but of course he still wouldn't be next, so that didn't make sense. Then I wondered if his plan was to have William Fitzwilliam accused of his crime, but surely that was too feeble a premise to stake his future on.' He looked at his audience: the earl in his great chair, flanked by Sir Geoffrey and Sir Gilbert, with Martin, Adam and Eustace looming in the outer reaches of the light. The earl nodded for him to continue. 'It was when I accused him of poisoning the wine, my lord,' he winced at the memory of his humiliation in the great hall, 'he was so happy to drink it – surely an innocent man might have wondered if the wine really was poisoned, even if he hadn't done it himself? But he was so sure it wasn't poisoned that he must have *known*. And he could only know that if he was the perpetrator himself, and it was something else he'd tampered with. And then the sugar – the marchpane – I knew. He did want to kill Sir Gilbert, but he wanted to kill the rest of you as well. Then he and the lady M-M – ' he couldn't bring himself to say her name out loud, not in front of the earl – 'they would have your earldom now, my lord, your lands and your power.'

He stopped for a moment while they took this in. Eventually the earl nodded again and Edwin continued, his voice shaking at the enormity of what he was saying. 'So they needed you gone, my lord, and Sir Gilbert; they couldn't leave the Lady Isabelle in case she married again; and they needed to kill your other sister and goodbrother to make sure. The way the realm is at the moment they could talk their way out of a mass poisoning – especially if they'd made themselves a little ill at the same time – and especially if they promised all your lands and men in support of the king and the lord regent. Henry de Stuteville said himself, my lord, that he believes in forward planning, and I think they've been working on this ever since you announced that Sir Gilbert was going to marry the Lady Isabelle.'

The earl exhaled. 'And they were this close to succeeding.' Edwin knew he didn't need to bother answering that. The earl looked at his companions. 'But here we are, and we must move on from here.'

Sir Gilbert spoke first. 'What will you do, my lord?'

The earl shrugged. 'She is my sister, and he her husband. I can't execute my own blood, and nor will I deliver them to the lord regent to do so.'

Edwin was shattered. This was all happening like it had before. Nobody cared that Hamo was dead – his conscience pricked him a little, knowing that he hadn't had Hamo uppermost in his thoughts either – and a nobleman could escape being brought to justice because of his birth. But he didn't attempt to argue or protest: this was the way of his new world and he needed to get used to it.

The earl was continuing. 'But I will make sure they leave these shores and travel to their lands in Normandy, never to return.'

Sir Geoffrey nodded. 'He can't harm you in exile, my lord.' He paused. 'And Sir William?'

The earl looked up at Edwin. 'Well, from what you say he had nothing to do with it?'

Edwin nodded. 'Yes, my lord. When Hamo shouted for "William" in his death throes, it was his brother he was calling for, the brother he thought was dead but had seen in the hall.

Maybe he thought it was a ghost who was killing him, seeing as there was nobody else in the room. The noises weren't a struggle, they were just him kicking things over as he died. As you saw from the dog in the hall, my lord, it must have been very painful.' He swallowed. 'I thought at first that Sir William had persuaded Thomas to put the poison in the sugar, but I soon realised he wouldn't do that to his son. Then I found out that Henry de Stuteville had been seen talking to Hamo – I can't think that he tried to get Hamo to do anything deliberately, my lord, otherwise he would have said something – he wasn't popular in the household but he was loyal to you.' Maybe his conscience would rest a little easier for that. 'But there was probably some discussion of how Lord Henry would pay his donation for becoming a monk' – the earl looked surprised, but he didn't interrupt – 'if Hamo would assist him in some way. But obviously he didn't get anywhere, so he turned his attention to Thomas instead. My guess would be that he framed it as a joke, as Thomas loved – loves – a prank. And when Hamo ate his meal that night, he just couldn't resist the temptation to help himself to some of that sugar to go with it.'

There was silence for a moment before the earl spoke again. 'So, William shall go free. But I will not have that cursed boy in my household any longer, even if he doesn't turn up dead.'

The other knights indicated their agreement. 'But how will we find him, my lord?' asked Sir Gilbert.

Edwin couldn't help interrupting. 'I think I can help you there, my lord. I mean – I don't know where he is, he ran away when he realised what he'd done, but he's been gone so long that he must have found a hiding place or we'd have found him by now. And I know someone who knows every haven for a small boy for a mile around.'

The earl nodded once more, then stretched his arms out and yawned. 'Good. Search again at first light. If you find him, send him to me, and you yourself report here after dinner tomorrow morning.'

Edwin bowed, a little less awkwardly than he had a few weeks ago, and left the room.

At the outer gate he had to rouse the porter to let him out, and then he walked down the road to the village. For the first time in many nights the moon was covered by cloud, so he couldn't really see, but he was used to the walk and didn't stumble. It would be light within an hour or two, so there wasn't much point in going to bed – he didn't think he'd sleep, anyway. He made his way back to the cottage and sat down outside it, under the eaves, his back against the daub wall. Families. What terrible things could be hidden within them. It was almost worth not having one. But, as he leaned against the wall which his father had made, lovingly, as a shelter for his beloved wife and son, he realised that wasn't the answer either. His parents had been two halves of the same whole, and he wanted that for himself, he knew that now. Not for him the life of the priest, or even that of the man so dedicated to his work that he didn't marry, like Hamo, who had died alone and in pain.

He put his head back and allowed himself, finally, to bring Alys fully into his mind. He could see her so clearly that it was as if she were there. He savoured her smile as he savoured the quiet of the sleeping village. There was something oddly comforting about being the only person awake, as though he were watching over them. Slowly, he allowed himself to relax as he waited for the sun to come up.

He must have dozed off, for the light came more quickly than he expected, and the sounds of waking issued from each cottage. He rose stiffly. He put his head round the cottage door to let his mother know he was alive and well, and then set off back up the castle road. Thank the Lord the day was cloudy and overcast, and he could smell a certain dampness in the air.

As he drew near to the outer gate, he met the minstrel coming the other way, a pack over his shoulder. He was singing to himself, but the same few lines over and over again, consulting a piece of parchment as he did so. *Li ciels est clairs, li airs est purs, Ades s'en vait li tans oscurs.* Very appropriate, thought Edwin: the sky is clear, the air is pure, and the dark time is receding. He called out a greeting and the man stopped.

The minstrel smiled. 'Ah, it's you. I heard about what happened – by the time the tale got round the whole place it turned out you saved the lord earl and his family by fighting off a hundred men at once.' He grinned. 'Maybe I'll write a song about it.'

'It wasn't quite like that, but yes, I helped the earl, thank the Lord. Where are you going now?'

The minstrel waved his arms expansively. 'Who knows? I've the open road, a purse of money and a new song to learn. What could be better?'

For just a tiny moment, Edwin envied him. No cares, no responsibilities, no master. But then again, no employment, no security, no home. No wife. That life was not for him.

'Well, I'll bid you farewell then. I enjoyed your performances, and I wish you luck on your journey, wherever it is you're going.'

The minstrel shook his hand. 'York, probably – there's always good pickings there. But I'll stop off at a few places on the way. Good luck to you too.' And he was off, with the easy loping gait of a man who walked many miles, looking down at his parchment and up to the sky as he sang his new lines. *The earth moves from death to life, the lark sings of love ...*

Edwin watched him as he took the road north, before turning back and entering the castle.

He might have known that Sir Geoffrey would be up already, although he couldn't work out from the knight's tireless face whether he'd napped for a couple of hours or not slept at all. He explained his plan and Sir Geoffrey nodded in approval and pointed, so Edwin made his way to the guest quarters. He'd never been in here before, and God forbid he should knock on the wrong door and wake an angry noble.

One door had three guards standing outside it, so he murmured a greeting and crept past – he didn't think they would be enough to protect him if he came face to face with Henry de Stuteville. He reached the end of the passageway and tapped softly on the door there. After a moment it was opened by Peter, who put his finger to his lips and pointed at Sir Roger, who was on his knees praying. Edwin waited until the knight had finished and crossed himself, and then he entered.

Sir Roger smiled. 'Ah, a hero again, I hear?' He stood and clapped Edwin on the shoulder.

Edwin smiled back. 'Thank you, Sir Roger. But there's one part of the mystery yet to solve, and I think Peter can help.'

They both looked at the little boy, who was standing open-mouthed. Sir Roger laughed. 'Come now, Peter, this is your chance to be a hero too. You'll help Edwin for me, won't you? There's a good lad.'

Peter nodded eagerly and followed them outside, where they found Sir Geoffrey and Martin. Edwin saw him flinch a little, but Martin patted him encouragingly and Sir Geoffrey made an effort to look less stern.

'Now, Peter. As you know, Thomas, the lord earl's page, went missing three days ago. We've looked in all the obvious places, but we haven't found him. So I thought that you might be able to help – nobody will know all the places he might be hiding better than you.' Edwin hoped he was right and wasn't about to look foolish just as he'd managed to redeem himself with the earl.

But Peter was already looking about him keenly, and then, without a word, he trotted off out of the inner gate. The men looked at each other and followed him.

Edwin almost lost sight of the boy in the outer ward, for the sun was properly up now and the business of the day was beginning. But there he was, slipping past the stables. He hesitated briefly outside the doghouse, and waited for Edwin to catch up. 'Three days?' Edwin nodded. 'They'd have found him in there by now. No, he must be …' Peter darted off again, almost skipping through the crowds. He reached the smithy and stopped uncertainly in front of the imposing figure of Crispin, who stood scowling with his huge burn-scarred arms folded.

The smith relaxed when he saw who was following the boy. 'What can I do for you, Sir Geoffrey, Sir Roger?' He nodded at Edwin and Martin.

Sir Geoffrey was perplexed. 'To be honest I am not quite sure.'

Edwin looked at the smithy. Other than the stables it was the largest of the buildings in the outer ward, but it was all open inside, with plenty of room for the forge, the anvil, the racks of tools and the finished weapons and implements. A leather curtain marked off the small corner where Crispin slept, but Thomas couldn't possibly be in there. And the building backed directly on to the castle's outer wall, the thatch sloping up to it, so there couldn't be any room behind it either.

They all watched in some confusion as Peter inserted himself in the gap between the smithy and the building next to it, the lean-to which belonged to the fletcher. They followed him to the mouth of the alley and saw him reach the outer wall. He looked up at the smithy roof, high above his head, then put his hands and feet into dents in the wall – barely perceptible toe-holds; he climbed up and disappeared into the thatch. Edwin squeezed himself down the alley and looked up, seeing a small opening in the straw. There was silence for a moment, then a squeak and a loud scrabbling. Then two small boys fell out of the thatch, rolling over and over. Thomas, for it was he, kicked Peter in the belly and managed to get away; he streaked past Edwin and towards the mouth of the alley – only to thump into Martin, who caught him easily and lifted him off the ground, still shrieking and protesting.

Edwin helped Peter to get up. He was a little winded but fine. Edwin peered up towards the – now bigger – hole in the thatch. Peter gestured. 'Go and have a look.' Edwin made a very clumsy attempt, nothing like the boy's nimble climb, and managed to haul himself up far enough to put his head inside. What he saw surprised him. Although the thatch sloped up towards the wall on its narrow laths, there were heavier beams supporting the roof which were level, creating a triangular space. A board had been laid across them, and a small nest of straw was on top. It wasn't very big, but it was easily large enough to house a small boy with room to turn around and even to store food; Edwin saw the remains of what looked like a stale loaf in the far corner. But it also stank, so he lowered himself to the ground again and looked at Peter. The boy wrinkled his nose. 'Yes. When I used it I was only there for a few hours at night time. If he's been there two or three days, then ...'

They made their way back up the alley. Martin and Sir Geoffrey were hauling the protesting Thomas away, but Sir Roger and Crispin were still there. The smith looked down at Peter. 'So you used to live in there, did you?'

Peter stepped back to shelter next to his master. 'Yes. When I was ... alone. But not all the time – I moved around in case anyone found me.'

Crispin crouched, lowering his huge bulk, his knees cracking, so his eyes were on a level with Peter's. He looked steadily at him, making Peter flinch away even more, but then he softened. 'And there was I thinking it was rats. And so it was, but a different kind. Warm, was it, with the forge going?'

Peter nodded.

Crispin put out a huge, burn-scarred hand, dwarfing the boy's shoulder. 'Aye, well, I'm glad it kept you alive in the winter. And I don't suppose you'll need it no more.' He stood once more, a towering figure but one less frightening, and moved away to start his day's work.

Sir Roger looked at Edwin over Peter's head and shrugged. 'Well, you never really know … I shall say a prayer for our good smith. But in the meantime,' he ruffled Peter's hair, 'well done, young man. Come, let's find you something to eat.' Peter unclasped his hand, which had been clutching the knight's tunic, and looked up at him adoringly. Then they moved off together.

Edwin stood in the doorway of the earl's council chamber. He could feel his knees shaking, which was odd, as surely his lord would have only good things to say to him. But the presence of so much authority in a confined space was still too much to be taken easily, as he suspected it would be for some time, if not always. The earl sat in his chair, his robe arranged around him, looking formal. Dear Lord, to think he might be dead now, the castle and lands in uproar, and a murderer sitting in his place. A murderer whose first act would have been to get rid of him, Edwin, as well.

The earl nodded to him and he entered. He looked at Sir Geoffrey, standing to the earl's right, and received an almost imperceptible nod of the head. He looked at Adam, who was holding the door open, and received a smile. He looked at Brother William, sitting at a small table where the light from the window fell, who bent his head over his parchment and dipped a quill in the inkpot. In short, he looked at everyone except the earl. As he moved forward he glanced at Martin, who was standing behind the earl, and wondered what he was gesturing about. Then he understood, and sank to his knees in front of the chair, his eyes down. The rushes were fragrant, but the floor underneath was hard and cold.

'Look at me.'

Edwin dared to raise his head.

'You have served me well, Edwin Weaver.'

Edwin managed a whisper. 'Thank you, my lord.' So why did he feel like some kind of axe was about to fall?

The earl continued. 'You risked my wrath and indeed your life because you knew you were right. Disobeying me is not commonly something I countenance, but you have my leave to do it if a similar situation should arise again.'

Edwin wasn't sure if he needed to reply to that, but the earl hadn't finished.

'It is … unusual for me to accept fealty from someone who does not hold lands from me, and you can't exactly give homage, but … hold out your hands.'

Confused, Edwin raised his hands, palm upwards and apart. He saw Sir Geoffrey mime to him, and quickly changed to put his hands together, as though in prayer. The earl put his own hands around them.

The earl was touching him. Actually touching his hands. These hands, with their golden and bejewelled rings, had dispensed justice and made knights. They had been in contact with bishops and kings. And now they were enfolding his own, which he could feel quivering. The earl's hands were warm, dry and steady.

He looked straight at those slate-grey eyes as the earl spoke. 'Do you, Edwin Weaver, swear to be my liege man, faithfully serving me and no other – saving only his Grace the king – until the day of your death?'

He couldn't take it in properly. What was the correct response? What if he said the wrong thing? 'I swear it, my lord.'

Thank God, that must have been right. The earl continued. 'I accept your oath. In return I pledge that I will protect you and yours from injustice and harm. You are my liege man.'

Edwin felt his hands released, and he sank back on to his heels, stunned.

There was silence, and then the earl threw back his head and laughed, looking more informal and somehow younger. 'Come now, Weaver, no need to look like a cornered hare.

Stand up and name your reward for your service these past days.'

Edwin managed to get his feet under him and his body into an upright position. 'My lord, I – '

The earl looked him up and down. 'I think we'll start with new clothes and a proper belt for that rather fine dagger. Anything else?'

Edwin opened his mouth but no words came out. Fortunately the earl seemed in a good mood and gestured to Adam for wine while he watched and waited.

As Edwin saw him sip from the goblet, an idea came to him. Could he possibly ask …?

'Ha!' Something must have shown in his face, for the earl was leaning forward. 'Spit it out, Weaver. I'm sure you're not going to ask me for the crown.'

'Uh, my lord … Might I have your permission to get married?'

There was silence for a moment as the earl's face registered surprise. Then he put his cup down and slapped the arm of his chair. 'I like it.' Edwin's relief nearly overwhelmed him. The earl smiled. 'Others might have asked for gold, but you … yes, you have my permission, and good luck to you. In honour of my sister's wedding I will also add to your bride's dowry and furnish your marital home. Done?'

Edwin could hardly believe his good fortune. 'Thank you, my lord, thank you.' What else could he say?

The earl flapped a gesture of amused dismissal. 'Take him away, Geoffrey, and get him a drink before he falls over.' Sir Geoffrey bowed and Edwin felt himself being steered out of the chamber and into the stairwell.

By the time they left the keep he had recovered himself enough to see where he was going, at least. Sir Geoffrey took him to the great hall, which was empty except for one or two serving men finishing the clearing up. Sir Geoffrey spoke to one of them, and soon Edwin was sitting with the knight at the end of one of the long tables, a cup of cool ale in front of him. He was still dazed, but in the jumble of thoughts about clothes, furnishings and weddings something else surfaced. There was one more thing he needed to know before he could let go completely.

'Sir Geoffrey, was my father ever a weaver?'

The knight put down his own cup and wiped a hand across his beard. 'Godric? No, lad, he was the bailiff's apprentice and then the bailiff, never a weaver.'

'Then why did he have that name? The earl always called him by it, and now he does it to me.'

Sir Geoffrey looked thoughtful. 'He never told you? Mind, I don't suppose there was any reason why he should.'

'Tell me what?'

Sir Geoffrey took another swig before settling himself more comfortably on the bench. 'Gossiping is not a manly thing to do, but you've a right to know about your father's past.'

Edwin was intrigued. He leaned forward and put his elbows on the table, hands under his chin.

The knight laughed. 'It's not all that interesting, Edwin, and it won't take that long to tell. Many years ago we had another Godric in the village, so to tell them apart we called them Godric the tall and Godric the bailiff. Your father was new in his position then, and the name hadn't stuck very well when we started to have a spate of nasty happenings. The old earl, may he rest in peace, set Godric to sorting them out, and he did. When he was commending your father afterwards, he made a joke that Godric had put the different strands of those happenings together better than any weaver, and that he would henceforward call him the weaver in memory of his deeds. And it just stuck, really. Our lord the earl grew up calling Godric 'Weaver' long after Godric the tall had died, and never knew him by any other name. I expect he calls you the same as you're helping him in the way your father once helped his father.' He looked at

Edwin and Edwin felt himself being appraised. 'You're more like him than you know.'

He couldn't have chosen any words which would have made Edwin more proud than he felt now. His heart swelled and he could hardly choke out the words. 'I'll try to live up to him, Sir Geoffrey.'

The knight smiled and patted him on the shoulder. 'You made him proud while he was alive, and you'll keep doing so now he's looking down from above. So go now and get about your tasks so our lord will continue to know you as the weaver of webs.' There was a slight pause. 'One other thing your father had, which made his life richer, was a good woman. Marriage is a game of chance – you never know what hand you'll be dealt. But in that respect he was the luckiest man I've known. I hope to see you so fortunate.'

The smile which Edwin had been trying to push down since the earl had given him permission finally broke through, and Edwin felt it reach his face. 'I hope so too, Sir Geoffrey.' He stood and moved towards the door. 'And one day, will you tell me more about my father and these deeds that he did?'

Sir Geoffrey nodded even as he stood himself. 'One day, yes, but it will be long in the telling and today is not that day. Just be assured that he's looking down on you and is proud of the man you've become. Now go.'

Edwin smiled, more confident than he had ever thought he could be, and walked out into the ward, where a soft, refreshing rain was starting to fall.

Epilogue

It was five days later when Turold arrived in Lincoln, deep into the afternoon. He was often employed to carry messages for the earl, as he was a nimble rider and a discreet man who had some small knowledge of reading and writing. He was used to travelling to castles and large estates, but now he found himself in the middle of a town, delivering a letter to somebody he'd never heard of, and to be honest he was a bit confused. Why on earth would his lord want to contact anyone here? But he hadn't become one of the earl's most trusted envoys by asking questions: he simply obeyed his orders and did his duty, so here he was.

Lincoln was a place of much activity that afternoon, with traders bawling their wares in the sunshine, trying to entice customers towards them; there also seemed to be a fair amount of building work going on in various places. He'd already got lost twice in the maze of streets, before enquiries at a local tavern – which looked inviting enough to be his home for the night – had set him in the right direction. As he guided his horse down a steep slippery hill he looked again at the missive. He was looking for someone called Alys, who was the daughter of the late Nicholas Holland, and she would be running a fabric shop in a street called the Drapery.

He found the street, and after further enquiry about where to find the Holland shop – not to mention a number of curious glances from the townsfolk at the livery he was wearing – he arrived at the building and saw two small boys playing in the street outside the door. On seeing him, the younger of the two fled inside, but the elder stood and looked at him boldly.

Turold hailed him. 'You look to be a likely lad. Is there somewhere near here where my horse can drink?'

'Yes sir,' came the reply, 'there's a trough just down the road which the pack animals use.'

He dismounted and tossed his reins to the boy. 'Take him there and bring him back, there's a good lad, and you shall have a halfpenny.'

Looking as though he could hardly believe his luck, the boy caught the reins and led the horse down the street, standing tall and proud to be the focus of his neighbours' attention.

Turold stepped into the shop, adjusting his eyes to the darkness after the bright light of day outside, and after a few moments a girl who looked to be about sixteen or seventeen years of age stepped through from the back room to greet him.

He looked at her, glanced once more at the direction written on the letter, and looked up again.

'Are you the mistress here?'

She nodded. 'Yes sir. How may I serve you?'

'I have a letter for you.' He held it out.

She looked uncertain and did not extend her hand to take it. 'A letter? For me? Begging your pardon, sir, but I'm sure that can't be right. Would you mind waiting a moment while I fetch my husband?'

ḥistorical note

Although this story is fictional, it takes place against a backdrop of real events. England was an unstable place in June 1217; the victory at Lincoln depicted in *The Bloody City* had led to the capture of a number of French and English rebel leaders, and the retreat of the invading forces towards the south-east, but Louis himself was still free, still at the head of a sizeable army, and still backed by his all-powerful father, the king of France, not to mention his formidable wife, Blanche of Castile, granddaughter of Henry II and Eleanor of Aquitaine. Many of the nobles whose allegiance had wavered – Earl William de Warenne among them – were now firmly back in the royalist fold, but that didn't mean that everyone trusted them. And the chaos caused by having two proclaimed kings meant that there were plenty of opportunities for those who wished to gain land or power by less than honest means. What was one more suspicious death in a land riven by civil war?

The earl is a real person, as are his sisters and their husbands, although I have made the whole family a few years younger than they probably were in real life (hard facts such as birth dates are difficult to come by for people living at this time), in order to feature their children as youngsters. There seems to be some doubt about the order of their birth: most scholars agree that the earl was the eldest, but as to the sisters, the *Dictionary of National Biography* gives it as Isabelle, Maud and Ela, while the *Plantagenet Roll* has Ela, Isabelle and Maud, and other sources vary. I have therefore felt free to compromise with my own order of Isabelle, Ela and Maud.

All four of the siblings were or had been widowed, and by the summer of 1217 all the sisters were married again to the husbands you see in this book. Isabelle had actually already married Gilbert de l'Aigle of Pevensey by this point; I only realised this after writing *The Sins of the Father*, so I thought I'd better introduce them to each other sooner rather than later! Ela was the widow of Robert of Naburn, and her second husband really was called William Fitzwilliam of Sprotborough; Maud was the widow of Henry, Count of Eu, and she and her second husband Henry de Stuteville (sometimes spelled d'Estouteville) did leave England permanently to settle on his lands in Normandy.

Those familiar with the layout of Conisbrough castle will notice that I have put the chapel (as I did in *The Sins of the Father*) on the lower floor rather than in its true position higher up in the keep; I have also allocated as the armoury the stone building next to the inner gatehouse whose origins are obscure.

Mediaeval weddings differed in some respects from modern ones. There were of course no civil services: all services took place at a church. The wedding itself was solemnised outside the door in order to make it as public as possible, and then the party would go inside for the nuptial mass afterwards. Brides wore their best dress, but not white (white bridal gowns didn't become popular until the early nineteenth century). Noble weddings in particular were more of a business arrangement between two families than a statement of affection between two people – it would not have been unusual for the bride and groom not to set eyes on each other until after the match had already been arranged by their relatives, especially if they were young. The declarations the couple made were more about lands than love. If they happened to care for each other (or at least to have the potential to do so) then that was something of a bonus – and we do have evidence of couples forming very strong bonds during their married lives – but it was by no means a prerequisite to the match. This is probably the only instance I can think of where the lower orders in the thirteenth century might have been a little better off than their noble counterparts; although arrangements did often involve family negotiations over lands or chattels, the peasant couple were much more likely to know each other and to have formed an attachment before their wedding day.

Once in a marriage, a noblewoman had very little power, or at least not officially. She was, in effect, owned by her husband – all her goods became his and she was obliged to obey him in all respects. Marriage was not a partnership of equals. Of course, not all couples featured a domineering male and a cowering female, but nobody would question the idea that the husband had the right to beat his wife if he saw fit. I thought hard before writing the scene in which William Fitzwilliam hits his wife: to me it is a repellent act, but in a noble household in the early thirteenth century nobody, frankly, would bat an eyelid. It was, in effect, the 'happy' ending for all concerned, or at least for the men in the room, in that what they saw as the natural order had been restored. The wife would do as she was told in future.

Although they had few legal rights, noblewomen did have some pleasures available to them. Hawking was one of these: although women did not take part in the fast-pursuit hunting of larger animals such as boar and stags, hawking was considered a more ladylike activity where men and women could ride out together in search of their prey. This must have been a rare and enjoyable experience for those women who did not appreciate their normal sequestered living conditions.

Another form of leisure available to the nobility was the enjoyment of literature. A wide range of narratives in a variety of genres were produced at this time; they were meant to be performed in public rather than read privately, and professional minstrels would travel the country visiting castles, cities or fairs in order to perform texts they had rehearsed. The feats of memory required to memorise stories which were thousands of lines long were astonishing, so minstrels would have trained from an early age. Although the constant travel would have made for a hard life, a good minstrel with a decent repertoire would have found a warm welcome almost anywhere.

Among the most popular texts were *chansons de geste* (literally 'songs of deeds'), long poems which told epic tales of knightly heroes and their feats in battle. The *Song of Roland* is one of the great examples of the genre, depicting the battles of the ninth-century French emperor Charlemagne and his nephew Roland against the Saracens. It was probably originally composed in the eleventh century, but it enjoyed enduring popularity for hundreds of years throughout western Europe. There are nine original manuscripts of it still surviving, and the text has been edited by numerous modern scholars. The quotes from the poem in this book are from F. Whitehead's 1942 Blackwell edition; translations are my own.

The target audience of *chansons de geste* was aristocratic and male (i.e. the people who could afford to pay writers and performers), so the stories were full of scenes featuring the brotherhood of heroic knights, descriptions of luxury armour and gory combat details, which the knightly listeners would have appreciated. It might seem odd to us now that depictions of men wading through entrails or walking round with their brains dribbling out their ears classed as entertainment, but that just demonstrates how different our society is from the world of the thirteenth-century nobleman.

———•◦•———

Life for the peasant community at this time was very different to that of their overlords, with little time for leisure. Although some opportunities may have arisen for young men to leave their birthplaces and seek advancement elsewhere (particularly if they lived in a place such as Conisbrough where the earl's household offered opportunities), most people worked on the land in a never-ending annual cycle of drudgery. Margins were small, and many were 'harvest-dependent', a euphemistic term which basically means 'liable to die after one or two bad harvests'. Most families would owe service in their lord's fields each week, the number of days of which would increase near harvest time; depending on family situation and local custom this might have been the householder himself, or he may have been able to send an able-bodied substitute.

Contrary to popular belief, midsummer was actually the leanest time of the year for food. The grain from last year's harvest would be almost gone, being eked out by the careful housewife, and the new year's crop wouldn't be available for a number of weeks. Cows did not produce milk all year so the supply of dairy food would be drying up; chickens had ceased laying, and livestock would not be slaughtered until the early winter.

The mortality rate for all classes and ages was much higher than it is today. People died of diseases and infections which would be curable now, as well as being subject to a frighteningly high possibility of accident or injury. The perinatal period was particularly dangerous: women had roughly a one in eight chance of dying in labour or shortly afterwards, and something like one in six newborns did not survive. Women were generally shriven of their sins as a precaution before they started labour, and a newborn could be baptised straight after birth in the home, as waiting even the usual day before a church baptism might be too long. Unbaptised infants were denied burial in consecrated ground and it was believed that they could not enter heaven as, although personally innocent, they still had the stain of original sin on them. They would spend eternity in limbo: they were not subject to the physical torments of hell but were forever denied the eternal bliss of heaven.

Those lovely people who read early drafts of this book raised a number of queries about some things which puzzled or surprised them, so to conclude this note I would like to offer clarification on some points which relate to daily life in the early thirteenth century.

Sugar was a hugely expensive luxury item which had to be imported from the Middle East. It arrived in the form of cones or loaves and was generally brown, not having been subjected to the modern refining processes which produce white sugar. It would have been available only to the rich and would certainly have been reserved for special dishes, and kept under lock and key. Honey was the main sweetener in general use, although even this would have been a rare treat for many villagers.

Mealtimes varied according to class and occupation. The main meal in the castle was dinner, which was served in the hall late in the morning and ran to numerous courses for the nobility; there would also have been a less elaborate evening meal. Dinner was deliberately a public affair where the lord could show his generosity to his household, and the household in turn had the honour of eating in the same room as him. Our earl still takes his evening meal in public as well, but some fashionable nobles were starting to retire to a more private chamber, or solar, for theirs. Villagers were more likely to take some bread with them to their work in the fields and then to eat a hot meal of vegetable pottage, probably with more bread, at home in the evening at the end of the day's labours. Breakfast was not a formal meal, being generally considered fit only for infants and the old or infirm, but those who could afford it may have had a little something.

Some readers were surprised to see Joanna riding astride her horse when she went hawking. Side saddles were not seen in England until over a hundred years after the events depicted here; the first documented example, a chair-like affair with a footrest, is credited to Anne of Bohemia (1366–1394), wife of Richard II. Before this, if women were sitting pillion behind men and/or they were travelling at an amble and being led, they could sit sideways on the horse, and there are depictions of this happening in the twelfth and thirteenth centuries. However, this allows no control of the mount, so in any situation where a woman had to control her horse by herself she would have needed to ride astride.

Something a little more esoteric which confused a few readers was the mediaeval perception of time. We are used to our structured, scheduled days of twenty-four hours split with precision into minutes and seconds; to those in the early thirteenth century this would have been an alien concept. In a world with no clocks or watches they had no way of dividing time so precisely, so a day consisted of twelve hours which ran from sunrise to sunset, meaning that hours could indeed be longer or shorter depending on the time of year. *Sext* ('the sixth hour') was at noon; the day was further subdivided by *terce* ('the third hour') mid-morning, and *nones* ('the ninth hour') mid-afternoon. For any division smaller than that people would need to use other measures, for example 'the time it takes to walk a mile' or 'the time it takes to say three paternosters'. Something you certainly wouldn't hear, if you arrived in Conisbrough in June 1217, is anyone saying, 'I'll be there in twenty minutes'!

And finally, I have been asked why Edwin and his fellow villagers weren't out practising their archery on Sunday morning, as this is something often depicted in mediaeval-themed books or films. Bows and arrows were certainly in general use (although bows were not as large as the classic 'longbow', taller than a man, which developed later) and some of the villagers might have been out practising for recreational purposes, but the law making it compulsory for all men to equip themselves with a bow and arrows was not passed until 1252, and Sunday practice didn't become compulsory until 1363. As Edwin isn't terribly keen on anything involving weapons, I've let him off. For now.

Further Reading

Richard Almond, *Medieval Hunting* (Stroud: The History Press, 2011, orig. 2003)

Frances and Joseph Gies, *Marriage and Family in the Middle Ages* (New York: Harper and Row, 1987)

Roberta Gilchrist, *Medieval Life: Archaeology and the Life Course* (Woodbridge: Boydell Press, 2012)

George C. Homans, *English Villagers of the Thirteenth Century* (London: Norton, 1975, orig. Harvard University Press, 1941)

Ann Hyland, *The Horse in the Middle Ages* (Stroud: Sutton, 1999)

Wolfgang van Emden, *La Chanson de Roland: critical guides to French texts* (London: Grant & Cutler, 1995)

Acknowledgements

One of the joys of publishing a book is being given the opportunity to say thank you to all those people who helped, in many different ways, during the creation of it. So here goes …

My editor Matilda Richards is a huge supporter of my work, and it's brilliant to be able to talk to someone who empathises so completely not just on series direction, but also on vital things such as the correct placement of commas. Jamie Wolfendale and Maria Fallon, also of The History Press, have worked tirelessly to promote my books, and neither of them minded being contacted, probably more often than absolutely necessary, by an author who is a bit clueless about marketing.

Stephanie Tickle and Andrew Bunbury, my two best critical friends and readers, neither of them afraid to call a spade a spade, went through early drafts of *Whited Sepulchres* in great detail and offered many helpful insights and suggestions. The fact that they frequently came up with completely different and opposing comments about the same passages only made the redrafting process more interesting.

I'm very grateful to Sarah Jones, equine vet, for her advice on horses. My questions on how to train and ride them, and how they might react in certain circumstances, were probably fairly straightforward; the one on how somebody might go about putting down a crippled horse with only a hunting knife to hand probably less so.

My fellow historians (and fellow devotees of bacon sandwiches) Julian Humphrys and Sean McGlynn have been hugely supportive in all sorts of ways, with words of encouragement, practical advice and the sourcing of presentation and review opportunities. My non-mediaevalist colleagues at work, particularly Susan Brock, Caroline Gibson and Nick Monk, are also owed a debt of gratitude, basically for putting up with me going on and on about stuff which probably doesn't interest them in the slightest …

Last but certainly not least, my thanks and love go to my husband James (who also added another map to his collection!) and our children. I couldn't do any of this without you.

About the Author

C.B. Hanley has a PhD in mediaeval studies from the University of Sheffield and is the author of *War and Combat 1150–1270: The Evidence from Old French Literature*, as well as the historical works of fiction *The Sins of the Father* and *The Bloody City*. She currently writes a number of scholarly articles on the period, as well as teaching on writing for academic publication, and also works as a copy-editor and proofreader.

Also in this series …

The Sins of the Father: A Mediaeval Mystery
C.B. HANLEY

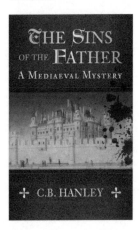

1217: England has been invaded. Much of the country is in the iron grip of Louis of France and his collaborators, and civil war rages as the forces of the boy king try to fight off the French. Most of this means nothing to Edwin Weaver, son of the bailiff at Conisbrough Castle in Yorkshire, until he is suddenly thrust into the noble world of politics and treachery: he is ordered by his lord the earl to solve a murder which might have repercussions not just for him but for the future of the realm.

978 0 7524 8091 6

The Bloody City: A Mediaeval Mystery
C.B. HANLEY

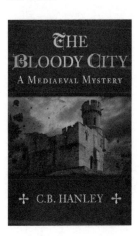

1217: Lincoln is not a safe place to be. A French army has captured the city, and the terrified citizens huddle in the rubble of their homes as the castle, the last remaining loyal stronghold in the region, is besieged. Edwin Weaver finds himself riding into grave danger after his lord volunteers him for a perilous mission: he must infiltrate the city and identify the traitors who are helping the enemy. Edwin is pushed to the limit as he has to decide what he is prepared to do to protect others. He might be willing to lay down his own life, but would he, could he, kill?

978 0 7524 9704 4

Visit our website and discover thousands of other History Press books.

www.thehistorypress.co.uk